# "I'd like to ask you out."

Penelope's throat dried. She couldn't feel her fingers and had to lock her knees to remain upright. Date? Leo? Absurd. They were too different.

And she was afraid she wasn't nearly enough.

She leaned her hip heavily against the desk. "I don't think—"

"Or we could start slow. Have lunch. Or even just coffee." His voice dropped to a husky, sexy tone that could strip a woman of her inhibitions. And her good sense. "It doesn't matter to me. Just a few hours. I'd like to get to know you better."

"Why?"

The word hung in the air, bald and loud and yes, desperate-sounding. Too bad. She wouldn't take it back even if she could. She was too curious to hear his answer.

"Because I find you interesting." Leo stepped forward, his body and her own pride trapping her between him and her desk. "Because I'm attracted to you."

A thrill raced through her before she could stop it. He was attracted to her? That...that was impossible. Implausible. Incredible.

And terrifying.

Dear Reader,

It's been seven years since I sold my first book to Harlequin Superromance. Seven years isn't all that long, but oh, how things can change. Then, I was waiting for my first book to hit the shelves, my youngest daughter was in grade school, my older daughter had just entered the teen years and my son was learning how to drive. Now, my fifteenth book is out, my baby is a high school senior, her sister is a college sophomore and my son a college graduate.

He's also a married man. Which makes me old enough to be a mother-in-law! How that happened, I'm not sure, but I feel incredibly blessed to have such a sweet and beautiful daughter-in-law.

So much has changed. Yet there are many constants, too. Family who give love and support. Dear friends who bring joy and laughter, and the familiar faces of the people in my hometown. Maybe that's why I love writing the In Shady Grove series so much. Not only do I get to revisit previous characters, but I can also share some of my favorite things about small-town life.

In *Charming the Firefighter*, Penelope Denning moves to Shady Grove hoping to find a safe environment to raise her teenage son. When she meets firefighter Leo Montesano, she finds much more. Love, of course, but also a place where she truly belongs.

I hope you enjoy Penelope and Leo's story and that you'll look for the next book in the series, out next year. Please visit my website, bethandrews.net or drop me a line at beth@bethandrews.net. I'd love to hear from you.

Happy reading!

*Beth Andrews*

# BETH
# ANDREWS

---

## Charming the
## Firefighter

HARLEQUIN® SUPERROMANCE®

Recycling programs
for this product may
not exist in your area.

ISBN-13: 978-0-373-60886-7

Charming the Firefighter

Copyright © 2014 by Beth Burgoon

**Printed in U.S.A.**

www.Harlequin.com

When Romance Writers of America RITA®
Award-winning author **Beth Andrews** was a
young wife, she started a gas grill with the lid
down. The small explosion left her with singed
hair and a lifelong respect for propane. While no
handsome firefighters came to her rescue that
day, she will never forget that particular incident.
Mainly because her husband reminds her of it
every summer. Learn more about Beth and her
books by visiting her website, bethandrews.net.

## Books by Beth Andrews

### HARLEQUIN SUPERROMANCE

#### In Shady Grove

*Talk of the Town*
*What Happens Between Friends*
*Caught Up in You*
*Small-Town Redemption*

#### The Truth about the Sullivans

*Unraveling the Past*
*On Her Side*
*In This Town*

*His Secret Agenda*
*Do You Take This Cop?*
*A Marine for Christmas*
*The Prodigal Son*
*Feel Like Home*

Other titles by this author available in ebook format.

For Hannah Grace.
Welcome to the family!

# *CHAPTER ONE*

PENELOPE DENNING GLANCED behind her, left, then right, then left again. Still alone. She was safe.

Shaking her hips to the Fray's latest song, which streamed from her laptop, she danced from the pantry to the center island and set down the bottle of olive oil. She wiggled her shoulders and moved side to side to the beat, the tile floor cool under her bare feet. At the catchy chorus, she sang along under her breath.

And Andrew said she couldn't sing. She may not be in Beyoncé's league, but Penelope could hold her own against the likes of a few of those *American Idol* finalists. She was definitely good enough for the church choir, no matter what her son said. It wasn't as if she'd have to stand in front of the entire congregation under a spotlight, performing solo and, no doubt, sweating and nauseous. She'd be a part of the group.

She sang louder. She'd finally be a part of something. Would have a place where she belonged. Maybe she should audition for the choir.

Unless Andrew was right. In which case she'd simply make a fool of her—

Something creaked. Penelope froze, the tiny hairs on the back of her neck standing on end, the tune dying in her throat.

She turned, her chest tight with trepidation. Only to exhale heavily to find the room still empty.

Oh, thank goodness.

She was being paranoid, that was all. But she stopped shimmying and two-stepping. Sang silently with only her foot tapping.

No sense tempting fate. If Andrew caught her dancing around the kitchen, he'd undoubtedly give her one of the smirks he'd perfected over the past two years. Then flay her with some sarcastic comment, one meant to hurt her. To anger her.

She hated to admit how often he was successful.

But not today, she assured herself, layering circles of fresh mozzarella and thick slices of tomato on a rectangular white plate. Today there would be no drama. No arguing. None of the angst, heartache or soul-crushing doubts that came with raising a teenager.

All she wanted was one day where she and her son weren't at each other's throats. Where they spent time together—in the same room—conversing and, perhaps, even laughing a few times. One measly day where she wasn't the bad guy who'd ruined his life.

And he wasn't an ungrateful, mouthy brat.

Surely that wasn't too much to ask for.

She checked the caprese salad with a critical eye. Gently patted the tomato and cheese slices together so they lined up perfectly—two neat rows alternating white and red, each layer set exactly halfway on top of the one before it. Exactly. She wiped her hands on a clean towel, then drizzled a thin stream of olive oil over the dish.

The midday sun shone brightly through the dining room's huge windows, illuminating the dust mites dancing in the air. One reason she'd bought the house, a midsize Victorian that had been remodeled, was the open floor plan. The entire first floor flowed, from one room to the other—foyer to living room, living room to dining room, and dining room to kitchen. She liked the sense of roominess. Of freedom.

After spending too much of her life cooped up in hospital rooms, waiting rooms and doctors' offices, all she wanted was space. Space to stretch out. To move around.

Space to breathe.

A warm end-of-summer breeze ruffled the lacy curtain adorning the window above the sink and brushed against the back of her neck. Shutting her eyes, she inhaled deeply. Held it, just…held it in her lungs, the clean scent of the fresh air, the pungent aroma of olives and basil. Feeling this satisfied, this content, was all too rare. At least, it had been rare for her.

Might as well soak it in while it lasted.

She exhaled—mainly because she had no other choice, not if she wanted to keep living. She tore the top off the small bunch of basil on the cutting board, rolled the leaves up and began slicing. That sense of peace and contentment was fleeting. Life was too fluid. Always changing, always shifting, moment to moment, milestone to milestone.

She couldn't do anything about those shifts taking her in new directions, those moments fading into the past, the milestones passing.

It was so annoying.

But what she could do was control how she responded to being set off course. She'd moved to Shady Grove to give her and Andrew a fresh start. It'd taken a while—going on eight months—but they'd finally settled in this small town so far away from everything they'd known. *Everyone* they'd known.

A fact Andrew never let her forget.

It hadn't been an easy transition. There had even been times when she'd considered giving up and moving back to California.

If only to stop her son's complaining.

In the end, she'd held firm and, more important, had stood by her decisions. Hooray for her. Hand over that shiny gold star, because she'd persevered against Andrew's miserable attitude and constant griping.

This parenthood thing wasn't for sissies, that was for sure.

She did her best to keep her son safe and healthy. Made sure they commemorated his milestones, no matter how small or insignificant, from getting his braces off to his voice cracking before it deepened to passing his driver's test. Every stage of childhood, every rite of passage of adolescence, was cause for celebration.

For too long she'd worried he'd never get—

*Clang! Clang!*

She glanced up, just to make sure the weights Andrew was lifting—and dropping with such careless abandon—didn't crash through the ceiling onto her head.

There was more clanging followed by a loud thump, which had her praying he hadn't dinged the hardwood flooring.

Again.

Pressing her lips together, she carried the salad to the fridge and tucked it alongside the heaping bowl of fresh-cut fruit. She wouldn't worry about the floor. She'd ignore the fact that she'd told him, at least one hundred times, not to drop his weights.

How hard could it be to set the dumb things down gently?

That was what her life had come to. Ignoring the parts she couldn't control, couldn't fix. Andrew constantly texting, even during dinner. His spending most of his time in his bedroom. How he took three showers a day—and there was no way she was even going to think about why, or what he was doing in there for so long. His new fixation with lifting weights and getting—as she'd overheard him tell one of his friends—cut, when he should be focusing on his schoolwork.

And, of course, his surliness, rudeness and out-and-out bad attitude.

The joys of motherhood. Someone should have warned her about this.

Not that she'd change anything, she assured herself quickly, kneeling to retrieve her favorite serving platter from a lower cupboard. Her son was going through a stage. A two-year-long stage that seemed to have no end in sight.

But that was all right. She could handle it. Andrew was fine. Not quite happy, but that would come in time. There were more important things than happiness. Security. Safety.

He was healthy and that was most import—
*Clang!*

She reared up, whapping the top of her head against the counter. Her vision blurred and tears filled her eyes. She fell onto her butt with a thud. Rubbed the spot and prayed like mad those tiny stars circling her head weren't real.

When the dizziness passed, she gingerly climbed to her feet. She wouldn't yell, she thought, as she carefully climbed the narrow staircase leading from the kitchen to the second floor. She'd approach him calmly. Rationally. Explain why he needed to be more careful.

She knocked on his door. Behind it metal clanged. He grunted in exertion.

It sounded like torture.

"Andrew?" she called, knocking again, making sure to keep her tone friendly and pleasant, as if she wasn't sporting a possible concussion due to his negligence. "Honey, could you open the door?"

Nothing. Her eyes narrowed. She widened them, blinked a few times. No. She wasn't going to get upset. Wasn't going to jump to conclusions. For all she knew, he hadn't heard her.

His next doctor's appointment, though, she would make sure his hearing was checked.

Using the side of her fist, she pounded on the wood. "Andrew!"

No matter how hard she glared at the door, it remained shut.

She tried the handle. Locked. She jiggled it, frustration building. Still locked.

There was only one thing to do, one surefire way to get his attention. She pulled her cell phone from her shorts pocket and sent him a text.

Open the door. Now.

Andrew could, and often did, ignore her. Her insights and opinions, her attempts at civil conversation and questions about his thoughts, his feelings.

But he never ignored his phone.

A moment later, the door opened and her son—her sweaty, disheveled son, the child who used to look up to her with such adoration in his eyes—scowled down at her. Yes, down at her because, thanks to a growth spurt last year, he now towered over her by a good six inches.

He wiped the back of his hand across his forehead. "What?"

Her mouth tightened. Her head pounded. Then again, dealing with her son usually left her with a headache, pondering where she'd gone wrong.

"Take out your earbuds," she said slowly, over-enunciating each word in case he'd suddenly learned how to read lips.

His frown deepened. "What?" he shouted.

She jabbed her fingers at her own ears, mimed pulling something out.

With an eye roll, he pulled the earbud from his left ear. Half his attention was better than nothing at this point. "What do you want?"

Her entire body stiffened. She wouldn't lose her cool. She would not lose her—

Oh, who was she kidding?

"The first thing I want," she said in a mom voice guaranteed to let him know he was messing with no ordinary mortal, "is for you to speak to me civilly and politely."

Another eye roll.

How on earth had her well-behaved, sweet boy

turned into this…this…closing-in-on-six-foot, shaggy-haired, sarcastic, ill-mannered man-child?

And what did she have to do to get the old kid back?

"Really?" she asked, crossing her arms. "No apology?"

He turned, walked to the weight bench in the corner, laid back, and started pumping a barbell up and down. Up and down.

Stubbornness was just one of the new, and many, unattractive traits he'd acquired and perfected since puberty hit him full force.

She stepped into his room and wrinkled her nose at the scents of stale sweat, dirty socks and only God knew what else. Maybe it was a good thing he kept the door shut all the time.

Holding her breath, she crossed to the window, stepping over a pile of clothes she knew darn well had been clean and neatly folded two hours ago. Mainly because she was the one who'd washed, dried and folded them.

She opened the window. "I guess you've had enough of your phone privileges then."

Privileges he'd just gotten back after she'd shut off his account for the past two weeks thanks to his smart mouth.

Some days she felt more like a parole officer than a mother.

He set the weights on the support bar with a clang, his face flushed, either from exertion or irritation.

Heaven forbid he actually be embarrassed or ashamed of his behavior.

"Sorry," he muttered, already moving on to bicep curls, his elbow resting on his knee as he pumped the weight with slow, deliberate movements.

She smiled. A small, forgiving smile, though his apology was halfhearted at best. Forgive and forget—her life motto.

"It's okay," she said, but he kept his head lowered, eyebrows drawn together in concentration, lips moving as he counted his repetitions.

He'd changed, and more than his personality. The raging hormones she blamed for his bad attitude had also broadened his shoulders, deepened his voice. His face, a blending of her features and those of his father's, had lost its roundness. His hair was darker—nearer in shade to her own than the sandy-blond he'd had as a grade-schooler—and badly in need of a trim. He was a tall, darkly handsome, soon-to-be-cut young man.

God save her when the teenage girls started coming around in earnest.

She picked up three clean shirts and carried them to his closet. "Why don't you jump in the shower?" she asked, shaking the wrinkles out of the first shirt before placing it on a hanger. "I'm about to put the burgers on the grill so we can eat in half an hour."

"I'm not hungry," Andrew said, sweat sliding from his hairline down the side of his forehead.

Yuck.

She hung the shirt, then slid a hanger into the next one. "You're always hungry."

It was the main reason her grocery bill surpassed the gas, electric and cable bills combined.

With a shrug she had no idea how to take, he switched hands and started doing reps on that side. "I'm eating at Luke's."

She blinked. Blinked again. Kept the smile on her face. "Why would you eat at Luke's?"

"He invited me over. His family's having a picnic."

"So are we. I made all your favorites. Taco dip and potato salad." Both with light versions of sour cream and mayonnaise instead of nonfat. For him. Because he claimed the nonfat tasted like crap, which wasn't even true. "And brownie sundaes for dessert. With whipped cream. I even got bacon for the burgers."

He snorted. "Turkey bacon. Tastes like shit," he said under his breath.

But loud enough that she could hear.

She pretended otherwise. "*Real* bacon." She'd read it was better to use that instead of turkey bacon, which often had more additives.

He eyed her suspiciously, his blue eyes—his father's eyes—narrowed. "Real burgers? From a cow?"

Full-fat beef burgers? Did he have any idea how bad all that grease was for him? "Turkey burgers. They taste just as good."

"No. They don't." He switched sides again, didn't bother looking at her. "Like I said, I'll eat at Luke's."

"But I want you to eat here. With me."

"No, thanks."

She squeezed the shirt in her hand. She'd made a trip into Pittsburgh yesterday to get all the ingredients she needed to have a special picnic for the two of them. A trip that had taken all afternoon, which meant she'd had to stay up late to finish the laundry and housework, not to mention that profit-and-loss statement for work. She'd spent the morning cooking and baking, wanting nothing more than to enjoy a leisurely, pleasant Labor Day. With her son.

And all he had to say to her was *no, thanks?*

She didn't think so.

"You're eating here," she told him, her tone brooking no argument—though that never stopped him before. "With me. We'll eat, play some board games or maybe watch a movie. It'll be fun."

It would be like it used to between them. Before he started hating her.

His expression darkening, he stood. Let the weight drop to the floor. "I want to go to Luke's."

"I understand that," she said, letting him know she heard him. That she was taking his wants and needs into account. Just as the therapist she and her ex-husband, Todd, had seen for marriage counseling had taught her. Not that it had worked out so well— they'd separated a month after their last session—

but at least she'd learned a few valuable tools for dealing with conflict.

"After we eat," she told Andrew, "you can go over there for an hour or so."

See? That was completely reasonable. Completely rational and, if she did say so herself, a very nice compromise.

"Everyone will be gone by then!"

So much for trying to meet him halfway. No good deed and all that.

"I want to spend the day with you," she said. "We hardly ever see each other."

"That's not my fault. You're the one always working."

"That's a bit of an exaggeration, don't you think? It's not as if I spend every waking moment at the office. I'd say the bigger issue is that we're on opposite schedules." When he wasn't bussing tables at Wix's Diner in the evenings, he was *hanging out* with his new friends.

Andrew tossed up his hands. "But I already told Luke I'd come over."

"I guess the next time you'll wait until you have permission before you make plans. Especially on a holiday."

"It's not Christmas," he grumbled.

He stared at her, all resentment and anger. The dark stubble covering his sharp jaw and chin mocked her, sparse though it was. A visible reminder that he wasn't a little boy anymore.

That he no longer needed her or, it seemed, wanted her around. Ever.

When she looked at him, love swamped her. Threatened to drown her.

And he looked right through her as if he wished she were already gone.

His phone buzzed. He grabbed it from the bed and checked the screen. "It's Luke. He says I can come over whenever I want."

Luke Sapko was a good kid. A nice kid.

Actually, he was nicer—and certainly more polite—to her than her own son was. The thought left her feeling guilty and inadequate.

Maybe she was too hard on Andrew. Maybe she wasn't hard enough. She had no idea. All she knew was it shouldn't be this difficult. It wasn't rocket science, for goodness' sake. By all accounts, humans had been raising children for two hundred thousand years. Surely she could guide her own son into adulthood. She had only two more years to go.

"Come on, Mom," Andrew whined. Funny how he could look like a grown man—or pretty darn close to it—and still act like a five-year-old. "A bunch of the guys are going. I don't want to be the only one stuck at home."

She winced. *Stuck at home.* Guess that summed up how he felt about spending a few hours in her company.

She tried not to take it personally. "Andrew, I—"

"Please?"

The rest of what she intended to say dried in her throat. *Please.* There was a word she didn't hear from him often.

He was working her. Or trying to. She knew it. He probably even knew she knew it. But he didn't care as long as he got his way.

She found herself softening. Luke was the first friend Andrew had made since moving here, and she didn't want her son to miss out on a chance to interact with his peers. Not when he actually seemed excited to be doing something in Shady Grove instead of complaining about how the kids were all small-town hicks, the weather was too cold and the beach too far away.

Maybe this was a step in the right direction. A sign that Andrew was finally settling into his new life.

And maybe she was just sick and tired of arguing with the boy.

"Fine," she said, though she sounded as if it was anything but. Since she'd wrinkled his clean shirt, she tossed it over her shoulder to iron later. "You can go. But I want you home by nine."

His triumphant grin collapsed. "Nine? I'm sixteen."

"I'm well aware of how old you are, Andrew. I did give birth to you. And yes, nine. Tonight's a school night." He'd started his junior year at Shady Grove High last week. "I don't want a repeat of what happened last year with your grades."

"Whatever," he mumbled, as if she hadn't given in to him. As if he couldn't care less that his grades last semester showed a marked lack of effort.

He sent a text, his fingers flying over the buttons.

Used to be a time when she could brush his hair back, make him smile and laugh. Those days were deader than her marriage vows.

"I'm gonna shower," he said, tugging off his sweaty shirt. He dropped it on the floor—two feet from his clothes hamper.

With a grimace, Penelope picked it up by the hem, the fabric pinched between her thumb and forefinger. "Do you have some sort of genetic defect that stops you from putting your clothes where they belong?" she asked, tossing the shirt into the wicker basket. "Or do you leave them scattered all over simply because you know it bothers me?"

"That's just a side benefit." And he rapped out a *da dum dum* on his dresser.

A joke? Wow. Give the kid his way and suddenly he was a comedian. She turned. Her smile froze, her breath locked in her lungs. The safe, secure world she'd worked so hard to build for them shifted, leaving her thoughts tumbling.

*No. Please, God, not again.*

"Andrew," she wheezed on an exhale, and worked to keep her voice calm as she closed the distance between them. Focused on clearing her expression. No sense worrying him. Not when she wasn't sure what was going on. "What happened to your back?"

He glanced over his shoulder. "What do you mean?"

"You…you have a bruise." Clearing her throat, she lightly touched his lower back, to the right of his spine. "Here."

Turning to the mirror, he twisted so he could see what she was talking about. He shrugged. "I must've bumped into something."

"I think you'd remember bumping into something hard enough to leave that big of a mark." It was at least the size of her fist, the center a dark purple, the outer edges bleeding into yellow. "Do you…do you have any other bruises?"

Another shrug. "Not that I know of."

But he had this one. One he'd seemingly been unaware of. Fear rose in her throat, threatening to choke her. "Do your joints hurt? Have you noticed being more tired lately? Have you been getting headaches?"

He rolled his eyes. "No, no and yes. Right now. A big one."

"Not funny," she murmured. This was serious. Couldn't he see that? Spinning him around, she searched his body for more bruises. His appetite was still strong and he'd put on weight, not lost it. She reached up to check the lymph nodes in his neck.

He jerked away. "Jesus! Knock it off. I'm not sick again."

"I know you're not," she said quickly, as if her words alone could make the statement fact. But she'd already learned the hard way that all the wishing, hoping and praying in the world couldn't change what was. She tried to smile. "But I'll make an appointment with Dr. Franklin tomorrow to—"

"I'm not going to the doctor." He stabbed his fingers through his hair, making the strands stand on end. "Look, the truth is, I didn't bump into something. I got it playing dodgeball in gym the other day."

Relief made her knees weak. Her head light. He wasn't sick. The leukemia hadn't come back.

Thank God.

But he had been hurt. Could have been injured even worse. What if he'd been hit in the head and gotten a concussion?

"No school district should be allowing a game like that to be played in gym class," she said, her fury and indignation growing. "First thing in the morning I'm going to call the school—"

"That's why I didn't want to tell you! I knew you'd freak out about it and it's nothing. It doesn't even hurt. And the last thing I need is you making it into some big deal." He yanked open a drawer, grabbed a pair of socks and underwear, then shoved it closed hard enough to shake the dresser. "It's a bruise. Not the end of the world. Not cancer. So don't even think about calling and bitching out the gym teacher, because I'm the one who'll have to take a bunch of shit if you do!"

He stormed out of the room, across the hall and

into the bathroom. Slammed the door shut as if to punctuate his little tantrum.

She hunched her shoulders. Bit her lower lip. A moment later, the shower started.

He didn't understand that she was simply doing her job as his mother. He resented everything she did for him. The healthy food she prepared, the doctor appointments she dragged him to, the tests and blood work. Even a simple question about how he was feeling set him off.

She worked so hard to keep him safe. Healthy.

And all it did was make him mad. But she was the one who suffered. She had to live with him, had to deal with him, day in and day out. His choices, actions and rotten, disrespectful, ungrateful attitude were her problems.

She just prayed they weren't her fault.

## CHAPTER TWO

"You GOING TO lie there all day?" James Montesano asked, tossing the basketball from one hand to the other.

Rolling onto his back, Leo Montesano squinted at the people peering down at him, their heads shifting as if they'd been detached from their bodies. Huh. Floating heads. That would make a great name for a rock-and-roll band.

James kept up with the ball tossing. Back and forth. Back and forth.

It drove Leo nuts.

He wanted to tell his brother to knock it the hell off, but the breath had left his lungs when he'd done his face-plant, and he couldn't speak.

Next to James, their brother, Eddie, wiped his forehead with the hem of his T-shirt, dislodging the frayed brim of his black Pittsburgh Pirates baseball cap. On Leo's other side, their younger sister, Maddie, smirked.

All three had dark hair, heavy eyebrows and deep, end-of-summer tans—traits Leo shared. About the only resemblances between him and his family.

Because if the situation had been reversed and one of them were flat on their back, he'd be offering a helping hand.

They just waited for him to get his own ass up off the ground.

You'd think there would be a time or two when the odds were even among the Montesano siblings, but more often than not it was three against one.

Them against him, usually.

That was what he got for following his own path, being his own person. Freedom, yes. But also a lot of grief.

"Well?" James asked, as if Leo's being bruised and sporting a possible head injury was ruining his entire day.

Leo squeezed his eyes shut, but as soon as he did, flashes of memory from last night's accident scene bombarded him and he opened them again. At least when he did, everyone's heads stayed put. And the images disappeared.

He shot James the middle finger.

"Guess he'll live," Eddie said before walking away.

James gave the ball extra spin as it moved from hand to hand, his dark eyes hidden behind a pair of aviators. "Too bad. I was hoping we could find a sub for you."

"Your concern is touching," Leo muttered as he shifted into a sitting position, the blacktop burning the palms of his hands, the bright sun warming his bare shoulders. He and James were both shirtless—no big deal when it came to playing a game of shirts versus skins, but not so great if you were pushed to the freaking pavement. His knees and palms—which had taken the brunt of his weight when he'd gone down—were scraped and stinging. He rubbed his hands against the sides of his shorts and glared at his brother. "Really. Warms a man's heart to know his family cares so deeply for his well-being."

"You want concern? Stop trying to turn a fun pickup game among family and friends into a grudge match."

"Hey, don't blame me. I'm the innocent victim here." He jabbed a thumb in Maddie's direction. "She's the one who tripped me."

"I'm not sure what you're accusing me of," Maddie said with a sniff and a lift of her chin, all affronted and lying through her teeth. "I was merely setting a screen."

Eyes narrowing, Leo got to his feet. "You're not supposed to move when you set a screen. Or stick your foot out."

She lifted a shoulder and sent him a small, evil grin. "Oops."

"You could at least try to pretend it was an accident and not a blatant act of aggression."

James's eyebrows rose above his sunglasses. "*Blatant act of aggression?* What have we told you about watching CNN? It's only for grown-ups."

Leo snatched the ball from James, and considered—

briefly and with much relish—shoving it down his brother's throat. Instead, he took three steps and heaved it over the ball hoop into the yard.

"I'll get it!" called Max, Eddie's eight-year-old son, scrambling after it.

Leo lifted a hand but couldn't risk having his attention diverted. Not when Maddie, wearing a pair of cutoffs and a red Montesano Construction T-shirt, was sauntering closer and closer to him, her stride aggressive, her long dark ponytail swinging in agitation.

She was moody, unpredictable and capable of turning on a man at a moment's notice.

"An accident?" she repeated, her tone cold, her shoulders rigid. "Like you 'accidentally'—" she made air quotes, her brown eyes flashing "—rammed your elbow into Neil's stomach when he went in for that layup?"

Now it was Leo's turn to grin, although he was pretty sure his was way more charming and, yeah, even more smug than hers had been. "Incidental contact."

"That is such bull."

"I was guarding my man. A little jostling for position is part of the game."

He didn't know what she was bitching about. Her boyfriend—or whatever title she preferred to give Neil Pettit—played in the NHL. He got pushed, rammed into and hit for a living. Now he couldn't handle someone playing tough defense on him in a friendly game of three-on-three?

Was it any wonder Leo couldn't stand the arrogant bastard?

"How about we save this discussion for another time?" James asked in his calm, big-brother-to-the-rescue way. "Let's finish the game before it's called on account of darkness."

Leo broadened his smile, knowing it would irritate the hell out of his baby sister. "Truce?"

He held out his hand. She looked as if she'd rather bite it off at the wrist and slap him with it a few times than shake it. "Do you really think I'm dumb enough to buy that?"

"That hurts." He slung his arm around her shoulders. "I'm nothing if not sincere—"

"A sincere, and sweaty, pain in the ass," she said, shoving his arm off.

He put it right back on her shoulders. Squeezed her to his side.

"And," he continued, having learned early on it was best to ignore much of what his sister said, "I have nothing but the highest regard for you and your intelligence. You're one of the brightest people I know."

All true. But her taste in men sucked.

This time she ducked out from under his arm and stepped back. "Save it. I'm not one of your brainless bimbos—"

*"Bimbos?"* He laughed, hoping it didn't sound as forced as it felt. "Did we time-travel back to 1952?"

"Yes, bimbos. Who hang on every word you say, simpering and sighing and batting their lashes."

"I got it!" Max called, his round face red, his breathing heavy as he ran to the edge of the driveway, the ball clutched to his chest. "I got it, Uncle Leo!"

Leo held his hands out and neatly caught Max's wobbly pass. "Thanks, bud." He spun the ball on the tip of his forefinger. Winked at Maddie. "Can I help it if women think I'm amazingly witty and incredibly charming?"

"That's only because they don't know you," she grumbled before walking to Neil and accepting the bottle of water he held out to her.

Leo let his smile slip. He bounced the ball twice—hard—then forced himself to tuck it against his side instead of winging it through the air again. Made sure his movements were easy and casual as he grabbed his own water and drank deeply.

He wished it were a beer. Or better yet, the slow, smooth burn of a Jameson. After the night he'd had, he could use a drink. But he had to report to work in a few hours.

And he was afraid once he started drinking, he might not stop. At least not until he had a decent buzz, one that blurred his thoughts and dimmed his memory. Until he could no longer remember the pain in Samantha Coles's eyes. Could no longer hear her voice pleading for him to help her.

His fingers tightened on the bottle, the sound of crushing plastic loud to his ears. He finished the water and tossed it aside. Pushed all thoughts of last night from his head.

A drop of sweat slid from his hairline and down his temple before disappearing behind his ear. He wiped his forearm across his brow. The bright, late-afternoon sun burned the tip of his nose. It was hotter than usual for Labor Day in southwestern Pennsylvania, and his parents' picnic was in full swing.

Family, friends, neighbors, coworkers and even a few college coeds—his mother's classmates in her pursuit of finishing her degree—littered the wide, open yard, and spilled out of the two-story house and onto the large deck. The air smelled of grilled steaks and burgers. The muted sounds of Foreigner's "Head Games" could be heard under all the conversation. The occasional good-natured cheer and burst of laughter rose from the group playing volleyball in the side yard.

Another successful party. Even though she was now a full-time student, having enrolled in Seton Hill University in Pittsburgh last year, Rose Montesano still found the time to entertain the masses.

Which was why Leo went to more than his fair share of gatherings, picnics and mandatory Sunday dinners. Having a large family who all lived in the same town had its share of perks—free meals being at the top of that list.

Across the driveway, Maddie and Neil stood so close together, you couldn't get a breath between them. She rose onto her toes and said something in Neil's ear. He grinned at her, then slid his hand to settle on her ass.

Leo's right eye twitched. Having family close by also had more than a few drawbacks.

Such as watching your baby sister get back together with the loser who had broken her heart.

"Are we playing ball or what?" he called.

Facing him, Maddie readjusted her ponytail. "Just waiting on you, Princess."

They resumed play, Maddie, Neil and Eddie against Leo, James and Ryan Pyatt, one of Montesano Construction's employees. After fifteen minutes of hard play, the score was tied, twenty all. Whoever made the next basket would win the game. Maddie dribbled, looking for an open player while James guarded her.

"Switch, switch," Leo told Ryan when Neil set a screen on the kid.

Ryan veered left and blocked Eddie while Leo spun right to guard Neil. They fought for position under the basket, pushing, shoving and bumping.

Maddie passed the ball to Eddie, who shot. It bounced off the rim. Leo went up for the rebound, shoulder to shoulder with Neil. He had a few inches more in height, but Neil had the advantage of being a professional athlete. He came down with the ball and pivoted and Leo knew he was going up for the shot.

The restlessness, the edge of frustration and anger Leo had tried to keep contained since last night built, bigger and bigger, until he was afraid he was going to explode with it. His muscles tensed, his body shook. He wasn't going to lose. Not today.

Not to Neil.

Leo leaped up and with a low growl, spiked the ball out of Neil's hands.

That he almost took Neil's head off in the process was, to Leo's mind, merely a bonus.

Breathing hard, Leo sent the son of a bitch a cocky grin. "You should stick to hockey."

As he walked past him, he bumped into Neil's shoulder with enough force to knock him back a step.

Leo grabbed the ball, then jogged over to the edge of the driveway. He bounced the ball at Maddie. "Check."

"What the hell is your problem?" she asked, which was a neat trick seeing as how her lips barely moved.

"No problem. Just playing the game."

"That how you want it to be?" She gave a sharp nod, then got into a crouch, her mouth set. "Fine. Don't say you didn't ask for it."

And she shoved the ball into his stomach.

She'd always had a mean streak.

Eyes on her—because despite popular opinion, he wasn't a complete idiot—he dribbled, keeping the ball low to the ground, his knees bent. James and Ryan worked to get open, James lifting his hand.

Maddie swiped at the ball, but Leo sidestepped. She was fast, he'd give her that. What she lacked in finesse and actual talent, she more than made up for in grit, determination and aggression.

They'd taught her well.

He faked left, then went right. Maddie stuck to him like a second skin, bumping and shoving as he made his way to the basket. He went in for the layup. Maddie jumped to block him.

And punched him in the jaw.

His head jerked back. His teeth snapped together and he landed awkwardly on the side of his foot. He stumbled, then caught his balance, juggled the ball, but it was too late. Maddie snatched it and sent Neil a beautiful bounce pass as he ran to the basket.

The show-off dunked it.

Bastard.

"Foul!" Leo waved his arms as if to erase the point from the imaginary scoreboard. "No basket. That was a foul."

Maddie blinked at him innocently, which he didn't buy for a minute. "Was it?" She made a show of looking around the driveway. "Funny, but I don't see a ref here. And I certainly didn't hear any whistle so I guess you're wrong—which, as you know, is one of my very favorite things to say to any of my brothers, but right now I'm taking extreme pleasure in saying it to you in particular." She patted his cheek. "You lost. Deal with it."

He edged closer. She, of course, wasn't the least bit intimidated. "You punched me."

"I wouldn't call that a punch," James said as if he had the right to stick his fat nose into their conversation. He turned to Maddie. "If you're going to jab, keep your elbow in. And don't tuck your thumb under your fingers or you'll break it."

Something they'd told her at least a hundred times. She was just too stubborn to listen to them.

She stretched and bent her fingers. Shook out her hand. "Everyone's a critic. Should I try again? I promise to have better form this time."

Leo gingerly touched the tip of his tongue to the cut on the side of his mouth. Tasted blood. "You deserve a broken thumb for that sucker punch."

She wrinkled her nose in faux concern. "Looks like it hurts. A lot."

"It does."

"Great. Then my job here is done. Now maybe you'll stop being such an ass."

"I doubt that," James murmured.

Leo bit back a snarl and kept his focus on Maddie. "If I need stitches, I'm going to be pissed."

"It's a scratch. Suck it up. Although it would be a real shame, messing up that pretty, pretty face with an unsightly scar." She edged closer and lowered her voice. "But nothing less than what you deserve for trying to antagonize my boyfriend all the freaking time."

"Just because you've forgotten what he did, how he treated you, doesn't mean I have."

"Yes, I've completely lost any and all memories from the past thirteen years," she said drily. "Look, Neil and I both made mistakes. It's not forgetting. It's forgiveness."

He couldn't believe someone as smart and self-assured as Maddie was willing to put herself in the same situation she'd been in at sixteen. Loving Neil Pettit. Trusting him to be there for her and Breanne, their twelve-year-old daughter.

"Maybe I'm not in a forgiving mood," Leo said.

"You don't have to be. Neil didn't ask for your forgiveness. And if you don't stop acting like such a jerk, Neil, Bree and I will be forced to skip these family get-togethers."

"Blackmail, Maddie? That's beneath you."

She nodded, not looking the least bit guilty. "And you acting like some overprotective brother is getting old. It's awkward and irritating to listen to your snide remarks and put-downs to Neil every time we get together. Don't think Bree hasn't noticed, too. Or that it doesn't bother her."

Leo's shoulders wanted to hunch so he jerked them back. But he couldn't stop himself from glancing toward the deck, the last place he'd seen Bree. She was still there, her chubby legs curled under her as she read a book, the sun glinting off her short cap of dark hair.

Though many, many women had fallen hard for him, there were only three he could truly say he'd ever loved. His mother and his sister were near the top of that list. But the number-one spot was held by the only female who'd ever had him wrapped around her little finger.

His niece, Breanne.

Ever since he'd held her as a red, squalling newborn, he'd been hooked. He'd been eighteen and she'd been his first in many ways—first baby he'd ever held. First bottle-feeding and diaper change. First time losing his heart.

He'd do anything for her.

Too bad she didn't need him any longer. She had her father back in her life.

For now.

"Do you really think Neil's going to stay this time?" Leo asked harshly. "Just because he's stuck it out this long doesn't mean he won't change his mind or take off again."

It had been over a year since Neil and Maddie had reconciled, but nothing had really changed. Neil still played professional hockey. Sure, he'd recently been traded to the Blue Jackets, but they were based in Columbus—a three-hour drive from Shady Grove.

"I know he's going to stick," Maddie said.

Leo shook his head sadly. "I feel sorry for you for believing that."

Her eyes got all squinty. Never a good sign. Swear to God, if she hit him again, he was dumping her crazy ass in the pool. Luckily, she kept her hands at her sides.

"I trust him and what we have," she said. "Neil and I are together and we're going to stay together so I suggest you grow up and get over this stupid, adolescent rivalry or whatever it is you have with him. Or be prepared to lose me and Bree."

She stomped off, headed directly to Neil and into his arms. He kissed the top of her head.

Leo wanted to punch something himself.

"He abandons her and Bree," Leo muttered when James joined him, "and I'm the one she socks in the jaw?"

"Quit whining," James said. "It's a scratch."

Leo jabbed a finger at his injury. "Does this look like a scratch?"

"Yes. Rub some dirt on it and we'll start another game. Get some of our pride back."

"Easy for you to say." Leo carefully ran his tongue over his bottom lip, wincing when he reached the gash at the corner. He bent and retrieved his T-shirt from the grass. "You're not the one bleeding."

"You deserved it."

Leo snagged James's water bottle and took a drink. Swished it around his mouth while Eddie joined them.

Leo spat onto the grass. "Deserved to be viciously

attacked?" Eddie rolled his eyes. Leo narrowed his own. "You have something to say?"

"It was a foul," Eddie said, like some freaking Zen master brushing aside Leo's dark scowl and low growl with his own calm expression and quiet tone. "Not a mugging."

Leo's free hand fisted. "Who asked you?"

"What are you?" James muttered. "Thirteen?"

Eddie's mouth turned down, his shoulders rigid. Maybe not so Zen, after all. "You asked, you idiot."

Stepping between them as he had so many times in their lives, James made a tsking sound. "Name calling." He faced Eddie, tossed him the ball. "Just walk away. You know this isn't about you."

"Maybe not," Eddie said, "but he's obviously jonesing for an ass-kicking. I'm happy to oblige."

Leo shifted to the left, but so did James. He peered around James's shoulder. "You want to go, Eddie?"

"That really something you want to do in front of Max and Cassidy?" James asked Eddie.

Eddie glanced at Max, who sat cross-legged on the grass raptly watching the unfolding scene, one small, grubby hand petting Zoe, James's German shepherd/husky mix, the other holding a dripping red Popsicle.

"Cass is in the pool with Harper," Eddie said, the latter being his girlfriend, Cassidy her three-year-old daughter. He spoke in his usual irritatingly slow way, as if thinking through each word before letting it out of his mouth. "And I could always send Max into the house for a few minutes."

Max scrambled to his knees, and the action had Zoe jumping to her feet as well. "You always send me somewhere when you fight with Uncle Leo. Why can't I watch?"

"Because you'll lose respect for your uncle when you see him cry."

Leo stepped forward. "We'll see who ends up crying."

Though he was honest enough with himself to admit there was a chance it would be him. Eddie was built like a tank, had fists like bricks, and could take a sock to the nose and keep coming at you.

Without so much as a glance Leo's way, James slapped the back of his hand on Leo's chest, stopping him in his tracks. "I'll talk to him," he said to Eddie. "See what bug is up his butt."

Frowning, Leo glanced at Max. "Did I suddenly turn invisible?"

Wide-eyed, his dark hair in a newly minted Mohawk, his mouth stained red, the boy shook his head. "I can still see you."

With one of his laconic shrugs, Eddie turned and walked away.

Leo sneered. "Wuss."

James sighed, and before Leo could evade, wrapped his arm around Leo's neck and squeezed. Hard. "Let's chat."

Leo struggled, but it was no use. James may have

been the poster boy for mild-mannered good guy, but he knew how to put a headlock on someone and make it stick.

"James," their mother said in the exasperated tone she'd perfected raising four children—Leo figured it was the teen years that had done her in, "what are you doing?"

James turned, dragging Leo along. Leo raised his head as much as possible to see Rose staring at them from her vantage point on the deck, her hand shielding her eyes from the sun. A small crowd had gathered around her, including James's wife, Sadie; Sadie's sister, Charlotte Ellison; and Breanne.

"Just going to have a heart-to-heart with Leo," James said, sounding way too cheerful for the situation.

Then again, if their positions were reversed, Leo would be feeling pretty damned chipper himself.

"You," Leo spat out as James sent their audience a jaunty wave, "are a dead man."

James whirled them around, forcing Leo to scramble for balance or wind up on his knees. With his free hand, James gave Leo a noogie. "Actually, I've never felt more alive."

As if to prove it, he started whistling and didn't stop until they turned the corner behind the garage.

Leo shoved James, stumbling when his brother's arm suddenly loosened. "What the hell is your problem?"

"My problem? You're the one going all rogue on

the basketball court. Far as I can tell, I just saved you from getting your fat head beat in."

"I can handle Eddie."

"I wasn't talking about Eddie."

"Neil won't do anything." That was the problem. No matter how much Leo baited the other man, he never lost control.

"Neil's not the one I was talking about, either. Maddie's pretty pissed at you."

Leo twisted the lid onto his empty water bottle. Untwisted it. "She'll get over it."

She couldn't stay mad at him. No one, especially not anyone female, ever could.

"You've been acting weird ever since you got here," James said, watching Leo carefully. "What's going on?"

He began to pace, but couldn't rid himself of the edginess riding him like some howling monkey. "Nothing's going on."

Christ, couldn't a guy have an off day? Just because he wasn't all charm and humor didn't mean something was wrong.

"Charlotte was telling me and Sadie about that car accident on Langmaid Lane last night. The one involving those two college girls."

Leo's stomach pitched. The water he drank threatened to come back up. His brother's tone was neutral, his expression clear, as if they were discussing something as irrelevant as the Steelers' chances of making the playoffs this year.

"She mentioned how upset she was, how upset everyone in the E.R. was that they lost the driver."

A cold sweat formed between Leo's shoulder blades. He pulled his shirt on, but still felt chilled. Sick with unnamed emotion. With regret. "Char's an E.R. nurse. She understands they sometimes lose a patient."

As a firefighter and EMT, Leo knew that as well.

But knowing it sure as hell didn't make it any easier to accept.

"She said you were at the scene of the accident," James continued, drilling for information, trying to get inside Leo's head, inside his thoughts. Wanting Leo to spill his guts—as if that would do any of them any good. "First one there, actually. And you stayed with the victim the entire time."

Leo's hands shook. He curled his fingers, once again hearing the crackle of plastic from the water bottle while his nails dug into his other palm until he felt the bite of pain. *Victim.* That's all she was to James. All she'd be to most people who would read about the single-car accident in tomorrow's edition of the *Shady Grove Times.* A faceless victim. A tragedy.

"She had a name," Leo managed to say, his voice hoarse. He cleared his throat. "Sam. Her name was Sam."

Samantha Coles. She'd been young, barely twenty-two, her cheeks still holding the softness of youth. When he and his partner had arrived on scene, she'd been trapped, the front of her crumpled car wedging her between the steering wheel and her seat. Leo had assessed her injuries, and kept her calm while the rest of the team had worked to free her.

Blood had stained her clothes, her brown hair. Her face had been bruised, her body cut and broken. But her green eyes had been clear. Through it all—the horrible noise and her own pain—she'd kept calm.

Had trusted him to help her. Had believed him when he'd said she'd be okay. That he'd save her.

"I wasn't with her the entire time," he continued, his voice strained, though he fought to sound casual. "Once we brought her to the hospital, the E.R. staff took over."

"Charlotte also mentioned that when you heard Sam hadn't made it, you punched the wall."

Leo opened and closed his fist. It still ached.

There had been no censure in James's tone, no judgment. Only compassion and pity.

And that was even worse.

"You ever see someone die?" Leo asked quietly, knowing the answer before James shook his head. "I have. More than a few. It gets to you sometimes, but you deal with it. Compartmentalize it and move on to the next case, the next person who needs help."

It was what he did, what he lived for. It was what made him different from his siblings—carpenters, all three. What made him who he was.

James clapped a hand on Leo's shoulder. "Want to talk about it?"

Hell, no. What good would talking do? It wouldn't turn back time so that they reached Sam and her friend earlier. Wouldn't stop Sam from checking her phone or taking that curve too fast. Wouldn't bring her back to life.

No, rehashing it wouldn't do anyone any good. Least of all Leo.

"Can't," Leo said, stepping back so James's hand fell to his side. "I need to get home and grab a shower before I go to the station. Tell Mom and Dad I had to leave for work, would you?"

Without waiting for James's response, Leo walked away, kept his stride unhurried and relaxed, though he wanted to run, wanted to escape as quickly as he could before James tried more psychobabble crap. Or worse, dragged a few family members in on his attempt to get Leo to open up to them, tell them all his thoughts and feelings.

A young woman had died last night. He'd witnessed it. How the hell did they think he felt?

He passed Maddie's truck and pulled his keys from the front pocket of his cargo shorts. The only reason he'd even come to the picnic was because he hadn't wanted to be stuck at his place alone with his thoughts and memories. He'd figured being surrounded by people and conversation, laughter and food, would help settle the unease rolling through him, the tension, the feeling that, while he'd done all he could for Samantha, he should have found a way to do more.

He slid behind the wheel of his car, turned on the ignition. And wished he'd stayed home.

WHEN ANDREW BOUNDED down the stairs, Penelope was sitting at the dining-room table. His hair was still damp and curling at the ends, a tiny piece of toilet paper stuck to a cut on his chin. He'd changed into loose gray shorts and one of the clean T-shirts she'd hung in his closet, his favorite sweatshirt slung over his shoulder.

"It's curious to me," she said, her voice sounding surprisingly loud to her own ears, "how anxious you were to leave and yet it took you over an hour and a half to get ready."

He gave her one of his ill-mannered shrugs. "Car keys."

Raising her eyebrows, Penelope took off her reading glasses. "Is that a declarative comment? Or an inquiry into the keys' whereabouts?"

"Can't you talk like a normal person instead of a librarian? *Curious. Anxious.* And no one says *declarative.* Or *inquiry.*" He frowned and scratched his cheek. "Except for judges and lawyers and stuff."

"Thank you for that." She picked up her wineglass only to discover it was empty. Well, that would just not do. She leaned forward, the edge of the table digging into her sternum, the tips of her fingers grazing the bottle of chardonnay. Grunting softly, she stretched and snagged the bottle by its neck. Dragged it toward her, then waved it in her son's general direction. "It is so enjoyable to be critiqued on my vocabulary by a child who calls everyone *dude*— including his mother—and uses the word *duh* as an answer to most questions, as well as a pithy response to any conversation someone beyond the age of twenty might attempt to have with him. Next you can educate me on the finer points of eye-rolling, sarcastic comebacks and a general disrespect for authority. It'll be *such* a good time."

He went still. Studied her. "You're acting weird," he finally said. "I mean, you know, more than usual."

Lovely.

She started to roll her eyes, but then realized she couldn't very well lecture him on the disrespectful gesture if she did it herself, so she pretended to find the ceiling extremely fascinating.

"I'm fine," she said, feeling no desire to assure him when, in all honesty, he didn't sound worried, but more…put out. Then again, when was he ever concerned about her feelings?

She poured wine into her glass, the bottle significantly lighter than when she'd opened it not thirty minutes ago. How had that happened? She'd only had a glass…or had it been two? She gave an inner shrug. And took a healthy sip.

Having lost her appetite knowing she'd be dining alone, she'd opted to catch up on some of the work she'd brought home. Unfortunately, she hadn't been able to concentrate, not with her out-of-control emotions clouding her thoughts. Wine was a surprisingly effective remedy for what ailed her.

Even if the numbers on the laptop screen were now a bit blurry.

It was an interesting discovery, and one she could have made years earlier had she ever allowed herself to have more than one glass of the wonderful stuff.

"Mom!"

She jumped and, horror of horrors, had wine sloshing over the edge of the glass and onto her hand. She sucked it from her fingers. "Why are you yelling?"

Andrew gaped at her as if she were the one who'd lost her ever-loving mind. "Because I've asked you the same question twice and you haven't answered me."

She blinked at him. Why was he so upset? Teenagers. Lord only knew what got into their heads sometimes. "I already told you, I'm fine."

Better than fine. She actually felt…good. Light and floaty and sort of free. As if all her worries had simply drifted away. Although oddly enough, for all her floaty feelings, her eyelids were becoming heavy. It was increasingly difficult to keep them open.

Andrew's narrow gaze flicked from her, to the glass, to the bottle. "Are you…are you drunk?"

She whipped her head around and leaped to her feet, but had to grab the table so she didn't topple over. Just a rush of dizziness from standing too quickly, she assured herself. "Of course not. I do not get drunk. I have never been drunk. Not once in my life."

And why she was speaking so slowly and carefully, she had no idea.

Andrew smirked—oh, how she hated it when the boy smirked. "Whatever."

She bristled and straightened, lifting her hands from the table as if to prove to both of them she was not only capable of maintaining her balance, but sober enough to do so. "Andrew, you know how I feel about drinking to excess."

"I know how you feel about everything. Every. Damn. Thing."

What was wrong with that? She made her expectations clear, let him know her thoughts, views and opinions on the matters that were important. Her views on drinking—especially underage drinking—smoking, drug use and sex may be conservative, but there was nothing wrong with making good, smart, responsible choices and respecting your body.

"Why all this concern about my sobriety?" A thought occurred to her. "Will there be drinking at this picnic?"

"You caught me," he said as he flipped his sweatshirt from one shoulder to the other. "I'm just trying to divert attention from the fact that Luke's mom bought a keg so her son and all his friends can get wasted. Too bad she drew the line at hiring those strippers we asked for."

"The scary part is I'm not entirely sure you're joking."

His answer to that was, yes, one of his impressive eye rolls. "Keys?"

"On the hook by the door." Where they always were. Well, where she always put them. He, on the other hand, seemed to have a hard time remembering to hang them up after using her car. One time she even found them in the freezer.

She prayed he remembered to brush his teeth every day. No need to worry about him using deodorant, though. Or aftershave. The child splashed the potent stuff on like it was some sort of muscle-building, beard-growing, girl-catching elixir.

The room spun. Which was incredibly strange as she hadn't actually moved. Maybe wine on an empty stomach hadn't been the best idea. Lesson learned.

She'd always excelled at learning her lessons. And not making the same mistakes twice.

While Andrew texted someone, she pulled the raw turkey burgers from the fridge, then crossed to the double doors and stepped out onto the patio. Inhaled the warm air. There. That helped. A little food, a little fresh air and her head would clear right up.

She set down the plate, then knelt and turned on the gas to the grill.

"Bye," Andrew said, stepping outside.

"Hold it." She straightened—too fast, it turned out, as the world pitched and spun. "Were you born in a barn?"

"Seeing as how you were there, you'd know that better than me."

"Ha-ha. Close the door."

While he did, she shut her eyes for a moment, got her bearings. "I don't recall you asking for permission to take the car."

"I figured you wouldn't mind," he said, jiggling the keys, "since you're not going anywhere."

Irritation pricked her, dimming some of her previous glow. She couldn't fault his logic—after all, she had nowhere to go. But did he have to rub it in? Her foot began tapping in agitation as if of its own accord. She wasn't jealous of him. That would be ridiculous. She was thrilled beyond measure he'd made friends. That he didn't have her shyness, her awkwardness around others. And it wasn't as if she was a complete social pariah. There were a few women in the office she chatted with. Sometimes.

When they initiated the conversation.

"I'm not going anywhere, but seeing as how it's my car, it'd be nice if you asked first."

She winced. That had sounded close to…well… whiny was the only way to describe it. She pulled her shoulders back. She wasn't a whiner. She was a doer.

A doer with absolutely no social life whatsoever. How wonderful.

Andrew shifted, impatient to be gone. "Can I take the car?"

She wanted to say no, but that would be petty. Besides, if he didn't drive himself, she'd have to take him. And she was seriously considering a third glass of wine, since what she'd had already was making her feel…not quite happy…but certainly no worse for the wear. "I suppose."

He brushed past her. "See ya."

"At nine," she reminded him, since he'd had a hard time lately remembering when his curfew was. He didn't even acknowledge she'd spoken, just descended the two wooden stairs and crossed to her car in the driveway. He climbed in, buckled up, then, with the sound of the radio thumping much louder than was necessary, he carefully backed into the road.

"You're welcome," she muttered. So glad to see he appreciated her letting him go to Luke's, use her car and avoid her company for yet another day.

Didn't matter, she assured herself. She was fine on her own. She'd have a nice dinner, catch up on her work and maybe even finish the bottle of wine. Why not? Everyone else seemed perfectly content to indulge in bad behavior once in a while.

Maybe it was time she joined the party.

Besides, it wasn't as if she had to worry about giving her teenager the wrong impression since the child preferred to spend his time anywhere and with anyone but her.

Frowning, feeling more than a little sorry for herself, she jabbed at the grill's ignition button, though something in the back of her mind told her not to.

Too late. There was a loud boom and the lid flew open as a wall of flame engulfed her.

# CHAPTER THREE

"I THOUGHT YOU were dead."

With a groan she fervently hoped wasn't audible, Penelope eased onto one of the two high-backed stools at her wide kitchen island. "So you said," she murmured. "Several times."

More like twenty, but who was counting?

Well, yes, *she* was counting, but she doubted her young guest was.

"No," Gracie Weaver said somberly, shutting the door to the deck. The girl had gone out to make sure the grill was off. "I mean I seriously thought you were dead. Really, completely dead."

Penelope frowned, but her face felt sunburned and any movement or twitch hurt so she schooled her expression. "Is it possible to be sort of dead?"

She winced—another painful moment—and wished she could see her words floating in the air so she could grab them back before they reached Gracie's ears. The last thing she wanted was to encourage her neighbor's sixteen-year-old daughter to continue this inane conversation.

Maybe if she pretended to die—really and completely—the teen would go on her way.

"Oh, it's very possible." Gracie opened and shut several cabinet doors, her movements comfortable, as if she went through a stranger's cupboards on a daily basis. "I once read an article in *Reader's Digest* or *National Geographic* or something about this man who was in a coma for two months, but, get this—" she stood on her toes, the heels of her bright pink flip-flops lifting from the ground as she reached for a glass on an upper shelf "—he could hear everything going on around him. His brain was completely working the entire time. Can you imagine, being trapped in your own body, your mind working, but being unable to get your body to do what it wanted? Not being able to escape?"

Penelope glanced wistfully at the door. "I think I have a pretty good idea."

Gracie filled the glass at the sink and carried it over to Penelope. "Here. You should drink something so you don't go into shock or get dehydrated."

"I'm not sure that's how it works." But to appease—and hopefully silence—the girl, Penelope took a small sip of water, the trembling of her hand barely noticeable.

She still wasn't sure what had happened. One minute she'd been having a nice little alcohol-induced pity-fest and the next, she'd been flat on her back, the scents of propane and singed hair filling her nostrils. Her head had spun, her face stung and a low, annoying thrum filled her ears. But it hadn't been all bad. She was, for the most part, unharmed. And lying on the sun-warmed deck, blinking at the puffy white clouds drifting across the sky, her thoughts still pleasantly blurred by that last glass of wine, had been sort of calming. Peaceful.

Until Gracie arrived.

By then, Penelope had struggled to a sitting position and had only been catching her breath, getting her bearings. But Gracie had insisted on helping Penelope get inside—though Penelope took great pride in standing on her own two feet, on making her own way.

Now her little savior wouldn't leave her alone. And Penelope, never any good at asking for what she wanted, had no idea how to get rid of her.

"I really am fine. I appreciate you checking on me," she added in case she'd come across as ungrateful. Or worse, rude. "I'm sure you have better things to do today than worry about me."

*Worry. Annoy.* Why quibble?

"Not really. Besides, you shouldn't be left alone. You might have a concussion. Or internal injuries."

"I don't."

"But you could," Gracie said, studying her with a gaze that was way too direct, way too adult for someone so young. It was unnerving. "And you wouldn't even know until you fell unconscious or started coughing up blood or something."

"That's a disturb—"

"Are you hungry?" Gracie asked. "I could make you something to eat."

"I'm—"

"That's probably stupid, huh? I mean, you just had a near-death experience—"

"I wouldn't say I was anywhere near—"

"The last thing you want is a snack, right? Then again, you might want to celebrate being alive and I noticed you have brownies—"

"Really, I don't—"

"—and what better way to celebrate still being among the living than with some chocolate?"

Penelope wanted to cover her ears and beg Gracie to be quiet, just for a moment, but the determined and talkative girl walked over to the pan next to the stove.

Humming the same Fray song Penelope had danced to earlier, Gracie brought the brownies to the island, then once again invaded Penelope's privacy by searching through several kitchen drawers.

Penelope slumped. She surrendered. A woman had only so much fight in her, and she'd used up her stores with her son.

Her home was being overrun by a five-foot-two-inch wisp of a girl in cuffed jean shorts and a floaty white peasant top. A thick floral headband held back Gracie's light brown hair, the riotous curls reaching her waist.

Penelope couldn't imagine the time and effort needed to take care of that much hair. Her father believed long hair was nothing more than vanity. Her mother—whose own hair was still kept in the same short, layered style she'd worn since her college graduation in 1970—thought it was too much work.

Touching the ends of her chin-length hair, Penelope set her elbow on the counter. Even after she'd been on her own, independent in every possible way, she'd never let her hair grow past her shoulders.

Almost as if she was trying to gain her parents' approval.

Still.

She dropped her hand and straightened. Absurd. Years ago she'd realized she no longer needed to prove anything to her parents. She didn't care what they thought of her if they were proud of her.

If they loved her.

She could grow her hair as long as she pleased. Could color it and wear makeup and dress in any manner she so chose.

Except thirty-eight counted as middle-aged. Long hair would now be inappropriate.

Wonderful. She was old, haggard, divorced and unappreciated by her only child. Gracie was right. She really did need a brownie.

With a soft aha, Gracie faced her, waving a small spatula in the air. "Molly says chocolate is the perfect food, good for any and all occasions. Celebrations… commiserations…breakups and makeups…"

Using the spatula, Gracie cut into the dessert, whacking away at the chocolate all willy-nilly so that a few brownies were huge, a few were tiny and none were all-four-sides-are-perfectly-equal squares, as brownies should be.

Curling her fingers into her palms, it was all Penelope could do not to grab the pan and save her dessert from such butchery. How difficult was it to cut straight, neat lines?

Gracie dug out a huge, misshapen brownie and set it on a napkin. "Here you go."

Penelope glanced from the dessert in Gracie's hand up to the cheery, expectant grin on her face. "Thank you."

Then she broke off a corner and popped it into her mouth because Molly—Penelope's neighbor and Gracie's stepmother—was right. There was never any occasion that didn't go well with chocolate.

Even occasions such as suffering first-degree facial burns, being ditched by your own son, and, oh, yes, being alone while everyone else had somewhere to go and people who actually wanted to spend the day with them.

The bite stuck in her throat so she took another one to try to push it down. No need to feel sorry for herself. She was fine. Things could have been much worse, after all. She was healthy and whole and not seriously injured.

She ran her fingertips over her eyebrows. Still there.

See? She was just dandy.

But she'd been careless. Stupid. She really could have been seriously injured. Or killed.

All because she'd let her emotions get in the way of her good sense. Had let Andrew's behavior and attitude upset her to the point where she'd been unable to think of anything else.

She couldn't be an effective parent if she took things so personally. If she let him hurt her feelings or make her angry. Composure. Control. Those were the traits she needed to focus on. They would help her do her job of raising a productive, well-adjusted, hardworking human being. One she could send out into society without guilt, doubts, regrets or fear.

She shoved more brownie into her mouth. It wasn't helping. Maybe chocolate didn't make things better. What she needed, she decided on a brilliant flash of insight, was another glass of wine.

And possibly one of the Valiums she'd been prescribed during the worst of Andrew's illness. Of course, she'd had way too much pride to ever take any of the pills. Pride that was currently crumbling faster than her brownie.

Wine was definitely the lesser of the two evils.

She slipped off the stool and crossed to the table, snagging her glass and the bottle. On her return trip she wove a bit, her steps not exactly steady. Perhaps Andrew was right. Perhaps she had imbibed a little too much alcohol.

Except she didn't feel drunk. She felt quite good— other than her twinges of self-pity, her stinging face and her sore rear from landing so hard. She certainly wasn't acting drunk. No dancing topless on the table, no wearing a lamp shade on her head. She had complete control still.

She set down the bottle, then sipped from her glass. Glanced over to see Gracie staring at the pan of brownies with undisguised longing. "Would you like one?"

Gracie smiled and it lit her entire face. She wasn't what Penelope would call a pretty girl—took one plain Jane to know a plain Jane, after all—but she was cute with her wild hair and big gray eyes.

"I'd love one, but I'm a vegan. I don't eat any meat products, and that includes eggs and dairy. Well," she continued, as if Penelope had asked her to go on, which she definitely had not, "actually, I only decided to start practicing veganism last week. My dad, of course, thinks it's stupid, but then he's a carnivore right down to the barbaric practice of hunting animals—like going out and shooting a helpless deer makes him some sort of alpha male. Molly says it's his way of providing for his family, but I figure it's easier and costs less for him to go down to Pineview Market and pick up a package of ground beef, you know?"

No, Penelope didn't know. Just as she didn't know how to respond to Gracie. How to act or react with the girl around. She was much happier on her own, taking care of herself and Andrew. She didn't need or want help.

"I'm not sure—"

"Besides, no one I know even likes the taste of

the animals he brings home. I mean, who eats rabbit, squirrel or venison? If it was that good, they'd have it in the stores, am I right? But he just laughs, like my beliefs and ideas are some big joke, so I decided to counterbalance his overabundance of meat consumption by going vegan." Gracie slid another longing look at the brownies. "I've been good, too. I mean, Friday it was super hard because I forgot my lunch and it was pizza day—which is the only decent food they serve at school—but I held firm and I was really proud of my willpower."

"Well," Penelope said, shifting in her seat. Did the girl want a pat on the back or the go-ahead to forget her convictions this one time? "If you're sure—"

"Then again, I haven't eaten dinner yet on account of my entire family going to my grandmother's for a picnic, which, let me tell you, Molly was not happy about. Not that I blame her. Grandma can be so mean. Like last time she actually told Molly she was gaining too much weight even though she's the same size she's been at this stage with all the other pregnancies. Molly started crying, right then and there, and Dad just sort of stood there like he had no clue what to do or say. I mean, how hard is it? Your mother insulted your wife. Your pregnant wife. The woman who popped out five—and counting—sons for you. Say something. But he didn't so I had to step in and then I got in trouble for being mouthy and disrespectful to my grandmother. Where's the justice in that?"

Was Penelope supposed to answer that? "Thanks again for helping me. I really am feeling—"

"So, I'm sure a brownie would make me feel way better about being abandoned on a holiday by my own family," Gracie continued, as if she had no intention of ever running out of steam, breath or words. "And it's not like you actually told me you used eggs or butter to make these."

She stared at Penelope as if waiting for something. Penelope had no idea what. Denial? Confirmation? She couldn't read minds, after all, and was horrible at deciphering expressions. Oh, how she hated these situations. Social situations, which, oddly enough, this one definitely qualified as. She was always insecure and out of her element. It didn't help that her hair smelled singed and the pleasant, buzzed feeling she'd had was fading to a pounding headache.

She gulped more wine, then refilled her glass.

She could tell Gracie that of course she'd used butter and eggs. Who made brownies without those ingredients? And why would you want to?

But she respected the girl's determination to stick to her guns and eat healthy.

Plus, if she told Gracie the brownies were definitely not vegan-friendly, maybe, just maybe, the girl would leave, go to her own house.

Her empty house. Then they would both be alone.

How depressing was that?

"No," Penelope finally said, "I didn't tell you there were animal products in the brownies."

"In that case, and without any verbal proof or confirmation, I'll have a small one." Wrinkling her nose, Gracie nodded. "Half a one. Just a bite, really." She cut a tiny piece from the pan and ate it. "Two bites. Two bites can't hurt, right?"

"Thanks, again, for the help," Penelope said, standing so she could usher the girl out the door. "I don't want to keep you from this gorgeous, sunny day."

Gracie waved that away. And ate another bite of brownie. "I was just reading in my room. I have to be careful because I burn really easily and with all the new research on the hazards of too much sun exposure, I prefer to stay inside."

Penelope hung her head. She felt foggy. Her thoughts not quite clear. If they were, she'd be able to think of a way to get rid of Gracie—in a polite, careful manner, of course. Her ears started to ring. No, she thought, frowning, not ring, more like... blare.

Like...she lifted her head, her eyes wide. Sirens.

"You called 911?" she asked, incredulous and horrified at the very idea, even as the small part of her brain that was still functioning logically wondered why it had taken the emergency responders so long to arrive. Definitely something she needed to take into account if something ever happened to Andrew.

Gracie, in the act of eating yet another brownie, dropped the spatula guiltily. Nodded. "When I was outside turning off the gas to the grill."

Penelope checked her watch, squinting to make out the numbers. Approximately eight minutes for them to get here from across town. Not bad, she had to admit. Though five minutes would have been better.

The siren got louder. And louder. Closer and closer.

She did a mini twirl, her mind telling her to escape, her feet having no idea what she was doing. No. No, no, no. The last thing she needed was everyone in Shady Grove knowing she'd done something so completely stupid. And they would. She'd lived here for less than a year, but she already knew the paper was notorious for printing things like this, usually smack-dab on the front page.

Oh, dear Lord, she could imagine the headlines: Local Accountant Left Heartbroken and Alone After Son Refuses to Spend Time With Her. Almost Blows Her Own Head Off to End Her Grief.

She'd die of embarrassment.

No. She definitely did not want the fire department here, parked in her driveway for the entire neighborhood to see. Did not want them trying to help her. She was fine. Slightly charred, yes, but overall no real harm done.

The sirens were close now, the sound incredibly loud. Gracie hurried toward the front door as if she owned the place, her flip-flops slapping in the most irritating way.

"This way," she told someone.

A moment later, she returned followed by a tall,

darkly handsome firefighter—in boots, a heavy jacket and even a helmet—looking as if he was ready to battle a raging inferno instead of dealing with a now stone-cold grill.

"This is a nightmare," Penelope whispered, shutting her eyes. "A complete and utter nightmare."

"Are you kidding?" Gracie asked breathlessly, her eyes dreamy as she stared at the good-looking man. "If I'd known the local firefighters looked like that, I would've let that stove fire keep burning last year instead of putting it out with the extinguisher."

Penelope doubted all the firefighters in town looked like the one approaching her. He was one of *those* guys. Too handsome, with dark, wavy hair visible underneath the helmet, deep brown eyes and a charming, boyish grin.

One that said, *why yes, I do know I'm God's gift to women. Drink it in, ladies. Drink it in.*

The worst kind to a woman's sense of self, willpower and virtue.

Not her, of course. Other women. She was too old for him. Had too many responsibilities and more important things to focus on in her life other than dating or, heaven forbid, a relationship.

Especially when she'd already proved she wasn't any good at them.

"Ma'am," he said, "I'm Leo Montesano with the Shady Grove Fire Department. Could you tell us where the grill is?"

*Ma'am.* See? Even he knew she was too old for him.

Why she was disappointed and a little ticked off, she had no idea.

It must have been that disappointment that had her taking a moment to realize what he'd asked—and that he wasn't alone. A huge bear of a man, his wide face as ordinary as the dark-haired one's was extraordinary, stood behind the younger firefighter.

All she could do was lift her hand and point to the door.

"I'm on it," the second fireman said, heading out the French doors.

"Could you tell me what happened?" Firefighter Montesano—or whatever title he went by—asked, taking his helmet off.

Even mussed, his hair was perfect, dark as night and waving sinfully, almost artfully, around that sculpted face.

"I was reading in my room," Gracie blurted, stepping between them. "I had the window open because it's such a nice day, when Leighann—that's my best friend—called. She was upset, again, over her boyfriend. I was talking her through yet another romantic crisis—I mean, it's obvious he only wants in her pants so I'm not sure why she's so shocked each and every time they're alone and he tries something and then he gets mad and storms off when she says no." She frowned at the firefighter. "Are all guys like that? Or is it just a teenage thing? Because most of my friends have the same problem."

Shedding his jacket, the firefighter raised his

eyebrows at that overload of information, but didn't seem embarrassed by the question. "I'm going to respectfully decline to answer that."

She sighed as if in resignation—or else she was simply taking in the firefighter in all his six-foot-plus glory. And what glory it was. Broad shoulders, narrow waist and biceps that proved the man spent a great deal of time in the gym.

"Fine." Gracie shrugged. "I'm only trying to get some insight into the inner workings of the adolescent male brain."

He grinned and yes, it was even more potent than Penelope would have imagined.

"Believe me," he told Gracie. "The last place you want to go poking around is a teenage boy's mind."

"Amen," Penelope muttered so fervently she wouldn't have been surprised to see a choir of angels drift down from the heavens to sing it with her.

Then again, if she could see into Andrew's head, she might have a better idea why he hated her so much.

Sending that devastating grin her way, the firefighter helped her sit.

"Anyway," Gracie said, "I was telling Leighann she needed to dump him when there was this big boom—"

"It wasn't that big—" Penelope interjected.

"It was! It shook the windows. I hung up on Leighann and hurried over. By the time I got here, Ms. Denning was awake but like, stunned. The grill wasn't burning or anything so after I helped her inside, I shut it off and called 911."

"Smart thinking," the firefighter told her.

"When you have five brothers under the age of eight, you learn the ins and outs of fire safety. The twins especially are fascinated with anything that burns. Or explodes," Gracie said, helping herself to another brownie. "Still, I was terrified I'd find poor Ms. Denning dead or in flames when I got here."

*Poor Ms. Denning?*

Penelope shut her eyes. She'd been called many things in her life—smart, reserved, aloof. Cold. But never poor Penelope. Not when she'd been a child and had moved ten times before her fourteenth birthday, forced to attend a new school almost every year, always the new, awkward girl no one wanted to sit with at lunch. Not when her marriage had fallen apart and Todd had found comfort in the arms of another woman. Not even when her son was so sick that many people, including his doctors, feared he wouldn't make it.

She wasn't someone to be pitied.

"I'd offer you a brownie," Gracie said to the firefighter, "but I can see you take your physical health very seriously and probably don't eat sweets or junk food or anything that, you know, tastes good. How many hours a day do you work out?"

Penelope caught his gaze. "Make it stop," she whispered. "For the love of God, make it all stop."

His grin broadened and he knelt in front of her. "I take it you're Ms. Denning?"

"Yes. Penelope Denning." She'd gone back to her maiden name a few months ago when her ex-husband had remarried. She hadn't felt right being Mrs. Freeman anymore. Not when another woman also claimed that title.

She held out her hand. "Nice to meet you, Mr. Montesano."

A look of bemusement in his dark eyes, he shook her hand. His grasp was firm and warm. "You, too, Ms. Denning. And Leo is fine."

She wondered if he was related to the people who ran Montesano Construction, a successful contracting firm in town. She assumed so, but hated to assume anything, and asking felt like prying. Small talk was part of the world, part of living and breathing and sharing the planet with other human beings.

It should be reserved for certain situations—workplace gatherings, social interactions such as parties and bridal showers that one couldn't get out of, and horrendous first, second and third dates.

But small talk should not be a part of her day off.

"Look straight ahead for me." He shone a light in her eyes. "How are you feeling?"

Stupid. Helpless. Both of which she hated. "I'm fine. Gracie is making it out to be worse than it was."

"She was acting spacey," Gracie said, peering around Leo's arm, her mouth twisted in contemplation. "I think she may have been in shock."

"I'm not in shock." Penelope looked at the fire-fighter. "I'm not in shock. All of this fuss isn't nec-essary." Yes, she sounded a bit…strident…but it couldn't be helped. "I did not almost die. I did not suffer any internal injuries or head trauma. All I want is to curl up on the sofa and relax."

Her voice broke at the end, a low, desperate sound that could have been misconstrued as a sob. It was horrifying. Humiliating.

She simply wanted to be left alone.

Now a bubble of laughter rose in her throat. She clamped her lips together to make sure it didn't es-cape. She'd lost her mind. That was the only ex-cuse for her roller-coaster emotions. For wanting to be alone when she spent so much of her time on her own.

When she spent so much time being lonely.

The events of the past hour started pressing down on her, pushing on her chest, an unbearable weight forcing the air from her lungs. She felt her compo-sure, her control slipping, sliding away from her grasp, faint as a wisp of smoke. Tears stung her eyes, made her throat ache.

"I think I left my cell phone on the deck," she blurted, praying her phone—safely tucked in her pocket—didn't ring. She looked at Gracie. "Would you mind looking for it?"

"No problem." But she seemed reluctant to leave. "I'll be right back."

Gracie stepped outside and Penelope grabbed

Leo's hand and tugged him forward so their faces were only inches apart.

"Help me," she whispered, her voice ragged and more than a little desperate. "Please, please help me."

# CHAPTER FOUR

PENELOPE DENNING WAS DRUNK.

Leo wasn't a detective, but it didn't take a shiny badge or a degree in criminal justice to figure out she'd enjoyed one too many glasses of the wine on the island. Her amber eyes were glassy and slightly unfocused, her speech slow and careful.

He'd give her a five on his personal Levels of Intoxication Scale. Not pass-out, blackout or even fall-down drunk. Just tipsy. And obviously careless with it.

He could have warned her that too much alcohol and gas grills didn't mix. Actually, alcohol didn't mix well with any item that contained a flammable liquid—lawn mowers and those damned turkey deep fryers especially, included.

He patted her hand, but she continued clutching him, her nails digging into his skin. "That's what I'm here for," he said soothingly. "To help you."

He tried to ease away but her fingers tightened on him and she leaned forward, scooting so close to the edge of the stool she almost slid off. She caught her balance, perched there like a bird about to take flight.

"No." Her clear voice trembled; her eyes took on a wild glint. "Help. Me."

She tipped her head to the left—and about toppled herself off the stool. He steadied her, then followed her pointed gaze out the door where his partner, Forrest Young, had been joined by fellow firefighters Casper Rhett and rookie Simon DePaul. The teenage girl lifted a chair cushion and said something that had Casper fighting a smile, Simon turning white and Forrest letting out one of his huge laughs.

The girl had a way with words—and wasn't afraid to use as many as humanly possible.

"While I'd love to help look for your phone," Leo said to Penelope, "my search-and-rescue training has taught me only how to find people."

His tone was easy and he even managed a grin, though he was sure it was strained. But then, he wasn't some damned bloodhound with nothing better to do than find lost personal items.

She frowned, looking so confused he bumped her intoxication score up to six. "Why would you look for my phone?"

He patted her hand again, both to reassure her and in the hopes she'd get the hint and let go. The woman had a grip like a spider monkey. "Because you lost it."

"I did not lose my phone," she said, all kinds of indignant. "I don't *lose* anything. I'm a very careful, responsible person."

He took in her disheveled dark hair, her pink face and wrinkled clothes. "That's obvious."

She nodded, her expression saying, *damn right*.

Finally releasing him, she shifted, lifting her hips off the stool in a pelvic thrust that was so awkward, jerky and unsettling, he shut his eyes and tried to erase the memory from his mind. No woman should ever, ever move like that.

"See?" she continued, dragging her phone from her pocket. She waved it at him and he was surprised she didn't stick out her tongue and add a triumphant *Ha!* "I told you I didn't lose it."

"Then why did you ask that girl to look for it?"

Penelope stared at him as if he was as simple-minded as his siblings always accused him of being. "You're a firefighter, right?"

"That's what it says on my shirt."

"Exactly. You're a hero. A real live-action figure. No one has a body like that except firefighters. And maybe marines. I mean…" She gestured at him. "Look at you."

The back of his neck warmed. He scratched it. He knew what he looked like. Hell, females had been hitting on him since puberty struck in full force at the age of fifteen. And while he'd admit to having a healthy ego, it wasn't as big as most people—mainly Maddie—thought. "That's a little hard to do at the moment. How about I find a mirror as soon as we get you checked out?"

She rolled her eyes then slapped her hand over

them. "Oh, my…did I…did I just roll my eyes?" she whispered.

"Yep."

She groaned, the sound way sexier than it should have been. It was totally inappropriate and unprofessional, but for a moment—a brief, heated moment—his body tensed. Interest, attraction stirred.

He pushed it aside.

He didn't flirt on duty.

"I hate when people do that," she said.

It took him a moment to realize she wasn't talking about men flirting with her. He cleared his throat. "Yeah, the eye-rolling thing is irritating as hell." And, luckily, not something Bree had perfected yet. Though a few of the boys he coached on Shady Grove High School's football team had it down to a science.

"I'm sorry," she said, finally lowering her hand. "But you were placating me when I'm trying to make a valid point."

He lifted her wrist, pressed his fingers against her pulse, tried to focus on the steady rhythm and not on how soft, how warm, her skin was. "Which is?"

She exhaled in exasperation, her breath washing over his cheek. "You're trained to do heroic things, like run into burning buildings when everyone else is smart enough to run out." She edged closer and under the cloying, lingering scent of propane, she smelled sweet, like lavender. "Leo, I want you to play hero for me."

Though her words were throaty and cajoling, he

doubted, very much, that she meant it the way it sounded. Which was fine. He wasn't interested in her. Yeah, she was pretty enough with her dark complexion and light eyes and that little mole next to the right corner of her mouth.

Okay, maybe he was a little bit interested. He wasn't dead, after all. And the image her words created in his mind—one of him, shirtless in only his uniform pants and suspenders, standing next to a bed where she reclined in a fire-red teddy that ended high on her tanned thighs—took hold and rooted deep.

He let his gaze skim down her legs to her bare, narrow feet, the toes painted a pale pink. She had great legs, curvy and muscular.

"I'm flattered," he told her, unable to count the number of times he'd said that to a female while on call. "But it's against regulations for me to fraternize with women while I'm working."

Or at least, it was highly frowned upon.

He wouldn't do so even if his captain gave him a notarized note telling him to go for it. His family thought he was a dog, some playboy who took any and every opportunity to make time with women. Not completely untrue, but he had his standards, whether they believed it or not. He didn't hit on women under his care.

"Flattered? What are you…" Her eyes widened and she blushed, the color staining not only her cheeks but also her throat and the sliver of skin on her chest visible in the vee of her shirt. "You think I...that I want..." She shook her head, then reached up and held both sides of it as if afraid it would fall off her shoulders. "I'm not...I'm not flirting with you."

He pulled his stethoscope from his bag. "My loss."

She twisted her fingers together. "I do not flirt with men."

"No? Just women?"

She laughed, a surprised, light burst of sound that washed over him, sweet and warm, like a ray of sunshine. He wanted to absorb that brightness, soak it into his skin, into his bones. Wanted it to dispel the coldness inside of him, to erase his memories of last night.

"I'm not gay. I just...I don't flirt with men *or* women. I don't flirt with anyone." Her voice trailed off in resignation. Or disappointment. "At all."

"That clears it up," he murmured, his voice inadvertently husky. He skimmed his gaze from her long, side-swept bangs to her prominent cheekbones, then lingered on that mole. "Like I said...my loss."

Her mouth opened on a soundless *oh,* her eyes wide.

He bit back a grin. Technically his comment, his demeanor, could be considered flirtatious, but he wasn't big on technicalities.

"I couldn't find it," the teenager said as she stepped into the room. She pulled her own phone from her pocket. "Do you want me to try calling it?"

Penelope blanched; her guilt over her little white lie couldn't have been clearer on her face if she'd written out a full-blown confession on her forehead in red marker. "Isn't it silly? I had it in my pocket all along."

The kid, a pixie in hippie clothes with hair to her waist, lifted a shoulder. "No problem. Are you sure I can't fix you something to eat? Or I could do your dishes," she said, crossing to the sink. "Maybe throw in a load of laundry for you?"

Penelope glanced at Leo. "Oh, I don't need you to—"

"And when I'm done, I'll grab a couple of movies from my house. You probably shouldn't be alone." The kid turned to Leo. "She shouldn't be alone, right? If she has a head injury?"

Penelope's sigh was as close to a whimper as Leo had ever heard from a human. She sent what could only be described as a long, yearning look at the bottle of wine.

And Leo finally got it.

Why the hell hadn't she just said she wanted him to get rid of the kid for her? Women. Always wanting a man to read their minds, know their every thought and react accordingly.

Only to give the poor sap hell when he didn't.

Wrapping his stethoscope around his neck, he stood. "I'm sorry. I didn't catch your name when I came in."

"Gracie Weaver," she breathed. But when she

shook his hand, she made eye contact and didn't send him any underage come-hither looks or step closer in order to brush against him. Unlike what a few of the bolder cheerleaders had done after their first scrimmage last week.

Thank you, sweet Jesus, for small favors and for young girls who didn't hit on him. Amen.

"Weaver?" he asked. "Wes's daughter?"

"The one and only."

Far as Leo knew, she meant that literally. Last he'd heard, Wes and his wife, Molly, had enough sons to form their own basketball team.

He took the girl by the arm and led her toward the door. "You did a great job," he told her. "Calling us, shutting off the grill and helping Ms. Denning inside. But HIPAA rules state that unless you're related, or a legal representative of the patient, you can't be present at this time."

All bullshit, and if he wasn't mistaken, something Gracie suspected, but unless she called him on it—and whipped out a copy of the HIPAA regulations—he was standing by his words.

He opened the French doors, avoiding Forrest's smirk as he deposited Gracie on the deck. "I'm sure Ms. Denning is grateful for all your help."

And he shut the door.

"You were a little rude to her."

He crossed back to Penelope, who was giving him the time-honored death stare of doom.

Some days, a guy couldn't win.

"Sometimes playing hero means being the bad guy." He unwound his stethoscope and put the ear tips in. "Just going to listen to your lungs, make sure they're clear."

She sat rigidly, her hands on her thighs, her fingers curled. Everything sounded good.

"Gracie meant well," she said.

"I'm sure she did." He wound the stethoscope around his neck and straightened. "But it seemed to me you could use a break from her good intentions."

"She was very helpful," Penelope said, glancing nervously to the deck as if worried Gracie was going to return. "But she was quite…chatty. And pushy."

"That can be a lot to take in. Especially when someone is having a rough day. She seems like a sweet girl, but it was obvious she was wearing out her welcome."

"I think she's lonely," Penelope said softly. "Her parents went to some picnic and left her home by herself."

"Wes—that's her dad—is a good guy. And Molly, his wife, is as sweet as they come. I'm sure they didn't abandon her. They love their kids."

Her ill-natured shrug told him she was firmly on Gracie's side in this imaginary battle she'd concocted between the teen and her folks—no matter that the kid had bugged the hell out of her. "So you're close friends with them?"

"Nope."

"Then how could you possibly know what emotions they do, or do not feel, toward their children?"

"I don't," he said simply. "But Shady Grove's a small town with all sorts of ties among the people who live here. Some of those ties are personal—friendships, marriage, family. Some are professional. But even if you don't know someone personally, chances are someone you know does. In this case, that someone would be my eldest brother and his wife. They went to school with Molly, hung out in the same crowd. And Wes is good buddies with my captain. So I know them well enough to say they wouldn't ditch their kid. They're decent, hardworking, caring people. And about as opposite as two people can be, which must be why their marriage works so well."

"That is ludicrous. Not to mention highly unlikely. I would surmise that if they truly are *as opposite as two people can be*, their marriage will eventually crumble under the pressure of trying to hold up unrealistic expectations of success."

Gripping both ends of his stethoscope, he leaned back. Tried to figure out what the hell was wrong with him. He should be put off by her prim and preachy tone, but he liked her light, clear voice too much, the way she spoke with such careful precision. And it was tough to get pissed at her haughty, patronizing expression when her hair was such a mess, her face pink.

Interest stirred again and this time, he didn't fight

it. Didn't plan on acting on it, not at the moment anyhow. But that didn't mean he could stop from finding her fascinating.

From wanting her to keep talking.

If only because, for the first time since he'd arrived at the accident scene last night, he felt…lighter.

Women had a way of doing that, of making a man forget his troubles and focus on other things. Things such as soft, sweet-smelling skin, lush curves and long kisses. All things he'd rather think about than what had happened last night to Samantha, the pain and grief her family was going through.

His sense of responsibility for their loss.

"I take it you're not big on the theory that opposites attract," he said.

"Hardly. Oh, people like to believe in that silly, romanticized notion, but in reality what holds a relationship together is commonality. Common interests." She ticked the items off on her long fingers, one by one. "Common views on religion, politics, finances, child-rearing—"

"And sex," he couldn't help but add.

Her flush deepened, but she held his gaze, her chin lifted as if to prove he couldn't fluster her. "Yes, naturally they should also have similar views about sex. What they shouldn't believe is that simply because they have a satisfying physical relationship, they can work through other problems. For a relationship to succeed, a couple should have similar intellects in order for them to enjoy scintillating conversation, as well as interesting and intriguing debates. If they have similar tastes, they can share hobbies and enjoy the same types of film, shows and music. All of which will make it easier for them to want to spend time together."

"That's quite the theory," he said, wondering about her romantic relationships. Was she in one? His gaze flicked to her left hand. No ring. No signs of a husband from what he could tell. But then, he'd seen only the hallway and kitchen. For all he knew, there could be a spouse lurking around somewhere, but something told him there wasn't. "Most women believe in love and forever and happy endings."

She snorted, then looked appalled, as if unable to believe the sound had actually come from her. "I'm all for love and forever. I also realize that happy endings require an immense amount of work and sacrifice, and if both people aren't willing to pull their weight, none of it will be enough to make a doomed relationship last."

She made relationships sound like a job, not something to be cherished and revered.

Like he'd said—fascinating.

She shook her head. "I don't see what any of this has to do with why you're here."

"Not a thing." But she was right. He needed to get back to work, focus on getting the details for his report, and make sure she really was as okay as she seemed and move on to the next case. He pulled out his notebook and pen. "Can you tell me what happened exactly?"

Her eyes narrowed. "Why?"

He tapped the notebook. "Gives me something to write in here. If I come back with blank pages, my captain gets cranky."

She slumped back and crossed her arms. "I had a glass of wine."

He waited, but when she didn't elaborate, he asked, "And the wine made the grill explode?"

She sent him a bland stare. "I was simply explaining the events leading up to the…the…incident." Chewing on her bottom lip, she cleared her throat. "I may have had more than one glass, but definitely less than three. I think."

Holding his pen over the paper, he raised his eyebrows. "You lost count?"

"Of course not. I'm an accountant. Counting is what I do," she said in an aggrieved tone. "Counting and adding and subtracting and reading tax law among other things. The point," she said, "is that I am not drunk."

"I didn't say you were."

She sniffed. "You didn't have to. I can tell by your face. You look all…smug. And amused."

"Smug?" he murmured. "That hurts."

"Let me tell you something," she continued as if she hadn't heard him. "While I may not be completely, one hundred percent sober, I am *not* inebriated." She spoke with the slow enunciation of the drunk, but she handled the word with impressive skill. "I'd realized I should eat something and that was why I lit the grill in the first place. I'm not drunk," she repeated, though way less vehemently. "I'm just…" Her voice dropped to a whisper, her eyes taking on a sadness that tugged at something deep inside of him. "I'm just having a really bad day."

Compassion swept through him. Nothing new there. Taking care of others wasn't just his job, it was his calling, one he was damned good at. He prided himself on his ability to sympathize with the people he helped, to understand what they needed most.

Penelope, with her sad eyes and that sexy mole, needed someone to make her day a little brighter, a little better.

She needed to know she wasn't alone.

"Excuse me a minute," he said before crossing to the French doors. He stepped outside and shut the door behind him. "Everything okay with the grill?" he asked Forrest.

"Hoses are still intact, no leaks or damage to them or the tank. Rhett and the rookie just left."

"Good. Hey, can you give me ten minutes? Ms. Denning isn't feeling well, but I think it's only low blood sugar." Low blood sugar. High alcohol content. Why split hairs? "I want to make sure she has something to eat, is feeling steadier before we take off."

Forrest shook his head sadly. "You saving the world again, partner?"

"Not the whole world," Leo corrected as he turned to go inside. "Just this one little corner."

WITH HER HEAD resting on her folded arms on top of the island, Penelope shut her eyes. She needed a moment to get her bearings, to gather her thoughts, then she'd get on with her day.

Her awful, horrible day.

She could hardly wait.

A moment later, she jerked upright. Confused and disoriented, she glanced around, then frowned at the fuzzy image of Leo Montesano taking food out of her refrigerator. She must have dozed off. The thought of Leo witnessing her impromptu nap should have horrified her, but she had too many other things on her mind.

Such as why on earth he was still there.

"What are you doing?" she asked.

"Getting you something to eat." He set the bowl of potato salad on the counter, reached back in for the caprese and taco salads. Carried them to the dining-room table, then crossed to her. "Let's sit at the table."

"This isn't necessary," she said, knowing she sounded ungrateful and prissy but unable to help it. "I'm perfectly capable of taking care of myself."

"That's clear enough to see, but everyone needs help once in a while."

"You don't even know me."

"I don't have to know you. It's my job to make

sure you're all right, and in a place like Shady Grove, we take care of each other." He studied her and for some odd reason, it took all her willpower not to fidget. "Let me guess. You're not from here."

"No." But she had been in town almost eight months. Long enough, she would think, to stop feeling like a tourist. An outsider. "But I lived here for six months when I was in middle school."

Many, many eons ago.

Out of the dozen-plus places she'd lived during her lifetime, the six months she'd spent in Shady Grove had been, by far, the happiest. She'd felt a sense of peace, of belonging she'd never experienced before. She wanted that for Andrew.

Was it so wrong to want it for herself, as well?

"Since you're new to town," Leo said, "let me show you how we take care of our own."

He helped her off the stool, kept his hand on her elbow, solicitous and polite, as he led her to the table. She sat, mainly because she had no idea what else to do. When he headed into the kitchen, she slid her hands to her lap, hid them under the table and pinched her forearm.

Yes, it hurt. This was real. She was wide-awake, sitting at her table while a man handsome enough to give a movie star a run for his money searched her cabinets.

What on earth had happened to her life?

"I hate to repeat myself," she said, "but what are you doing now?"

"Looking for…ah…" He pulled a plate from the cupboard. "Found it. Silverware?"

"Are you certain you don't want to open and shut every drawer?" she heard herself ask, then was appalled, not only that she'd say something so blatantly rude and antagonistic, but that she'd sounded so petulant doing so.

But she'd already had one stranger rummaging through her personal items—as personal as kitchenware could be. Her patience was threadbare.

"I could," he said, not sounding the least bit bothered by her rudeness. "But it'll save us both time if you just tell me."

"Next to the dishwasher," she muttered. Where else would they be? It was the most convenient place for them.

He pulled out a fork, knife and serving spoon, then walked toward her. He set the plate in front of her, laid down the silverware and began opening containers.

Maybe she was still in shock. Or tipsier than she'd originally thought, because she sat there like a helpless idiot and let him pile food onto a plate. Noticing that the potato and taco salads were touching, she grabbed the plate and pulled it out of his reach. Used the fork to separate her food.

"Thank you," she said stiffly. "But you really don't have to do this."

"That's what neighbors do. They help each other. Good neighbors, anyway."

Which let Penelope know, in a quiet yet still scolding way, that she was not being a good neighbor. Or, at least, a polite one. Shame filled her. See? She was horrible at this, this whole…social interaction thing. "I prefer to handle things on my own."

It was safer that way. No one could let you down if you didn't depend on them. And you couldn't disappoint them, either.

"Today," he said quietly, "you don't have to."

A lump formed in her throat and she dropped her gaze. She was being rude. Rude and inconsiderate and, worse, ungrateful, while he treated her with nothing but kindness.

She shouldn't want his sympathy. Surely she shouldn't be soaking it in, but it wasn't so horrible, letting someone else take the lead. Especially when she was so far out of her element. At work, she was fine dealing with people. She had her position and behaved accordingly. There were clear rules and guidelines of what was and wasn't acceptable behavior.

Personal relationships—whether casual or intimate—were different. It was too difficult to discern her role.

"Why are you doing this? I mean, beyond the good neighbor reason. This—" she gestured toward the food "—seems to go beyond the boundaries of your job description." She didn't consider herself a suspicious person, but she was old enough, and wise enough, to realize good deeds often came with strings attached.

"Because I'm a nice guy. And because it really is my job to make sure you're okay."

Of course. What did she think? That he wanted to spend more time with her? That he was flirting with her?

She was way too pragmatic for such nonsense. While she didn't underestimate her physical charms, she wasn't a great beauty by any means. Nor did she possess the type of overt sexuality that inspired flirtatious banter, longing looks or heated seduction. Especially from a man several years younger and at least three steps above her on anyone's looks scale.

Not that it bothered her. Much.

"Go on," he continued with a nod toward her plate. "Take a few bites for me."

Her eyes narrowed. She could do without that condescending tone, but if the only way to get rid of him was to eat, she'd gladly lick the plate clean.

"Would you care to join me?" she muttered, sounding about as ungracious and inhospitable as one could get. Sounding, she realized with an inner sigh, like Andrew.

Leo sent her a lethal grin and she couldn't help but think he was laughing at her. "Thanks, but I ate earlier at my folks' place." He rubbed the pad of his thumb over the slight bruise at the corner of his mouth. "Besides, my jaw's still sore. I'm not sure I'm up to chewing at the moment."

"Were you injured in the line of duty?"

"Nothing that dangerous. Or exciting. My sister punched me."

In the act of slicing a neat piece of tomato, Penelope froze. "Excuse me? Did you say your sister hit you?"

"Punched me," he said, as if that made a difference. "Don't worry. It wasn't the first time, and knowing Maddie's temper, it won't be the last."

She couldn't wrap her head around his words—or how nonchalant he was about the whole thing. What sort of woman physically attacked her own brother?

"Do you have any siblings?" he asked.

"A brother. Patrick." She couldn't imagine ever resorting to violence against him. She and Patrick respected each other, gave each other their space. Easy enough to do when they hadn't seen each other in two years...or was it three? She couldn't even remember the last time they'd spoken. Knew she hadn't talked with her parents since Christmas.

Did they ever miss her? Did they regret not having her in their lives?

She stabbed a chunk of potato, any appetite gone.

"Hey," Leo said, frowning at her in concern. "You okay?"

She couldn't even muster up a decent lie. Just shook her head. "I had all these plans for today," she heard herself admit, and blamed her uncharacteristic desire to confess on the wine. "And they're ruined." She swallowed, but it still felt as if she had a pebble stuck in her throat. "Everything's ruined."

Leo touched the back of her hand, a gentle, reassuring brush of his fingers. "I'm sorry your day didn't turn out the way you wanted."

The sincerity in his tone undid her. Her throat closed as tears threatened. *Tears*. She hadn't cried in years and had welled up several times today. But tears were useless. They didn't solve anything, only left her blotchy, red-faced, and feeling silly and pathetic. Giving in to them, in front of a stranger no less, was a weakness she couldn't afford. She had to stay strong. Control, of her life and her emotions, of her actions and reactions, was all she had.

She couldn't give it up. Not even for a moment.

Her lower lip quivered and she stood quickly, pushing back her chair with such force it wobbled precariously before settling on four legs again. "Excuse me, please," she murmured, already hurrying toward the small bathroom around the corner.

She'd just flipped on the light when the first tear escaped. Locking the door, she sniffed, tried to hold on to her composure, but it was no use. So she slid to the floor, hugged her knees to her chest, lowered her head and gave in.

# CHAPTER FIVE

LEO STARED AT Penelope's empty seat, then craned his neck to look around the corner where she'd disappeared. Scrubbed a hand through his hair. Hell. What had he gotten himself into? He had a habit—a bad one other people liked to point out—of jumping in with both feet, trying to do what was needed to fix any situation. It made him a damned good firefighter and EMT, but sometimes, his tendency to leap first got him into trouble.

Or into a weird, uncomfortable predicament. Like now.

Nothing he couldn't handle, though.

His phone buzzed. He checked the text from Forrest.

ETA?

Rubbing the bruise on his mouth, Leo considered his current circumstances, then typed in ten min knowing he could drag that estimate out another five minutes before Forrest got on his case about them needing to head to the station. But as long as they didn't get any emergency calls, Leo wasn't in a hurry to leave. Not until he'd made sure Penelope was okay.

Call it a personal defect, but when a woman ran from the room in tears, he had to find out what was wrong. Had to help her.

Telling himself he was just doing his firefighterly duty, and that his desire to somehow comfort her had nothing to do with the way his gut had tightened at the sight of her tears, he walked into the living room. No sign of her. He frowned. He doubted she'd gone outside. She didn't seem like the type of woman to let others see her in a vulnerable state—let alone someone who'd step out her front door looking anything less than completely put together.

Then again, he had only met her. For all he knew, she ran down the streets of Shady Grove barefoot and disheveled on a nightly basis.

But he doubted it. She was too self-contained. Too uptight.

And he was rarely wrong when it came to reading people. Especially women.

The sound of running water made him turn. He approached the closed door tucked under the stairs and tapped on the wood. "Ms. Denning? Are you all right?" When she didn't answer, he knocked again. "Ms. Denning?"

The water shut off. "I'll be out in a minute."

He pursed his lips. Not exactly a confirmation that her physical and mental states were A-okay, but at least he now knew she was conscious and capable of communication. He'd give her two more minutes. If she didn't come out on her own, he'd go in after her.

Deciding to give her some space and privacy, he returned to the kitchen. The counters were granite, the cabinets a glossy dark cherry, the tile floor Italian marble—or a really excellent facsimile—done in an intricate pattern. The walls were a soft yellow that carried into the bright and airy dining room. Splashes of green and blue accented both rooms in the form of knickknacks, wall hangings and a vase of cheerful flowers on the table. Whoever had done the remodeling did a good job—although his family would have done it better.

Just because he hadn't wanted to be a part of Montesano Construction, had never wanted to spend his life pounding nails, hauling boards and installing windows, didn't mean he wasn't biased when it came to the work they did.

He put the food in the refrigerator, then cleared the dishes—never let it be said all those lectures from his parents about responsibility and manners hadn't stuck with him.

"You're still here."

He turned as Penelope walked into the room, her eyes dry and clear, her chin lifted. No signs of distress or the tears he'd spotted earlier.

"Yes, ma'am." He set the plate in the dishwasher and tried to ignore how resigned she'd sounded. How disappointed. As if she couldn't wait to get rid of him when most women did everything in their power to keep him around.

He stuck a glass on the top rack of the dishwasher.

"You don't have to do that," she said as she rushed over and snatched the bowl from his hand, held it against her chest as if it were some precious treasure. "Really."

"Just helping out."

"Yes, well, I'm fine. And more than capable of doing my own dishes." And she proceeded to take out the items he'd put in and reloaded them herself. She shut the door, dried her hands on a towel, then faced him. "You can be assured that something like this will never happen again. I will be much more careful in the future." She picked up a pile of papers from the corner of the island, turned as if searching for somewhere to put them, only to set them on the spot where they'd been. Using the back of her hand, she brushed her bangs from her face. "I never should have let the gas build up like that, especially with the lid down. And then to ignite it? Well, that was just careless. Not to mention extremely dangerous."

"Even the most careful people can make a mistake sometimes."

That didn't seem to reassure her. Guess she didn't like being lumped in with regular folks.

"It's unacceptable to take such chances around something as dangerous as a propane grill. Before use, one should always check the level of propane left in the tank and make sure that tank is properly hooked up to the grill and that there are no loose or leaky hoses. With the lid open, then and only then should ignition be attempted. If it doesn't light, the propane should be shut off for a few minutes before trying again."

"You ever think about making a video and putting it up on YouTube?" he asked, fighting a smile. "Because you're really good at the safety tips."

She'd certainly captured his attention.

She flushed. "Of course not. I just wanted you to know I will be vigilant about grill safety from this day on."

*Vigilant.* Christ but she was adorable. He let his smile loose. Winked. "Glad to hear it."

The wink seemed to throw her. She stepped back, then straightened. "Thank you, again, for coming all the way out here."

He was being dismissed. Another new experience. The day had been full of them so far, most of them courtesy of the woman in front of him. He got her not-so-subtle hint—he wasn't an idiot. But he didn't want to leave. Not yet.

"That's what the SGFD is for." To take care of people. And answering this call had helped him, more than Penelope would ever know. It had given him a reprieve from the memories of last night's accident. A few minutes without his guilt. And his anger.

He should be the one thanking her.

Still, he couldn't stand here all day, not when he had no valid reason to stay.

"Don't hesitate to call your doctor's office or the Shady Grove emergency room if you're not feeling well," he said, gathering his gear. "Or if you experience a headache or nausea."

"I won't," she said so solemnly, he half expected her to cross her heart and hope to die. She held out her hand, polite to the very end. "It was nice meeting you."

He slung his coat over his left arm and shook her hand, holding on two heartbeats longer than necessary. She swallowed, her throat working, her eyes wary.

He edged closer, amused when she took a quick step back. "You take care of yourself."

Nodding like a bobblehead, she pulled her hand free and tucked it behind her as if afraid he'd reach for it again. "Goodbye."

He sent her a salute, grabbed his helmet then went out the patio door, jogged down the deck's steps and walked toward the ambulance. Behind the wheel, Forrest started the engine while Leo stowed his gear. He climbed into the passenger seat.

"You forget something?" Forrest asked as they idled in the driveway.

Buckling his seat belt, Leo glanced through the windshield at the house. "Nope."

Forrest leaned forward, resting his arms on the steering wheel. "You sure? Because the way you keep looking at the house it's like you're searching for something." His grin turned way too smug for Leo's peace of mind. "Or someone."

"Again…nope."

"I bet you were hoping to see our pretty patient with her nose pressed against the window, her eyes all starry and glistening and longing as she watched you walk away."

"If you're not capable of driving and talking," Leo said, keeping his tone bland, his face expressionless, "I'd be more than happy to switch seats with you."

Forrest laughed and shifted into reverse. "Don't worry. I'm sure she's in there, peeking out from behind a curtain as we speak, sighing and mooning over that pretty face of yours."

Leo couldn't help but check the house's front window, hating that Forrest was right about his wanting her to be standing there. Not because Leo's ego needed stroking.

But because he wouldn't have minded seeing her one last time.

ANDREW SAT ALONE at the picnic table, the setting sun warming the top of his head and bare shoulders as he hunched over his plate. The table had been set up on the edge of the yard away from most of the action.

Exactly why he'd sat there. He needed a few minutes of peace.

Everywhere he turned, there were more people, the Sapkos' yard filled with their family, friends and neighbors. He'd done the whole socializing thing, had played basketball with a couple of the guys, then messed around in the swimming pool for an hour.

He was getting better at it. Bullshitting and joking around with a group, being a part of it. He'd relax, pretend it was no big deal to have people wanting to talk to him, wanting to hang out with him. Then he'd remember all the years he'd spent alone and start worrying he was going to say something stupid.

Or worse, that they'd all somehow find out he actually liked reading the books assigned in English class. That he'd watched all the *Lord of the Rings* and *Star Wars* movies—even the prequels—so many times, he could quote them word for word. That he'd spent the first two years of high school in California as a social outcast.

That was when he'd duck out of whatever they were doing, take a few minutes to remind himself things had changed. *He'd* changed. He wasn't that kid anymore. He wasn't the dork who'd been too skinny, too awkward and weird to have any friends.

He'd never be that loser ever again.

"Hey," a girl said from behind him, trailing her fingers across his shoulders.

Whipping around, he about choked on his burger, but managed to swallow the bite in his mouth without coughing and spitting food all over Kennedy Hearst.

Thank God.

"Uh…hey."

"I've been looking for you."

His heart pounded. *Easy. She doesn't mean it the way you want her to.*

"You up for a game of Wiffle Ball?" she asked. "We could use you on our team."

"Sure." He sounded squeaky so he cleared his throat. "Yeah. That'd be great."

He ducked his head to hide a wince. *Great?* Jesus, could he get any more lame?

He started to get up, but she put her hand on his shoulder and swung one long, bare leg over the bench of the picnic table. "Finish your burger," she said, keeping her hand on his shoulder for a moment while she used him to balance herself before she sat next to him.

As in, right next to him, so close their thighs touched. Her skin was warm. And incredibly soft. His leg muscles tensed. His throat felt funny, but if he cleared it again, he'd sound like an idiot. Like he had some strange tic. So he sipped his soda, nodded. "Okay."

She nudged him with her hip and smiled, giving him a look from under her lashes. "I'll keep you company."

His palms started to sweat and he wiped them down the front of his shorts. "That'd be cool."

*Cool.* Yeah, that was one way to describe having the hottest girl he knew "keeping him company."

*Act like it's no big deal,* he ordered himself. *Do not be a spaz.*

*And whatever you do, don't stare at her boobs.*

Easier said than done when they were there—right there—in a tiny black bikini top.

A bead of sweat slid down his back. He focused on his burger, ate it, though it no longer tasted like anything. Which sucked since he didn't often get real hamburgers made of real beef and loaded with extra cheese. His mom would have a fit if she knew this was his second one—and that earlier he'd inhaled three hot dogs, plus as many side dishes as he could pile onto his plate, the cheesier, greasier and fattier the better. Not to mention he was on his third soda. The way his mom viewed soda, you'd think it was crack.

She was such a freak.

"God, you are like, so tan," Kennedy said, dragging the tip of one bright blue nail up his forearm. His skin prickling, he curled his fingers into a fist. "I laid out all summer and look." She stretched her arm out next to his, which meant she stopped touching him—damn it. "I barely got any color at all. Are you sure you're not, like, Hispanic?"

He stared at their arms. Next to him, hers was extremely pale and slender, her wrist delicate. He wanted to link his fingers with hers, feel her palm against his. "Uh…not that I know of. Just some Italian and even a bit of Cherokee."

"You are so lucky."

Lucky? He'd never thought so before. His DNA was just bits and pieces of genes brought in from people he'd never even met—except for his parents and grandparents, obviously. A body that had betrayed him once, had turned on him and almost killed him.

But, hey, if she thought he was lucky, who was he to argue?

"Meanwhile," she continued, "I got stuck with my father's pasty complexion. I mean, thanks a lot, right? I look like a ghost."

She didn't. She was a goddess. Her hair, a dark red, fell straight and thick past her shoulders. Her eyes were a light blue, her mouth full. She was taller than most of the girls in school, her legs long and toned from running cross-country.

She was everything he'd ever wanted. Everything he'd dreamed of.

She was also Luke's girlfriend.

Luke, who'd become the closest thing to a best friend that Andrew had ever had.

"You don't need a tan," he mumbled, sounding like an idiot, like a kid who didn't know what to say, how to act in front of a girl. "You look beautiful the way you are."

But it must have been the right thing because Kennedy smiled. Brushed her fingers over the back of his hand, her voice dropping to a husky whisper. "You're sweet."

He flinched. *Sweet.* Whoop-de-freaking-do. Sweet was friend-zone material. Sweet did not get a guy laid.

The last girl he'd had a thing for had thought he was sweet, too. Estelle Monroe was gorgeous, even prettier than Kennedy. They'd met in the spring, had gone out a few times while she'd been in town visiting her father. She'd been his first kiss, though he'd never admitted that to anyone.

Especially when it hadn't gone well.

Still, they'd worked through it and when she'd gone back to Houston with her mother, they'd tried the whole long-distance thing. But after a few weeks, they'd both lost interest. Last time she'd texted him, she'd admitted she was seeing some college guy. He told her to go for it. To be honest, it hadn't bothered him. He wanted a girlfriend he could actually see every day. Talk to. Touch.

Kennedy leaned toward him, her shoulder pushing against his arm as she helped herself to a chip from his plate. He froze, could barely breathe with her so close. She smelled amazing, like sunshine and sunscreen and some sort of floral scent that he figured was her shampoo.

"Did you try the cookies Luke's mom made?" she asked, nibbling on the chip. "They are, like, so good. I had two."

Then, her eyes on his, she slowly ran the tip of her tongue along the corner of her mouth, licking a speck of salt, then rubbed her lips together.

Andrew went rock hard.

Shit.

"Drew?" she asked, a small, satisfied smile on her face. "Did you hear me?"

He blinked several times, had to look down at his plate. What had she asked him? Oh, yeah. "Uh…I had a couple of the chocolate-chip ones."

"Those were good, too. But these were the spice ones with cream-cheese frosting."

He hated cream cheese. "I'll have to try one later."

She patted his arm. "I'll grab a couple for you." She climbed to her feet, once again using him to balance as she swung her leg around the bench, except this time, she pressed close to him and spoke directly into his ear, her breath washing over his skin. "Be right back."

*Don't watch her go. Do not watch her go.*

But he couldn't stop himself. When she disappeared around the corner of the Sapkos' one-story brick house, he jerked his attention to his food. Hoped no one had seen him staring at her, drooling over her like some dog.

Wanting his best friend's girl.

Andrew shoved his burger aside. Not that he'd ever come on to Kennedy or anything. Not while she was with Luke, anyway. There was a code, one he wasn't about to break even if he didn't understand it all that well. After she and Luke broke up—like, a few weeks after maybe—and when Luke was okay with it, Andrew would make his move.

Kennedy and Luke wouldn't last their entire high-school careers. They couldn't. It would burn out eventually, then Andrew could prove he was the right guy for her. She already liked him. Yeah, as a friend, but there were times he thought maybe she had a thing for him, too. Times he'd catch her watching him, interest in her eyes. And she was always touching him—when Luke wasn't around. Nothing major, just a quick stroke of his arm or hand. She stood close to him when she saw him in the hallways at school, her hip or thigh touching his.

She even texted him sometimes late at night, just to talk. Andrew didn't think she told Luke about any of that. He sure as hell wasn't about to.

Not because he felt guilty, he quickly assured himself. Or because they were doing anything wrong. It just wasn't any of Luke's business. They weren't messing around behind his back or anything so why make it into a big deal?

He lifted his head to see Kennedy walking toward him in her short cutoffs. Her waist was so narrow he could probably span it with his hands, her stomach flat. A light breeze lifted the ends of her hair; the sun made her skin glow. He couldn't look away.

"Here you go," she said, her voice husky as she set a thick cookie in front of him.

"Thanks." He took a bite, forced himself to swallow without grimacing. "You're right. They're good."

Sure they were. If you liked sour milk. But he'd eat an entire bowl of cream cheese frosting if it meant she'd smile at him the way she was now.

"Told you."

They ate their cookies in silence. The wind picked up and he considered putting his shirt back on, but Kennedy kept shooting looks at his chest and abs. He straightened and inhaled slightly, knowing it made the ridges of his stomach stick out.

He didn't quite have a six-pack, but he was close.

She leaned toward him, setting her hand on his thigh. "Do you want to go for a walk?" she whispered.

His mind blanked. Just…shut off with an audible click. She wanted to go for a walk? With him? "Everything okay?" he asked.

She rolled her eyes. "It's just…Luke. You know how he gets around all the guys."

Andrew had no idea, but Luke had obviously done something to upset her. It wouldn't be a big deal, them disappearing into the woods behind the house. She probably only wanted someone to talk to.

He flicked his gaze to her hand on his leg, liked how it looked against his skin. Imagined her sliding her hand higher, under the hem of his shorts, in between his thighs, those fingers curling around—

"Dude." Luke slapped him on the back. "You are one lucky bastard."

Andrew jumped. Kennedy slipped her hand to her own lap and edged away.

"What?" Andrew asked, knowing damned well he sounded guilty. He tried again, this time even adding a grin. "Why's that?"

Luke sat on Kennedy's other side and pulled her

in between his legs, linking his hands across her bare stomach. He kissed the side of her neck and murmured, "Hey, baby."

She wiggled out of his arms. "Oh, so you have time for me now?"

He tugged her back. "Come on. I always have time for you. And you're not going to be able to stay pissed at me once you hear how I found Drew the perfect girl."

Andrew glanced at Kennedy, who sat stiffly, her arms crossed, her mouth pulled into a frown.

"A girl?" Andrew asked stupidly.

Luke wiggled his eyebrows. "A hot girl."

"What are you talking about?" Kennedy asked, turning slightly to face him.

"I found our good buddy here a date." Luke grinned widely, proud of himself for somehow managing to find someone to go out with Andrew.

Andrew's hands curled into fists. Jesus, way to make him sound like a pathetic loser who couldn't get his own dates.

"Who?" Kennedy asked.

Luke took a drink from his water bottle. "Jessica."

Kennedy narrowed her eyes. "Jessica Constable or Jessica Wilber?" She slapped his chest. "It had better not be Jess Hanover. She is such a slut."

"None of the above. It's Jessica Kloss and I have it on good authority that she has a thing for the Freeman here." He held out his hand, leaving Andrew no choice but to slap it. "Congrats, bud."

Kennedy's mouth pinched. "Jessica said she liked him?"

Luke tapped his phone. "She texted me a few minutes ago asking if he was talking to any girls. I told her no and gave her his number." Luke nodded at Andrew. "Don't be surprised if she texts you tonight."

Andrew felt for his phone, but it remained silent and still. "Who's Jessica Kloss?"

Though this town and school were small, there were still close to eight hundred kids at the high school. "She's a sophomore," Luke said. "Dark blond hair to here." He motioned to his shoulders. "Plays varsity volleyball..." He scrolled through his phone, typed in something, then held the screen up so Andrew could see his Instagram feed.

"Cute," Andrew said of the sunny, smiling blonde in the picture.

Cute, but not Kennedy.

"When she texts you," Luke said, putting his phone away, "see if she wants to hang out this weekend. The four of us can go to the movies or something."

Andrew couldn't help but glance at Kennedy. She stared at the table. What had he expected? That she'd give him some sort of sign, a signal that she didn't want him talking to Jessica? Didn't want him with her?

That was stupid. Kennedy wasn't his girlfriend. She was Luke's. He had to remember that.

"Yeah, sure," he said. "That'd be cool. That is, if it's okay with you, Kennedy."

She lifted a shoulder but didn't meet his eyes. "Why wouldn't it be?" She shifted and wound her arms around Luke's neck, her hands in his brown hair. "I'm bored."

Luke hooked his finger under the strap of her swimsuit and ran it up to her shoulder, then down to the swell of her breast. "Yeah? I thought you wanted to play Wiffle Ball."

"I changed my mind." She arched her back and Luke's free hand settled above the curve of her ass. She wiggled closer. "Maybe we could find something...else to do?"

"We could always ditch the picnic for a few minutes," Luke said, his voice low. "Hang out in my room for a while."

Andrew wanted to stab his ears with a fork.

"I'll meet you there in five minutes." She stood and kissed Luke.

And when she straightened, she looked directly at Andrew. Held his gaze for one long heartbeat then walked away, her hips swaying.

"Dude," Luke said, "if my parents ask about me, tell them the last time you saw me was at the pool."

Andrew tried to smile. "Yeah. Sure."

Luke took off, keeping his own pace slow.

Andrew slumped in the seat. Someone called his name and he saw a couple of the guys near the driveway waving him over. He lifted his hand and stood.

The last thing he wanted was to sit there and think about what Kennedy and Luke were going to be doing in five minutes.

But the more he tried not to think about it, the more images filled his mind. Except they weren't images of Kennedy and Luke, but Kennedy and Andrew. Of her hands on him. Her mouth. Of what it would be like to be able to touch her whenever he wanted. Wherever he wanted.

His body stirred, his groin tightening. Damn it. Again? He quickly sat down, adjusted himself in his shorts. Some days he wished his penis had an on/off switch. It'd be less embarrassing that way.

"Having fun?" Luke's mom asked as she joined him.

And just like that, he went from turned on to contemplating never again even thinking about sex.

Mothers had that effect on people.

"Yeah," he said, his face warming as if she could somehow read his thoughts. "It's great. Thanks again for having me."

"Have you seen Luke around? He promised he'd help gather wood for the fire."

Andrew swallowed, forced himself not to so much as glance at the house lest she figure out what her son was doing in his bedroom. "Uh…he might be in the pool still."

Making a humming sound, she studied him, as if weighing his words on her bullshit meter. He must've passed, because she smiled, wrinkles forming at the corners of her eyes and mouth. She was very…round. Round face. Round body. Her short brown hair was half gray, but then she was pretty old. Older than his own mom, even. Like maybe… fifty.

"It's a shame your mother couldn't come, too," Mrs. Sapko said as she gathered the empty plates and glasses from the table. "I was looking forward to getting to know her better."

His mom wasn't exactly friendly at the best of times. She was awkward and unsociable and tended to put people on edge because she always had to be right. Had to be the smartest and best in the room. "She…uh…she already had plans. But she asked me to tell you thanks for, you know, inviting her."

"She's welcome here anytime, as are you. I'm glad to hear she's made friends in town," Mrs. Sapko said before walking away with the garbage.

Andrew snorted. His mom didn't have friends. Even before he'd gotten sick, she'd never gone to lunch with other women or had a night out. She spent her time with him and his dad or at work.

Period. No hobbies. No outside interests. He couldn't even remember the last time she went to the movies.

People avoided her. She was uptight, anal and uncomfortable with herself, and made everyone around her feel that way, too.

Was it any wonder he hadn't told her she'd been invited here?

The last thing he needed was his mommy hovering over him, telling him what he could and couldn't eat, watching him from the corner of her eye, as though she was afraid he'd take one misstep and fall off a cliff. She was way overprotective and too controlling. He just needed a few hours away from her.

But it bugged him, a little, how sad she'd looked when he'd asked if he could come here instead of hanging out with her all day. How weird she'd acted when he'd left. How unlike herself.

His stomach cramped. Not from guilt. Probably something he ate. His mom was fine. She liked being alone.

If she didn't, she wouldn't have left his dad.

She was probably doing paperwork or reading some book about the dangers of wheat or how dairy products were causing all of America's health woes or something else to make his life more miserable. It was better that she hadn't come. He didn't want her here. She'd ruin everything with her endless worries and constant nagging. He finally had friends. Was accepted into a group. They all thought he was just a normal kid.

He *was* normal. And he didn't want anything, or anyone, to take that away from him.

# CHAPTER SIX

By 9:33, PENELOPE HAD zoomed past worried, had a brief visit with anger, and was now firmly in frantic mode. She paced the width of the living room, stopping only long enough to peer out the front window to the street, but there were no signs of headlights, no sound of a motor. Where was he?

She called Andrew's phone. Again. It went directly to voice mail as had her other six calls. "Andrew, it's me. Call me. Now."

Chewing her lower lip, she considered her options. There was no sense calling the police—he was only half an hour late and she had no reason to think he was anything other than perfectly fine. That he was running late due to bad decision making and possibly a flat tire.

No reason except her overactive imagination and the fact that life didn't come with guarantees of safety or good health. She wasn't naive. Didn't fool herself into believing that nothing horrible could ever happen to her or her child. She was a realist, one who had faced every parent's worst nightmare and had, fortunately, gotten through it.

Because her child had lived through it. He had lived.

All she wanted was to keep Andrew safe. That was her job, the most important thing a parent could do. Protect her child. It would be a lot easier if he'd listen to her.

And come home on time.

What if something *had* happened? What if he'd had an accident on the way home and was, right this minute, lying in a ditch calling for help? Or had been knocked unconscious?

What if he needed her and she couldn't get to him?

Still pacing, she tapped her phone against her mouth. She hated this feeling of helplessness. Her son was missing. She needed to spring into action, take whatever measures were needed to find him and bring him home.

Then, when she knew he was safe, she'd kill him for turning her into a living-room-pacing, cell-phone-tapping lunatic.

Headlights flashed and she rushed to the door and threw it open, only to watch as a pickup turned left and drove down the road. She slammed the door shut, the sound amping up what was becoming an impressive headache.

She was never drinking again.

Probably.

She pressed the number nine on her phone. Andrew wanted to test the boundaries? Wanted to see how far he could push her? Well, he was about to find out. No more Miss Nice Mom. She was going to file a police report, say her car had been stolen. When they found her car, they would find her son. Problem solved.

*Great idea,* her inner voice said in a decidedly sarcastic tone. *The Shady Grove Fire Department already thinks you're careless and can't be trusted to light a grill. Might as well let the police department know you're also paranoid and can't control your son.*

Perching on the edge of the armchair, she frowned. Why did her inner voice always have to be right? It was so annoying.

Okay, she needed to think this through. Chances were Andrew was fine. He'd lost track of time or, more than likely, wasn't paying attention to it in the first place. And if the police found him hanging out at Luke's house, safe, sound and rebellious, she'd feel and look like a fool. Plus, they might charge him with auto theft.

That she briefly considered her son getting arrested a fitting punishment for missing his curfew had her dropping her phone as if it had caught fire.

Dear Lord, she was losing her mind.

Lights illuminated the room. This time she didn't move until the car pulled into the driveway.

She shut her eyes and sent up a prayer. *Thank you.*

By the time she reached the back door, Andrew

was strolling toward the house, whistling under his breath—whistling, for God's sake!—as if he didn't have a care in the world. When she constantly worried about everything, spent most of her time weighing options, planning for the next possible disaster.

It wasn't fair.

But then, who ever said life was fair?

She stepped onto the deck, the wood planks cold, the dampness soaking into her socks. "You're late," she snapped. "Where have you been?"

"Luke's." His tone suggested he wanted to add a *duh,* but thankfully, he refrained. He stepped inside, forcing her to retreat. "Why isn't the grill covered?"

She glanced at the grill and, sure enough, it was not only uncovered, but the plate of raw turkey burgers was still on the side table. "I forgot."

He tossed the keys onto the counter. She sighed and picked them up, hung them on the hook where they belonged.

"I thought after using it we were to always clean the grate, let the grill cool completely, then cover it," he said in that snide tone she hated. "No matter what."

"Funny how all of that escapes your mind when it's up to you to cover it, but the one time I forget it's suddenly deeply ingrained in your head."

He opened his mouth, probably to give her some grief, then narrowed his eyes. "What happened to your face?"

She bristled. She didn't consider herself vain, but

those were words no female wanted to hear. Ever. "When I lit the grill there was a small...flare-up."

His eyes widened. "You got burned? Are you okay? Did you go to the hospital?"

"I'm fine. It's a minor burn." Though it had hurt like the dickens when she'd showered, but the aloe she'd put on had helped.

"Are you sure?" he asked, sounding concerned and scared. For her. It was a new sensation, him worrying for her health and well-being. A nice one.

She unbent enough to pat his arm. Soften her tone. "I'm fine. Really. It was a stupid accident, which is why we always need to be careful when we're lighting the grill."

"I guess." He tossed his sweatshirt onto a chair and pulled out his phone. "Six calls? Overzealous much?"

*Overzealous?* Seemed she wasn't the only one who used their advance vocabulary words when the time was right. "You could have answered at least one of them."

"I was driving. No talking or texting while driving, remember?"

"I highly doubt you were driving the entire time as it takes less than ten minutes to get from Luke's to here."

"Your first call was at eight-fifty."

"I didn't want you to forget to be home by nine. Which, I might add, you weren't."

He texted someone, not even glancing at her. "I'm not that late."

She was so tired of this. So very, very tired of the fighting and lecturing. Of always having to be responsible, of being in charge. Of taking care of him.

To her horror, tears stung her eyes again.

Maybe she was having some sort of mental breakdown. After the day she'd had, she figured she deserved one.

"You are late. Over half an hour." Her voice shook, but she fought to maintain control. "And after I let you go over there, the least, the very least, you could do was be home on time."

He shifted his feet, reminding her of how, not that long ago, he'd hated getting into trouble, had hated making anyone feel bad or hurting their feelings. "Look, I'm sorry I was late, okay? We were playing Wiffle Ball and the game was tied. If I had taken off, my team would have had to forfeit."

Playing Wiffle Ball? In the dark? Highly doubtful.

But if she asked, he'd get defensive and accuse her of thinking he was lying.

Which she did. She just couldn't prove it. Didn't have it in her tonight to try.

"Fine." She stepped outside, grabbed the burgers and covered the grill haphazardly before returning, locking the door and turning off the outside light. "I'll let it go this time. But next time something like that happens, please do me the courtesy of calling me to let me know."

"I will." He studied her, his mouth twisting in concern. "You sure you're okay? Your hair looks funny."

No kidding. She brushed her bangs to the side. First thing tomorrow morning she needed to make an appointment to get the fried ends cut off. "I'm fine."

"I'm glad."

Then he did something so shocking, so out of character, all she could do was stare.

He hugged her.

*He* hugged *her*.

Oh, it wasn't a real embrace, just a one-armed sort of squeeze, but she'd take it, mostly because he'd initiated it. It was like her birthday, Mother's Day and Christmas all rolled into one.

Except on those days she was the one doing the hugging while he silently suffered through it.

He stepped back. "Next time, be more careful," he said, sounding so much like her she blinked.

Her lips twitched. Who would have thought she'd find a reason to smile today?

An image of Leo Montesano, all tall, dark and muscled, sprang to her mind. Yes, he could definitely put a smile on a woman's face, but he was like the moon. All golden and bright—and out of reach. She had no business thinking of him. He was pure fantasy.

Penelope preferred to live in the real world. No surprises. No changes in direction unless she was the one doing the navigating. No trips off course or to destinations previously unknown. Some, like her ex-husband, called her negative, but she preferred to think of herself as pragmatic. Did good things happen? Absolutely. But that didn't mean you could count on them. Better to be prepared for the worst and pleasantly surprised by the best.

"How was the picnic?" she asked as Andrew stuck his head in the refrigerator.

"Okay." He straightened, three plastic containers stacked in his arms.

"Didn't they feed you there?"

He set the food on the island. "Yeah. We had burgers and stuff, but they put the food away like, over an hour ago."

"An eternity," she said drily. He grabbed a fork, peeled open the taco salad and stuck it in, taking a healthy bite. When he went in for another round she grabbed the container. "Ugh. No. Just…no. Sit."

He did so and she got him a plate and dished out his food. Poured him a tall glass of milk, then sat next to him.

She never got tired of watching him, her boy. Even when he hunched over his plate and shoveled food into his mouth as though afraid someone would snatch it away and never feed him again. He was smart and handsome and complicated and strong. He was the one and only person to ever truly be hers.

She was terrified of losing him.

"You know," she said slowly, "I realize I have high expectations of you. I have them of myself, as well. I won't apologize for expecting you to do and be your best, but I understand that it might get frustrating, having someone pushing you all the time."

He shrugged, kept his head down. "It's okay. I mean, yeah, it's a pain in the a—er, the butt being told what to do all the time. But I know why you do it. I'll do my best to get better grades this year."

"That's all I ask." She wanted to ask for straight As, which she thought him perfectly capable of, but even she knew where her limits were. "I appreciate you putting in the extra effort. And to prove that, I'm willing to extend your weeknight curfew to nine-thirty—"

"Yeah?" he asked, grinning widely.

"After you prove to me you can meet the original curfew of nine o'clock for a month. If you do, and you're not late once, we'll extend it and your weekend curfew, too. Sound fair?"

She waited, breath held. If he thought it unreasonable, he'd explode, have one of his impressive tantrums or give her the silent treatment for days on end, using grunts as his only form of communication.

Actually, she didn't mind that one too much.

"Yeah," he said after a moment. "That's fair."

Her breath whooshed out. She smiled. Reached out to brush his hair off his forehead, but didn't want to ruin this moment by having him flinch from her touch so she lowered it to her side. For now, sitting with him like this, no tension between them, was enough.

For now, she'd enjoy being with her son.

THE NEXT AFTERNOON, Penelope looked up from her computer at the knock on her door. Before she could open her mouth, Emilia Moore, the company's receptionist, stepped into the office.

Penelope set her eyeglasses aside and pinched the bridge of her nose. She was lucky to have found a position at Stone, Bragg and Smithfield. They were one of the more successful accounting firms in southwestern Pennsylvania and she enjoyed the work and her supervisors.

But she couldn't get used to the lack of concern over the proper way of doing things. Such as waiting until someone actually bid you to come in before entering an office.

"There's someone here to see you, Ms. Denning," Emilia said, her tight white jeans leaving nothing to the imagination. Not that there was much left to imagine. The low-cut burgundy blouse bared a lot of the younger woman's assets.

Frowning, Penelope flipped through her daily agenda. As she'd thought. Blank. "I don't recall having any meetings this afternoon."

"You don't. Your calendar is wide-open," Emilia said, her voice, as always, cheerful and bright. It was enough to give anyone a headache. "Which is awesome since you'll want to give this particular visitor as much time as possible."

"Why? Who is it?"

Emilia paused and Penelope had no doubt it was only for dramatic effect. "Leo Montesano."

Penelope's mouth dropped. Literally dropped. Worse than that, she couldn't seem to do anything about it. Only God knew how long she sat there, jaw hanging wide open, gaping at the pretty brunette.

"You okay, Ms. Denning?" Emilia asked, her face scrunched up in what Penelope supposed passed for concern. "You look like you're about to pass out."

Penelope finally managed to shut her mouth and even stood, though her movements were jerky. "I'm fine. Thank you." She wiped her damp palms down the front of her skirt. Hated to admit her hands were trembling. "Did…uh…Mr. Montesano say what his visit pertained to?"

"Nope. But then, I didn't ask."

Of course she didn't.

"I'm sure he just needs help with a tax question," Penelope said, shooting for nonchalant, but suspecting she came across as slightly psychotic.

Emilia's smile had a sharp edge. "Well, yeah. I mean, why else would he want to see you?"

*Ouch.*

"Should I bring him in?" she continued as if she hadn't daggered Penelope in the ego.

And let everyone know he's come to see her?

She'd be the main topic of office gossip for the rest of the week. Her coworkers would speculate as to why Leo had come, how he and Penelope knew each other. Luckily, no one had heard about her misadventure with the grill. She'd like to keep it that way.

But refusing to see him would set off even more curiosity.

"Yes, please, bring him in. Thank you."

Emilia lifted a shoulder. "That's why they pay me the big bucks." And she sauntered out in her five-inch wedge sandals, her long, shiny hair swaying, hips swinging.

As soon as she was alone, Penelope whirled, right to left, her heart racing as she looked for an escape route. There wasn't one—unless she climbed out the window. An option she'd seriously consider if she weren't on the fifth floor. She was trapped.

And acting like a cornered ninny, exactly the reaction she'd had yesterday when Leo had arrived at her house, sirens blaring.

The low timbre of a man's voice reached her, grew louder from the hall. Frantic, she sat but misjudged the distance between her rear and the chair and almost ended up on the floor. Catching her balance, she straightened as Emilia opened the door fully.

"Here we are," Emilia chirped, both hands on the doorknob behind her back in a way that thrust her breasts out quite admirably. "Can I get you anything?" she asked Leo. "Coffee? Tea? My number?"

Once again, Penelope's mouth dropped. She felt like a ventriloquist's dummy.

If Leo was shocked by the girl's boldness, he hid it well. He grinned at her. "You tell your sister I said hi."

Emilia's sigh was a work of art, complete with forlorn expression and a full body exhalation. "Fine. But don't think I'm going to wait for you to come to your senses forever."

With a sharp *humph,* Emilia turned and walked out, shutting the door behind her. The walls started creeping in on Penelope, hemming her in.

She swallowed a burst of panic. Absurd. There was, as always, ample room in her office. It was actually quite large, with more than enough space for her big oak desk, the built-in bookcase to her right, and two leather armchairs for clients.

But somehow, today it seemed…cramped. As if there wasn't enough air to breathe, enough room for her to simply be.

Leo's fault, of course. He was too big with his tall, broad frame. Too male with his windblown hair and sharp jaw. He didn't belong here. This was her domain, the place she felt most powerful, most in control.

She couldn't let him take that away from her.

"Mr. Montesano," she said, putting on her cool, professional smile. "How can I help you?"

He walked toward her desk, all confidence and charm, his hands in the pockets of his dark dress pants, the sleeves of his crisp white shirt rolled up to the elbow. "First thing you can do is call me Leo."

"All right. Leo." And why did that sound too friendly? Somehow…intimate? She cleared her throat. "I'm surprised to see you."

Surprised. Flustered. Confused. None of which did anything for her equilibrium. And if a woman didn't have that, what did she have?

He grinned and she wished she was better at reading people because for a moment, he seemed self-conscious. Almost sheepish.

That couldn't be right.

"I'm a bit surprised by it myself," he said, casually glancing around, taking in her office. "Have you worked here long?"

He was surprised? What did that even mean? Did someone kidnap and blindfold him and drop him off in front of her building?

"Penelope?"

"Hmm?" She blinked. Realized he'd asked her a question. "Sorry?"

His dark eyes lit with humor. "I asked how long you've worked here."

She had no idea. Being around him killed her brain cells. Seeing him reminded her of how stupid she'd been last night, what a fool she'd made of herself. Embarrassment came rushing in, swiftly and sharply, heating her cheeks, turning her stomach.

She wasn't sure what to do with her hands so she picked up a pencil. Then, because she had, she was forced to hold it. "I started here just over seven months ago." There. That wasn't so hard. She even sounded normal. Hooray for her. "How did you know where I worked?"

"I looked you up on the internet."

"You looked…" She shook her head, finally laid the pencil down. "Why?"

"The usual reasons."

She almost sagged against her desk. Of course. She'd been right when she'd told Emilia he needed her professional assistance. He'd helped her last night and now he expected something in return for that kindness.

Nothing was free.

And if she was able to give him the help he needed, they would be even.

Smiling, she gestured for him to take a seat. "I usually handle only corporate accounts, but I'm sure if I can't help you with your problem, I'll be able to find someone who can."

He sat. "My problem?"

She waved a hand. "Whatever issue you're having with your taxes. Or your finances."

"I'm not here for business."

Her smile slipped. "You're not?"

"Nope. I'm here to see you."

That didn't make sense. "You're here to see me? But not for business?"

He nodded. "Now you're catching on."

She wasn't. She was afraid she was running way behind. "I'm sorry, but I don't understand."

He leaned back, looking for all the world as comfortable as you please. "I'm here to see you in a personal capacity."

"You want a personal favor from me?"

Leo laughed. The rich, low sound scraped pleasantly along her nerve endings. "I guess that's one way to put it." He sent her an easy smile, his gaze direct and open. "I'd like to ask you out."

"Out?" she asked weakly, the word muffled by the sudden roaring in her head.

"As in out on a date," he clarified. Must be he sensed that her brain had ceased working the moment he'd stepped into the room. Then again, he was probably used to having that effect on women. The power of a pretty face knew no bounds. "Dinner. A movie. Or we could go into Pittsburgh, see a show."

Her throat dried. She couldn't feel her fingers, had to lock her knees to remain upright. Date? Him? Absurd. They were too different. He was too good-looking. Too smooth. Too young. Too…everything.

And she was afraid she wasn't nearly enough.

She leaned her hip heavily against the desk. "I don't think—"

"Or we could start slow. Have lunch. Or even coffee." His voice dropped to a husky, sexy tone that could strip a woman of her inhibitions. And her good sense. "It doesn't matter to me. Just a few hours. I'd like to get to know you better."

She shut her eyes. Counted to ten. But when she opened them, he was still there, broad and earnest and, it seemed, completely sincere. "Why?"

The word hung in the air, bald and loud and yes, desperate sounding. Too bad. She wouldn't take it back even if she could. She was too curious to hear his answer.

"Because I find you interesting." He stood and stepped forward, his body and her own pride trapping her between him and her desk. "Because I'm attracted to you."

Her breath locked in her chest. A thrill raced through her before she could stop it. He was attracted to her? That…that was impossible. Implausible. Incredible.

And terrifying.

He edged even closer and she pressed against the desk, the rounded edge digging into the back of her thighs. "How about it, Penelope?" he asked, drawing her name out as if savoring each syllable. He trailed the tip of his forefinger up her forearm, his light touch like a flame along her skin. "Go out with me?"

Dear Lord, but he smelled wonderful, a mix of citrus and spice that made her want to breathe him in. And when he smiled at her, his eyes dark with intent, she wanted to believe in fairy tales. Wanted to believe in foolish dreams.

But fairy tales were for children. And dreams were for people who didn't know better. She wasn't some naive girl waiting for a handsome prince to sweep in and make her life complete. She was a mature, sensible woman with a teenage son who needed her time and full attention.

A mature, sensible woman who was wise enough to know when she was in over her head. Leo flustered her, and she hated being flustered. She doubted that feeling would ever go away, even if they went on a hundred dates. She needed to be the one in control. She liked knowing what the right thing to do and say was, and with him, she wasn't sure she'd ever have that ability again.

"No," she said, her voice firm. "Absolutely not."

# CHAPTER SEVEN

His smile slipping into bemused, Leo curled his hands into fists. He'd barely touched her, yet his finger tingled as if he'd been burned. "Excuse me?"

Her mouth turned down at the corners—not an encouraging sign. Nor was the little vee that formed between her eyebrows. He had an insane urge to smooth the wrinkle away.

As if reading his mind, she crossed her arms, her shoulders rigid, her body language pretty damn clear.

*Back off, buddy.*

Never let it be said he was a complete asshole. He shifted away and she exhaled softly, then circled the desk. His gaze dropped to the sway of her hips, the material of her gray skirt cupping her ass, the hem ending just above her knees.

She was all buttoned-up and untouchable, her hair a smooth, shiny cap, her black blouse tucked in neatly, her feet encased in a pair of ugly pumps. A far cry from the disheveled, tipsy, barefoot woman he'd helped yesterday.

He found that even more fascinating. Couldn't

help but wonder which one was the real Penelope Denning.

Couldn't wait to find out.

"Thank you for the invitation," she said, facing him, though her gaze landed somewhere above his right shoulder, "but I don't date."

He raised his eyebrows. "At all?"

Her gaze flicked to his, then away again. "No."

"Is that a religious thing?"

"It's a personal choice."

Or a convenient excuse, an easy way to brush him off. "Are you seeing someone?"

"I hope you're not one of those men who assumes that if a woman has no desire to go out with him, it must be because she's already involved with someone else."

At her scolding tone, the back of his neck warmed. He squeezed it. Hard.

"I'm not. I don't think that." But then, he wasn't used to being turned down, either. Christ, but that smacked of the big ego his brothers were always accusing him of having. He dropped his hand. "I'm just curious as to what I can do to improve my approach. Call me a lifelong learner. Always trying to up my game."

She sighed as if putting up with him was too much for her to bear. "I'm not seeing anyone else."

He grinned. "Then there's no reason we can't get to know each other better."

"Actually, there are several valid reasons."

He couldn't wait to hear them. He liked her voice, how she spoke in such clear, light tones. "Such as?"

She stared at him, began fiddling with the top button of her black blouse. Maybe not so unruffled, after all. She wasn't the only one. He couldn't tear his eyes away from her fingers; he imagined himself brushing her hand aside and undoing that button himself, parting the silky material to reveal what was underneath.

His blood thickened; his groin tightened, reminding him he hadn't had sex in over three months. Three long months. Oh, he'd had opportunities. When a guy looked like him, there were always opportunities, always women willing to warm your bed.

He just hadn't been interested in any of them.

Until now. Until Penelope with her vulnerability and sad eyes, her perfect posture and that sexy mole.

"Can't think of those valid reasons, after all?" he asked, liking how her cheeks turned pink when he teased her.

"For one thing," she said, sounding like a schoolteacher explaining why her students shouldn't run in the halls, "I'm recently divorced—"

"Yeah?" He picked up a palm-sized paperweight from the edge of her desk. Embedded in the glass was a black butterfly with an orange loop for its body, colorful wings and the word *Believe* scrolled underneath. He wrapped his fingers around it. "How recent?"

"I don't see what that has to do with anything."

He set down the paperweight. "You're the one who brought it up."

She stared at the paperweight, then huffed out a breath and moved it back exactly where it had been. "Over a year."

"Not all that recent then."

"May I continue?" she asked, her tone causing the temperature in the room to dip a good ten degrees.

He waved his hand, enjoying himself and her. "Please."

"Thank you. As I said, I'm recently divorced—" she glared at him as if daring him to argue with her; he wisely kept his mouth shut "—and concentrating on my career."

"I'm not asking you to quit your job. Just have coffee. During nonwork hours, of course."

"I'm focusing on my career," she repeated, "and my son."

*Son?* Leo glanced around, almost expecting the kid to appear out of thin air. "You have a son?"

"Yes. He's my top priority."

As he should be. He'd never dated a woman who had a kid before, but he would never ask someone to put him ahead of her child. "Kids love me," he said.

"How nice for you," she said, her tone bone-dry.

He grinned, realized he sounded like an arrogant ass. "I meant, I like kids. It goes both ways."

He was crazy about his nieces and nephew. Wanted kids himself someday. Kids, a wife, a big house and sprawling yard—the whole marriage-and-family deal. Someday.

Today, all he wanted was to take a pretty, smart, interesting woman out for coffee.

And that was a hell of a lot easier said than done.

"Looks like your reasons weren't so valid, after all," he said. "So, what day and time works best for you?"

"I'm older than you," she blurted.

He slid his gaze over her face. Gave a small shrug. "And?"

"I'm thirty-eight years old. You can't be more than twenty-seven—"

"I'm thirty-two."

She slapped the desk in triumph. "Exactly."

"It's six years. Not sixty." But it obviously bothered her. He didn't get caught up in age, though most of the women he'd dated were younger. Much younger.

But still, he made sure they knew where he stood. He never made promises he had no intention of keeping and he didn't string women along. He didn't have to use tricks, flattery or lies to get a woman into bed.

He knew the game, that push and pull between the sexes. Women held all the cards. The way they looked and smelled, how one caress could bring a man to his knees, one kiss could have him begging for more. Leo could play, had a few moves of his own, could work the angles as well as anyone.

But he preferred the direct route. Less chance of mixed signals. Or hurt feelings.

"Look," he said. "I'm not interested in trying to take you away from your son or career. I'm not saying we should run off and get married. I'm telling you I'm attracted to you and want to get to know you better. No strings. No commitment beyond a coffee date."

She made a sound, as if the air were leaking out of her. "At least you're honest."

If that was all he could get from her, he'd take it. "What do you say? Coffee? I'm off tomorrow."

She was tempted. For all her reasons and excuses, she was still tempted. He saw it in her eyes, in the way she nibbled on her bottom lip. But she linked her hands at her waist, as though afraid to reach for what she wanted.

"I see no reason for us to have coffee when neither one of us is looking for a relationship," she said, not sounding the slightest bit disappointed, damn her. "What other reason is there for dating?"

"Because it's fun? Because you get to meet new people, find out about their lives, get to know them?"

"I'm not interested in getting to know you."

Her words hit him, sharp and truthful. Her eyes widening, she slapped a hand over her mouth, her cheeks red.

Half grimacing, half laughing, he ran a hand

through his hair. "Wow. Nice shot. Please ignore any whimpering you might hear. It's just my ego dying a slow and agonizing death."

"I…I apologize," she whispered, looking as if she wanted the floor to swallow her whole. "That was uncalled for."

He lifted a shoulder. "If that's what you think, how you feel, then it's not uncalled for. But I am curious why you feel that way. As you pointed out, you don't know me so you can't possibly dislike me. My brothers say that takes at least a few hours of being in my company."

If she got the joke, she didn't show it. "There's no point in going through the whole ritual of dating. We're obviously ill-suited. We have nothing in common."

"That's a pretty big assumption considering we've only spoken for about an hour."

"On the contrary." She sat behind her desk, linked her hands on top of its glossy surface. "It's a perfectly logical conclusion. You're a firefighter. I'm an accountant. You run into burning buildings, I sit behind a desk and work with numbers. You probably have an extensive dating history while I was married for many years. You don't have children. I have a son who needs my time and attention."

"You've got this all figured out," he murmured. "Seems to me, we have quite a bit in common already. We're both single and live and work in Shady Grove. We probably know several of the same people, read the same paper and have maybe even watched the same films."

"All of that is superficial," she insisted. "After fifteen minutes we'd run out of things to talk about."

Who knew under that prim exterior lay such a stubborn soul?

"I take it you and your husband were opposites?" he asked, remembering what she said yesterday about people needing common ground to make a relationship work.

She bristled so much, he was surprised she didn't vibrate off her chair. "Not that it's any of your business, but we were very compatible."

"Yet it still didn't work out."

With a sigh, she sank into the chair, looking defeated. "No," she said softly. "It didn't."

"I'm sorry," he said, wanting to touch her, to offer her some small bit of comfort. "I didn't mean to hurt you."

She shook her head briskly. Refusing his apology? Wiping it away? He had no idea. "Your…interest… in me is…"

He rocked back on his heels, waited for her to continue. When she didn't, he asked, "Annoying? Flattering?"

"Misguided."

Not what he'd been expecting. "I honestly can't wait to hear why."

"My…behavior…yesterday at my house, how I acted…that wasn't me."

"It wasn't?"

"No."

"Don't tell me. It was your evil twin."

"I don't have a twin," she said and he wondered if she was always this literal. "Only an older brother."

He cleared the laugh from his throat. "My mistake."

"My personality, my actions and…chattiness… when we first met were all a side effect of too much wine, which came as the result of a disappointing day. So you see, you're not interested in me. Not really. The woman you came here to ask out doesn't exist."

"I don't believe that woman doesn't exist," he told her. "And even if I did, it doesn't matter because I'm finding this side of you, this woman in front of me, to be just as interesting."

She flinched. She actually flinched. Yeah, his ego was taking a hell of a beating today. Time to give the poor thing a break.

"But it's obvious you don't feel the same," he continued. "Can't blame a guy for trying."

She stood and walked around her desk to accompany him to the door, careful, he noted, not to get too close to him. "I'm sorry you wasted your time."

"It's my time and I don't consider it wasted."

Other than the repeated, brutal rejections, he couldn't remember when he'd enjoyed being with a woman more. When they were both still fully clothed, anyway.

"I really do appreciate the invitation," she said. "And that you went to so much trouble, seeking me out and dressing up…"

"The clothes weren't for you." He stopped at the door and faced her. "I was at the funeral home."

"Oh. I'm so sorry. Was it someone close to you?"

He could use that, he realized. Play on Penelope's compassion, the sympathy he saw in her eyes, to get her to go out with him. But he didn't want a pity date with the pretty Penelope.

And he'd never use Samantha's memory that way.

"No," he said. "I barely knew her."

Just as, it seemed, he wouldn't be getting to know Penelope, either.

He slipped out the door, loosened his tie as he made his way down the hall.

Sipping his beer, Leo surveyed his mother's dining room. His entire family—all twelve of them—were gathered around the antique oak table. Platters and bowls were passed, silverware clinked against dishes and Maddie bitched out James about some work problem.

Just another Sunday family dinner.

Leo loved his family. They were loud and nosy, always butting into each other's business or picking a fight. But when one of them needed help, be it a strong back for moving furniture, or a shoulder to cry on, the others were there. They shared a history. Had an unbreakable bond.

One that was currently around his neck choking the life out of him.

"I'm fine," he told his mother, who was doing the helicopter parenting so well, he was surprised she didn't make a *whap-whap-whap* sound when she moved. "Stop worrying about me."

Rose tucked her dark, chin-length hair behind her ear. "Not likely. Once you have kids that's what you do. Worry."

"Seems like a good reason to avoid it," he said, only half kidding.

"If you want to talk about it—"

"Nothing to talk about." He forced a grin. "But if there was, I know who I can turn to."

Even before she'd started pursuing a degree in social work and had taken the requisite psychology courses, his mom had always known when something was bothering him. It was as if she could read his mind.

Not that she needed psychic abilities when she knew everyone in Shady Grove. Leo should have known someone would tell her he'd attended Samantha's memorial service. Now she wanted him to talk about his feelings, for Christ's sake.

Spilling their guts over dessert was fine for his brothers and sister. Not for him.

Leo preferred to keep his professional and personal life separate. Preferred to get through the difficult times on his own.

Before his mom could regroup, or worse, mention

to the table at large that Leo was suffering from survivor's guilt and post-traumatic stress disorder—her dinnertime diagnosis—he scraped his chair back and stood. "I'll start the coffee."

Carrying his plate and beer bottle, he walked into the kitchen and was pouring water into the coffeemaker when Sadie and James came in.

"How much longer are you going to volunteer us for dish duty when we eat here?" James grumbled to his new wife as he set a stack of dirty dishes next to the sink.

"Until your mother realizes what a helpful, courteous and generous individual I am." Sadie opened the dishwasher and pushed up the sleeves of her neon pink fuzzy sweater. She loaded the machine, her movements quick and jerky, her long blond hair sliding over her shoulder. "That woman hates me."

"She doesn't hate you."

"No," Leo said. "Sadie's right. Mom hates her."

Sadie tossed up her hands with such force, water sprayed James's face. "See? Even Leo can sense it."

Glaring, James stepped back and used the bottom of his T-shirt to wipe his cheeks dry. "Leo's an idiot. What the hell does he know?"

"I know Mom's worried Sadie's going to break your heart."

They both stared at him as if he'd recited the Declaration of Independence. In Swahili.

Behind his grin, Leo ground his molars together.

They thought he was such a dumbass he couldn't see what was right in front of him.

"Did she tell you that?" James asked.

"She didn't have to. You've been jonesing after Sadie since you were, what? In middle school? And up until last year, Sadie didn't even realize it. Mom's not sure she'll stick around, that's all."

Rose had good reason to be concerned. For years, Sadie had popped into James's life whenever the mood struck her, then out again when she got bored or something better came along, leaving James heartbroken and wanting more.

"That's all changed," James said. "We've both changed."

Leo shrugged. "I know that and you know that. Hell, everyone in the family knows that. Except Mom."

"What should we do?" Sadie asked.

"Holy shit," James murmured. "We're asking Leo for advice. It's the end of the world as we know it."

Leo ignored him. "It'd probably go a long way," he told Sadie, "if you had a private conversation with Mom. Reassure her you have no plans on breaking James's poor, precious, sensitive heart ever again." He turned to his brother. "If that doesn't work, you could always step up and tell Mom in no uncertain terms that she needs to accept Sadie as your wife and her daughter-in-law and knock off the cold-shoulder routine."

James studied him through narrowed eyes. "Since when did you start giving good advice?"

"Hey, my advice is always good. You've just never heeded any of it before."

"Well, we're taking it now," Sadie said, shooting James an *agree with me or die* look. Rising onto her toes, she kissed Leo's cheek then hugged him. "Thank you."

Knowing it would piss his brother off, Leo wrapped his arms around Sadie and settled his hands on her lower back. "That's what I'm here for. General awesomeness."

She laughed. "I heard all about how awesome you are yesterday. Seems you were quite the hero a few days ago."

Damn it, why did his family always want to talk everything to death? All he wanted was to get over the accident and Samantha's death and move on. "You heard wrong," he said, dropping his arms and stepping back.

"Not according to Gracie Weaver," Sadie said with an eyebrow wiggle that made her look like she was having a seizure. "I had lunch with her and Molly yesterday and it's a safe bet to say you can now add Gracie to your long list of female admirers."

The tension in Leo's neck ratcheted up a notch. Sadie wasn't talking about the accident. She was talking about what had happened to Penelope.

That wasn't any better.

Antsy, he snagged his beer, took a long drink. Yeah, he'd thought of Penelope a few times since he'd left her office five days ago, had even considered calling her, but it wasn't as though he was obsessing over her.

He tipped the bottle again and frowned to realize it was empty. So she wasn't interested. No big deal; more fish in the sea and all that bullshit. He didn't beg women to go out with him. Didn't have to. Someone else would come along, make him forget he'd ever crashed and burned with the pretty accountant.

It couldn't happen soon enough.

"It wasn't that big of a deal," he said, grabbing a cold beer from the fridge. When he held it up to James, his brother nodded. Leo handed it over, then got one for himself.

"To hear Gracie tell it, you swooped into her neighbor's house like some sort of knight in shining armor. The only way it could have gotten any better was if you'd actually been on a horse. Or hadn't been wearing a shirt and had recently been sprayed with the fire hose."

"Give him an ax and put a constipated look on his face," James said, "and it'd be just like the pose he did for that calendar a few years back." He smirked. "Isn't that right, Mr. June?"

Leo shot James the middle finger. "It was Mr. July, hence the sparklers in my free hand. And that calendar raised ten grand for charity." He took a drink, then held the bottle between two fingers and spoke to Sadie. "Gracie deserves most of the credit."

The kid obviously wasn't holding a grudge about the way Leo had not-so-politely given her the boot. Though he felt like a dirty old man being the inspiration for a teenage girl's fantasies.

"Believe me, I heard all the details." Sadie went back to loading the dishwasher. "Molly's neighbor is lucky to be alive."

"What happened?" James asked.

"The Weavers' neighbor had a small flare-up with her grill," Leo said. "Gracie heard the explosion and called 911."

"She's a smart girl." Sadie closed the dishwasher, then dried her hands on a towel. "Not to mention brave."

"She did the right thing, turning off the grill."

"No, I meant the way she helped her neighbor into her house and stuck around to make sure she was okay." Sadie wrinkled her nose. "That is one unfriendly woman."

"She's not that bad."

"I don't know about that. Molly told me they went over when… What is her name? Patty?"

"Penelope," he murmured.

"Right. Penelope." Sadie took the bottle from James. Sipped. "Anyway, the whole family went over when Penelope and her son moved in and she wouldn't even let them inside, just stood there in the doorway talking to them through six inches of space."

"If they had all five boys with them," James said, "I wouldn't have let them in, either. Those kids are like a wrecking crew. But messier. And louder."

Sadie opened her mouth, then shut it and shook her head. "I was going to say they aren't that bad, but yeah…they're pretty wild. Still, Penelope didn't know that. Not upon first meeting them. And she refused the casserole Molly made." Sadie gave a quick nod as if that helped prove her point. "Just flat out said *no thanks*."

Leo thought of the food Penelope had in the refrigerator. It had seemed normal enough. Except for a package of ground turkey. Who ate turkey when they could have real beef? "Maybe she has dietary issues."

"Maybe," Sadie grumbled, crossing her arms then swinging them wide, the beer bottle tipping precariously. "All I know is that Molly has tried several times to be friendly. When she invited them over for a picnic, Penelope said she had too much work to do. When she asked Penelope if she was interested in joining their walking group, she claimed she got home from work too late." Sadie wiggled the beer in time with her tapping toe. "Every time Molly tries to initiate a conversation, Penelope can't get away fast enough."

James reached for his beer, but his wife moved it at the last second. "Maybe she doesn't like Molly."

"Please, Molly's a sweetheart. I think it's because she's…" She looked around, a wide-eyed sprite wearing painted-on jeans and that eye-searing pink sweater, then lowered her voice. "In the witness protection program. Or hiding from the mob. Or the law."

"She's not," Leo said, used to his sister-in-law's wild imagination. "She's an accountant at Stone, Bragg and Smithfield."

"Oh." Sadie made a face. "Yuck. Doing math all day would make anyone uptight, I guess. But still, there's no reason to be so secretive. No one even knows where she's from or why she moved to Shady Grove or what happened to her husband…if she even had one."

"She did," Leo said and wished he'd kept his mouth shut when he felt James's gaze, steady and searching, on him. It gave him the willies, like an itch in the middle of his back he couldn't reach. "She's divorced. And she's not really uptight, just… guarded." He thought about how uncomfortable she'd been when he'd gone to her office. "Maybe a little shy." Raising his bottle to his mouth, he caught James and Sadie staring at him as if he'd sucked his beer up through his nose. "What?"

"You know a lot about her," James said.

Leo rolled his shoulders, but the itch in the middle of his upper back remained. Relentless. A warning that he needed to tread carefully. "Not really."

"You like her," James said, his tone smug.

Leo shifted, then realized that would only make James think he was right. "Have we traveled back in time? Am I in middle school again?"

"Don't try to deny it. Why else would you know so much about a single, attractive—" James glanced at Sadie. "I assume she's attractive?"

"I've only caught glimpses of her a couple of times when I was at Molly's, but yes, she's pretty enough. Short dark hair. Nice figure. But she dresses like my mom. And, as was previously mentioned, she has a son."

"Doesn't sound like your usual type," James said to Leo.

"I don't have a type."

"Sure you do. Young, blonde and stupid."

Picking at the corner of the label on his bottle, Leo's mouth flattened. Maybe that had been his previous demographic, but things changed. People changed. "I don't limit myself when it comes to women. I love them all." He forced a grin, and promptly felt as if he was hiding behind a mask. "And they love me right back."

Usually.

James looked thoughtful, never a good thing. "What happened?"

"With what?"

"With this Penelope."

He raised his beer in a salute. "Not a damn thing."

James's eyes lit with humor. "She shot you down, huh?"

"What can I say?" He gave a self-deprecating shrug. "It was bound to happen sooner or later."

Though he would have preferred later. Much, much later.

With a laugh, James slapped Leo's back. "Chin up. I'm sure there are still plenty of women out there gullible enough to fall for whatever line you feed them."

That was the problem. He was getting tired of the lines. Of the casual hookups.

His family's fault. They'd started an epidemic of coupling the likes of which hadn't been seen since Noah and his ark. Maddie and Neil. James and Sadie. Eddie and Harper.

It was enough to make even the most die-hard bachelor wonder if he was missing out.

# CHAPTER EIGHT

STARING OUT THE passenger's-side window, Penelope tapped her fingers against the steering wheel of her car. Kids of all shapes, sizes and levels of fashion sensibilities trickled out the high school's front doors. But none of them were her son.

Late again.

She'd been prepared for this, she reminded herself. She'd told him his doctor's appointment in Pittsburgh was at four—when in truth, he wasn't scheduled to be there until four-twenty. She'd reminded him of the appointment that morning, told him she'd be at the school to pick him up at three o'clock.

It was now twenty after.

She picked up her phone and pressed his number. It went directly to voice mail. "Andrew," she said after the beep, "I'm out front waiting for you."

Five minutes later, the kids who had been milling around enjoying the sunny day had all but disappeared. With a huff of irritation, Penelope got out of her car, locked it and swung her purse over her shoulder. She marched up to the doors. Locked.

Of course. They locked them each day after the first bell rang. She pressed the buzzer. Nothing. She tried again.

"I think they left."

She turned to find Luke's girlfriend, a tall red-head wearing shorts and a T-shirt, smiling at her. What was with teenagers and the skimpy clothes they wore? It was barely sixty degrees for goodness' sake. Must be all those rampaging hormones making them hot-blooded.

"Hello, Kendall," Penelope said. "Nice to see you again."

"Actually, it's Kennedy."

Her face warmed at her blunder. She hated getting anything wrong, especially in front of others. "Oh, I'm sorry, Kennedy." She glanced at the doors. "So there's no one in the office?"

"They might be around, but I know sometimes they leave early if there's nothing going on."

"I'm looking for Andrew. He was supposed to meet me, but he must have forgotten."

Forgotten. Didn't care. Either way.

Kennedy waved at another girl who raced past. "Do you want me to find him for you? Or you could, you know, come with me. I just saw him actually."

"I'll walk with you if you don't mind." She was afraid if Andrew was told his mother was waiting, he'd give one of his annoying shrugs and go back to whatever it was he was doing. "Aren't your legs cold?"

Yes, that was a completely mom thing to say. Then again, she was a mom. Inane questions were to be expected.

"A little. I'm on the cross-country team and we have practice in, like, ten minutes." They walked down the sidewalk toward the rear of the school. "Once we get running, I'm more than warm enough."

All Penelope knew about cross-country running was that the course could be as long as seven or so miles and it encompassed different kinds of terrain. Still, it sounded like a nice sport. A nice, safe sport. She wondered if Andrew would be interested in trying it. He could use an outlet, both for his physical energy and for his emotional well-being. "Do you like it?"

"It's okay. My favorite sport is basketball, but that's in the winter. I like to have something to keep me busy."

Smart girl. Teenagers needed extracurricular interests in their lives, an activity or hobby to keep them socially engaged and focused. It developed a good work ethic, as well as time-management skills. She'd mention joining an after-school program or club to Andrew.

If she ever found him.

They approached the football field. Kids and adults littered the track circling it. Kennedy led the way down the paved walkway, then veered right, taking them behind the school toward another field, this one torn up and muddy.

"Your school has two football fields?" Penelope asked, carefully maneuvering the wide, concrete steps in her heels.

"This is the practice field. The football team only plays games on the turf field."

They were practicing now, bending at the waist and putting their hands in the mud. Penelope wrinkled her nose. It was completely unsanitary.

They all looked the same in their mud-streaked helmets, filthy pants that ended at the knee, mesh jerseys over T-shirts and spiked shoes. A ragtag bunch of testosterone-filled boys looking for an outlet for their aggressions.

She didn't know much about the sport other than it was barbaric, violent and dangerous. Boys and men ramming into each other as hard as they could headfirst.

There had to be an easier way to get concussed and break your bones.

Kennedy stopped to talk to one of her friends. Penelope wasn't sure which was worse, that the other girl had ruined her lovely blond hair by coloring the ends blue, or that she'd completely cut the sides out of a perfectly good shirt and now everyone could see her sports bra.

Not for the first time, she thanked God she didn't have a daughter. Then again, her son was such an enigma to her, maybe a daughter would have been better.

A potbellied man with a shiny bald spot blew a

whistle, the sound piercing the air and her eardrums. He must be the football coach. The boys stopped what they'd been doing and lined up in neat rows. Another whistle and they dropped flat to the ground in perfect synch, kicked out their legs, did a push-up, then jumped to their feet again and ran in place. Another whistle, another round of strange exercises. That whistle was like a magic wand.

She wondered if one would work on Andrew.

Another man approached the first, said something, then turned, facing her, though looking at the team.

Penelope's breath caught. Leo.

Ever since he'd left her office almost a week ago, she'd imagined seeing him several times around town—the produce section of the grocery store, in line at the drive-through at the bank. Even the hair salon where she'd gone to get her singed ends trimmed.

The man had seriously messed up her equilibrium.

She squeezed her eyes shut, then opened them again. Yes, yes, that was definitely Leo Montesano, his jeans faded at the knees, a black T-shirt molded to his broad chest, a backward baseball cap covering his dark hair, sunglasses shielding his eyes. He looked…well…certainly more casual than when she'd last seen him. But also younger. And very appealing in a basic, sexual way with his rounded biceps and lean waist.

She remembered how it had felt to have his hands on her, that light touch on her arm when he'd invited her out. It was pathetic how often she'd relived that moment, how she'd imagined leaning into him instead of pulling away. She'd even dreamed of him, she remembered with a silent groan. A heated dream where she'd touched him, kissed him, with no inhibitions, no fear.

Only to wake up burning with embarrassment. And need.

She sighed. Hadn't she already said he was fantasy material? He belonged in dreams.

He had no place in real life. Especially not hers.

She wasn't the only one affected, she noticed with a small smile. He was inspiring plenty of crushes in the young girls, who stared at him or whispered to their friends while sending him longing glances. To his credit, he didn't seem to notice any of the attention given to him, instead keeping his focus on the boys hopping up and down like puppets on strings.

"Oh, shoot," Kennedy said, looking at her phone. "I have to get to practice, but you can go on over."

The girl was gone before Penelope could ask where she was to *go on over* to. Turning toward the field, her gaze zeroed in again on Leo. Which was only reasonable. And to be expected. She was a heterosexual woman. A single woman. And he was a very attractive man.

No, she didn't regret turning him down the other day—she still didn't believe they would have enough in common to sustain even a coffee date. But that didn't mean she couldn't appreciate the sight of him on the sidelines as he grinned at something one of the boys said.

But staring at him, wishing for things she could never have, things that weren't good for her in the first place, wouldn't find her son and get them to the doctor's on time. Shielding her eyes with her hand, she scanned the area, left to right. Frowned. Nothing. Where on earth—

The coach blew his whistle again and the boys all started walking around, tugging off their helmets, their heads back, their hands on their hips as they caught their breath. Her eyes narrowed at a tall one in the back. There was something familiar about the way he moved, how he walked. She was shaking her head, denial flowing through her even as he took off his helmet and stabbed his fingers through his hair.

Andrew. Her blood chilled. Her mind blanked. But her feet were already marching her toward the field.

"THEY NEED TO RUN."

Leo glanced at Pops. "They'll run plenty during drills."

Pops made a *harrumph* sound. "How do you expect them to be able to play sixty full minutes if they don't build up their stamina?"

"I can't expect them to play any minutes if they're too exhausted from their warm-up."

"In my day, we did things differently."

Leo nodded. "Yeah, but this isn't your day. We've learned a lot about proper training and physical fitness." But he couldn't get angry at Pops, not when he was so excited to be helping out the team. Pops had coached Shady Grove High's football team for years before retiring after Leo graduated. No one was more excited than him when Leo accepted the head coaching job this past summer. "Could you take the defensive ends and work with them today?" Leo asked him. "We'll split the positions into different groups, work with them individually and then run through some plays."

Grumbling about the good old days, Pops went off to collect the kids.

"Don't look now," Bill Webster, his assistant coach, said quietly as he passed, his bald spot shining with sweat, "but you've got a mom bearing down on you. And she looks pissed."

Shit. Leo considered walking away, maybe ducking into the boys' locker room for the next…oh… three hours or so. He wasn't a coward. Just tired of dealing with whining, overbearing parents who were never happy with how much playing time their kid got, constantly questioned why Leo played someone over him, or complained about how hard their poor, precious son worked out during practice.

He loved coaching and the kids were great.

The parents drove him nuts.

He would have instituted a ban on them, at least

during practices, but the principal had told him that wasn't allowed.

Too bad.

Knowing there was no escape, he turned. And watched through narrowed eyes as Penelope stormed toward him, arms swinging, face scrunched up in a dark scowl.

Not a parent but the woman he hadn't been able to get out of his head. Penelope was here. She'd come to him. Had sought him out. His lips curved in a triumphant grin.

She'd changed her mind.

And didn't look too happy about it.

He shouldn't still be attracted to her after she shot him down. Should never find a woman wearing a freaking pantsuit—a gray one, complete with a buttoned-up blazer—sexy. But he did. God help him, he did.

He wasn't sure if that made him crazy or a masochist.

He could question it—and his sanity. But why? Some things just were. Hell, when he'd been hungry for a cheeseburger today for lunch he hadn't analyzed it. He'd ordered one and eaten it. When he'd known at the age of seventeen that he wanted to be a firefighter, he didn't sit down and consider his other options. He followed his gut. Went with his instincts.

No matter how much he would like to pretend otherwise, those instincts were screaming at him to try again with Penelope. That she was worth whatever effort he put in.

Something told him that when it came to her, his effort needed to be Herculean.

Setting his clipboard on the metal bench, he told Bill to take over for a few minutes, then climbed the short knoll to the track, meeting her at the end of the visitors' bleachers.

"Hello, Penelope," he said. "I'm surprised to see you here. Don't tell me. You made a list of pros and cons about going out with me and realized there are no cons."

He winked.

She practically growled.

Not the response he'd been expecting.

"Don't," she snapped, her voice low and angry, her hands curled into fists. "I'm not in the mood for your inept flirting or dubious charm."

He took off his sunglasses, hooked them in the collar of his shirt. "No," he murmured. "I can see you're not here to take me up on my offer of a coffee date. You look like you're here to rip my heart out with your bare hands. What I can't figure out is, why?"

She jabbed a finger at the field, her body vibrating, but her eyes were cool. "What is my son doing out there?"

Leo followed that accusing finger. He saw only his football players, not a younger kid. "Your son?"

"My son. Andrew."

Something niggled at the back of Leo's brain and he turned again, this time zeroing in on Luke Sapko and Drew Freeman. Even from a distance, he noticed Drew's wide eyes, the color draining from his face.

*That* was her son? The sixteen-year-old kid who could catch a bullet?

"Drew Freeman's your son?" he asked, just to clarify. When she'd mentioned she had a son, he'd assumed the boy was younger. Maybe ten or twelve at the most.

"Don't pretend you didn't know."

"How would I know?" he asked, keeping his own voice low, hoping she'd follow suit as they were starting to garner the attention of the kids, coaches and a few parents nearby. "You said your name was Penelope Denning, and you never mentioned how old your son was or his last name."

Color filled her cheeks, but he wasn't sure if it was because she was obviously pissed off enough for her head to explode or because she realized he was right. He hoped it was the latter.

"The question is, what is my son doing out there with the football team?"

Leo scratched his head and readjusted his cap. "He's out there because he filled out the proper paperwork and handed it in on time, passed the mandatory physical given by a local doctor, showed up to every summer workout and practice, attended the day camp we had for two weeks in July, and has put in the time and effort showing he deserves to be on the team."

"I want him off that field."

He waited for her to throw in a good foot stomp. It didn't happen. "Listen, if there's a problem—"

"Oh, you bet there's a problem," she said harshly. "The problem is he doesn't have my permission to play football, so get him off that field. Now."

Leo could only stare at her. What did she mean Drew didn't have permission?

Before he could ask, she sidestepped him and stomped away.

He caught up with her before she reached the bottom of the hill, grabbed her arm. "Why don't we—"

"I will not calm down," she said, yanking away from him, her chin in the air. "This is none of your business."

Irritation pricked. He fought it, didn't want to get into a shouting match in front of the kids. "I was going to suggest we go somewhere quiet and private to discuss this," he said, keeping his tone mild. "Somewhere without the chance of gaining a rapt audience."

She followed his gaze to the field, but seeing Drew out there must have beaten out her common sense because she didn't seem to care whether they had an audience or not. She took two more steps. "Andrew," she called. Loudly. "Come here."

All noise stopped, the boys and assistant coaches

and managers all looking their way. Drew's face flamed red and he hurried off the field.

"Mom," he said, his voice low, "what are you doing here?"

Penelope's eyes widened. "What am *I* doing here? What are *you* doing here?"

"Shit," Drew mumbled, shutting his eyes and tipping his head back. "I forgot about the doctor's appointment."

"That's not the only thing you forgot," Penelope said as the kids edged closer to be in better hearing range. "You seemed to have forgotten to mention to me that you signed up for football."

Leo stepped between then. "Why don't we take this conversation inside?"

She whirled on him, looking ready to slap the common sense right out of his head. "There's no need as we have nothing to discuss. My son does not have permission to play football, he never had permission to play football, and I'm going to make sure the school board, the superintendent and the principal all know that you allowed a minor to be on your team without his parents' consent."

Leo was getting tired of her attitude, especially when she was making Drew so uncomfortable. "Don't you think you're going overboard?"

*"Overboard?"* she repeated, her voice shrill. "My son has a bruise on his back the size of a fist because of this stupid, barbaric sport. He could have

been seriously injured, paralyzed or killed, and it would have been all your fault for letting him play."

"I *let* him play," Leo ground out the words, "because he had signed paperwork."

"You need to check your facts because I would never let my son participate in such a dangerous sport. Especially not one that requires a helmet! You had no right to let him on the team without double-checking with me." She turned to Drew. "And you. How could you do something so dangerous? So risky? And you lied—"

"I didn't—"

"Omitting the truth is the same as lying."

Drew's head hung, his hair falling forward. Poor kid. Leo turned to the rest of the team. "Back to work. Now," he added when they didn't move quickly enough. A couple of stragglers, including Drew's buddy Luke, hung back. "Sapko, you and Williams and Runyan seem to have so much free time, why don't you give me five laps."

"Aw, Coach, come on," Luke whined. "We're just sticking together. Isn't that what you said a good team does?"

"You're right. A team should stick together." Leo raised his voice so the entire team could hear him. "Listen up. Thanks to Sapko reminding me the true meaning of teamwork, you all get to run. Give me seven laps—"

"Seven?" Williams, thirty pounds overweight,

groaned. "I'm going to die." He turned to Luke. "Then I'm going to kill you."

Leo kept his eyes on the boys in front of him. "Make it ten. Unless anyone else wants to add a comment?" If there had been crickets out, they would have been chirping. "Good. Now get moving."

Leo turned back to Penelope and Drew. "Let's go inside and—"

"We're going home," Penelope said, reaching for Drew's arm, but he shifted away and her expression darkened.

Before things got worse, Leo stepped in front of her. Lowered his voice. "You've humiliated your son in front of his classmates and several of his teachers. No matter what he's done, there's no reason to embarrass him this way, not when you could have handled it in a quiet, private manner. Now, before you spew any more threats my way or piss off your son further, let's go inside and discuss this."

TEARS PRICKED PENELOPE'S EYES. She was humiliated and shamed to realize Leo was right. She glanced around. He'd gotten the rest of the football team moving, but there were still plenty of other people watching them. All who had witnessed her outburst.

She glanced at Andrew's sullen face. She swallowed. She wanted to reach for him. To apologize for yelling, for behaving in such an uncontrollable way, but didn't want him to think that gave him the upper hand, was afraid it would when he was the one who should be sorry.

Head high, she nodded at Leo. "Fine."

She followed him inside the school where he led her through the gym to a small office. He motioned for her to take a seat in one of the two vinyl chairs facing a small, cluttered desk. Shades of that day in her office, but reversed. They were now in his domain, a domain of man things with sports memorabilia on the walls, the scent of sweat and dirty sneakers in the air. He was the one in control here, as she'd proven by losing her temper outside.

She didn't like it. Any of it.

"Take a seat next to your mom," Leo told Andrew, who slouched against the wall by the door.

"I'm good," Andrew said.

Leo, in the act of pulling open a drawer, glanced at her son. "Sit down, Drew."

He did so, shooting Penelope a dirty look as he yanked the chair as far away from her as possible.

Leo opened a file, searched through it, then took out a set of papers and slid them across the desk to Penelope. "Here are the forms I received from Drew."

"His name is Andrew," she said, hating feeling as if she was the one in the wrong.

"You want me to call you Andrew or Drew?" Leo asked Andrew as if her opinion on what her son was called didn't even matter.

"Drew's fine," he murmured.

Since when? From the time he'd been a baby, he'd been Andrew. But she wouldn't quibble about it, not when she had bigger issues to fight over. "This isn't my signature," she told Leo, pointing to the illegible name on the line where the guardian was to sign the form.

Leo nodded, though why he thought he needed proof when she'd already told him she hadn't granted Andrew permission to play was beyond her. "Did you sign your mother's name on that form?" Leo asked Andrew softly.

She didn't think he was going to answer, but then he shifted and met Leo's eyes. "Yeah. But only because I knew she'd say no."

"Of course I would have said no." She couldn't believe her son would even want to play such a dangerous sport. "As of this moment you are off the team."

He rounded on her, his eyes wide. "That's not fair."

"It might not be fair," Leo said, all calm and rational. "But it's the truth. You lied about having permission, you lied to your mother and you lied to me. There's no way I could keep you on the team even if I wanted to."

Andrew blanched. "You don't want me on the team?" he asked, sounding small and scared.

Leo rounded the desk, sat on the corner and crossed his arms. "You think I want someone on the team I can't trust? What about the other players, your teammates and friends? This could come back to bite all of us on the ass. More than that, though, I need players who are honest. Players I can trust to make the right decisions, on and off the field."

Andrew swallowed and crossed his arms. Blinking his eyes, he ducked his head.

Why didn't it ever upset him when he let her down? When he disappointed her? What was she doing wrong?

Someone knocked on the door, then it opened, and an elderly man with thick, bushy eyebrows poked his head in. "Everything okay in here?"

"Not really," Leo said. He stood. "Could you take Drew and have him clean out his locker?"

The older man looked surprised, but just nodded at Andrew. "Come on, son."

Andrew went, head down, feet dragging.

"Meet me out front as soon as you're done," Penelope told him.

The older man clapped Andrew on the shoulder and walked him out. Through the window, she could see the man talking to him, his head close to her son's.

She rose, clutching her purse to her chest. What did one say after having a meltdown—and what could most certainly be construed as a temper tantrum—in front of fifty teenagers?

"I can talk to the superintendent," Leo said, obviously one of those annoying people who was never at a loss for words, "see if there's some way we can work this out."

"There's nothing to work out. Andrew is coming home with me and he won't be back."

"What he did was wrong. And he needs to face the consequences of those actions, but there might be a way for him to stay on the team. With your permission this time, of course."

"You have plenty of other boys out there willing to sacrifice their health and well-being for the satisfaction of your ego," she said stiffly. "You don't need my son."

One corner of his mouth kicked up but his eyes were cool. "My ego is just fine. I don't need a bunch of teenagers running around to build it up."

She believed him. From what she could tell, he had the looks, the charm and the confidence to handle any situation. Plus, he was obviously very comfortable with himself. Still, her pride wouldn't let her take back her words.

Her pride had always been her downfall.

"I refuse to allow my son to play a sport that's so dangerous," she told him.

He held his hands out and she bristled. She wasn't a wild beast needing to be tamed. "I understand you're upset he lied—"

"I'm upset because he could have been hurt." Leo didn't understand anything. How could he? As far as she knew, he'd never been married, didn't have any children. "Was already hurt."

"Football is a rough sport, but it's getting better—

better training, better equipment. If possible, I'd like to keep Drew on the team."

"His name," she said slowly and carefully, her words coming out from between her teeth, "is Andrew. And he is not playing, and never will play, football."

"That's your call, of course, but I think you should know he's a valuable member of the team. His teammates, the other coaches, they all like him. *I* like him. He's athletic and a hard worker. He made a mistake, but it's obvious he did it because he really loves the game and wants to play."

"He's a child. He doesn't know what he wants. That's what I'm here for." To help him. Guide him. Stop him from making a mistake.

Keep him safe.

"You only want him to continue playing," she said, turning toward the doorway, "so I don't report your neglect to the school board."

Leo's eyes flashed and narrowed, his expression darkened, and she got a very quick, very real glimpse of what he would be like if he was angry. "I want him to keep playing because I think it could be good for him. Because he enjoys it and the team loves having him. He's made friends and works harder than any other kid out there." He sent her a dismissive glance, his upper lip curled. "But then, you were right the other day at your office. You don't know me at all."

Shaken, feeling unsure when initially she'd been

positive of her position, that she was right, she
walked away, her legs unsteady. She kept going even
though part of her, a big part, wanted to turn around
and apologize for assuming the worst of him.

# CHAPTER NINE

His mom was such a bitch.

Fuming, Andrew glared out the car window, the houses they passed a blur. He hated her. Couldn't even stand being in the car with her, breathing the same air. She'd ruined everything. *Everything.*

Why couldn't she just leave him alone?

When he'd seen her at the field, he'd about shit his pants knowing she'd found out his secret. But then she had to go and rip into Coach, humiliating Andrew in front of his team.

His ex-team, he thought bitterly, his hands fisting. He was done playing football and now all the guys knew he'd had to lie and trick his way onto the team because his mom treated him like a goddamn baby.

"We need to discuss this," she said, her voice calm as she pulled to a stop at a red light.

That was her. Always wanting to talk every damned thing to death.

"I know you're upset," she continued.

He snorted. No shit he was upset.

"What you did was wrong."

"I wasn't robbing stores," he muttered. "I was playing football."

Her fingers tightened on the steering wheel, the knuckles going white. Good. He hated when he was upset and she remained so calm and cool as if it didn't even matter. "You lied. To me. And to your coaches."

"I had to."

"There's never a good reason for lying," she insisted, like some nun or something.

Even though she'd lied to him plenty. Had told him that everything would be fine between her and his dad, that they would work things out.

"Would you have let me play if I'd asked?"

She glanced at him, horrified. "Of course not."

"Exactly. That's why I lied. I knew you wouldn't let me play. You don't understand me or how important playing football is to me."

"It's just a game."

"It's not just a game. It's something I really want to do." It was something he was good at. Finally, something he excelled at that wasn't schoolwork, where the other kids didn't look down on him or call him a dork because he liked to read and usually got good grades. "I'm tired of you treating me like a baby. I'm not sick anymore and I need to make my own decisions. Stop trying to run my life."

His mom pulled to a stop in their driveway. Since they'd been so late for his appointment, she'd had to reschedule. Fine by him. The last thing he wanted was to drive into Pittsburgh and be poked and prodded so a doctor could tell his mom he was still healthy. He just wanted to get away. His skin was hot and itchy, his chest tight, like if he took too deep of a breath he'd crack. Like if he opened his mouth to say something, he'd never stop yelling and his brain would explode, just *boom* all over the car.

He jumped out before she'd even fully shut off the ignition and stalked down the driveway.

"Andrew," she said, loud enough for the whole neighborhood to hear. "Where are you going?"

"For a walk," he snarled, not even looking back.

"No, you're not. You get back here and go to your room. We'll discuss this later when you've had a chance to calm down."

He kept walking. Refrained, barely, from giving her the middle finger. But he wanted to. Oh, how he wanted to let her know how tired he was of her. How done he was with her endless rules and her constant questions. Of her hovering and that stick up her ass, which made it impossible for him to have any fun because she was too uptight to do so herself.

"Andrew," she called again sharply, her tone high and unsteady. "Andrew!"

He ignored her. Let her come after him. He snorted, shoved his hands into his pockets. He'd like to see that. Prim and prissy Penelope chasing her son down the sidewalk. Not going to happen.

He flipped his head to get the hair out of his eyes. Slowed his pace now that he'd put some distance between them. Anger simmered in his blood, heated his veins until it seemed to burn through his skin. He was pissed all the time, even more so than when he was sick. Then all he'd wanted was to be better. To be healthy. Normal.

Now he didn't know what the hell he wanted except to get away from his mom.

He kicked at a rock, but missed, his toe skimming the surface of it. He kept going, head down, the wind chilling his bare arms. Yeah, that was what he needed to do. Get away from her. For good.

Hopefully forever.

He pulled out his phone, dialed his dad's number. Voice mail.

Shit.

It beeped. "Dad." He cleared his throat because he sounded like a whiny baby. Tried again. "Dad. It's me. Call me."

He wasn't going to stay here. Not with her. He'd move back to California, move in with his dad. His steps slowed. Sure, his old man worked all the time, but so what? It wasn't like Andrew needed to be babysat constantly. He'd just have to make sure not to be any trouble. Keep to himself, get himself to school, get a job so he wouldn't need any spending money and help out around the house without being asked. That sort of stuff. As long as he wasn't some pain in the ass, his new stepmom probably wouldn't care.

His throat tightening, he shoved his hands into his

pockets again. Except they hadn't invited him to stay with them over the summer. When he'd brought it up, his dad had claimed he and Lorraine were still getting to know each other or some bullshit like that.

He clenched his fingers around his phone and considered throwing it, but he wasn't that stupid. He kicked an empty recycling container in front of a one-story brick house but it didn't help him feel better. So he kicked it again. And again.

"You might be better off finding a more constructive use of your time and a way to deal with your frustrations than abusing a helpless piece of plastic."

He whirled, breathing hard, and saw Gracie Weaver walking toward him, a huge black dog by her side.

His face flamed, warmth suffused his neck. "Mind your own business," he snapped, giving her a sneer.

She lifted a shoulder. "You're beating up a recycling container in the middle of a public street. Seems to me that is my business. But if you'd rather continue acting like a gorilla, be my guest."

She walked on, but her dog stopped and shoved his nose into Andrew's crotch. Andrew froze. He'd never been around dogs much. Especially not ones big enough to eat his face off with one bite. He considered shoving the dog's head away, but didn't want to get his hand that close to the animal's mouth and all those sharp teeth.

Gracie sighed, tugged on the leash, but the dog

was so huge, it didn't budge. "Seriously, Sauron? That is so disgusting and rude."

The dog lifted his shaggy head, glanced at Gracie, then shoved his nose right back into Andrew's balls. Finally, the dog sat on his haunches and stared up at him, his head tipped to the side as if asking if he could sniff Andrew's crotch some more.

"Sorry about that," Gracie said. "He has no manners."

Andrew couldn't answer, didn't want to take his eyes off the dog. But hadn't he read somewhere you weren't to make eye contact with them? That they took that as a sign of aggression?

Frowning, Gracie stepped closer. "You okay?"

He nodded.

She looked from him to her dog, then to him again. "Are you afraid of dogs?"

He whipped his head up. "No."

He sounded like a complete wuss. Maybe that was why she didn't look convinced. She set her hand on the dog's head and he noticed her nails were short and unpainted, her fingers slender. "It's okay. He won't hurt you."

Yeah, right. That was the same thing the nurses used to say right before poking him with a needle. They'd used that same stupid, soft tone, too, as if he'd believe their lies if they said it nicely enough.

"Really," Gracie went on, stepping closer to Andrew. "Sauron's big and dumb but really sweet and harmless." She cupped the dog's face in both hands, gave it a vigorous rub. "Aren't you, baby?"

People and their pets were so freaking weird.

Andrew's face was hot and probably red. He ducked it, hoped she didn't notice. Not that he cared what some dweeb like Gracie thought, but he didn't want it getting around that he was afraid of dogs.

He edged to the side, then froze when the dog shifted as well. "I just…I don't like dogs all that much."

She looked at him as if he was abnormal, which he hated. People had looked at him that way for half his life, and he never wanted to feel abnormal again. "So you're a cat person?"

"Like, am I part cat?" he asked before he could think of it. He held his breath and hoped she didn't give him a hard time for a lame joke.

She smiled. His stomach did a weird flip. Nerves because of the dog, he assured himself. Not because some wannabe hippie chick looked almost cute with her mouth curved up, her eyes sparkling.

"Ha. No. I mean do you prefer cats over dogs?"

Shrugging, his eyes on the dog, he moved to the left. "I've never thought about it. I've never had a pet."

His mother said they were too much work. See? This was all her fault. If she'd let him have a dog or a cat or even that parakeet he'd wanted when he was ten, he'd know how to act around animals. Not be stuck here waiting for this dumb dog to bite him.

Not forced to have this stupid conversation with Gracie.

"Oh, that's too bad," Gracie murmured, sympathy in her big eyes.

Great. Now Gracie Weaver felt sorry for him. Jesus.

"Whatever." He started walking. He hoped no one had seen them together. He'd busted his ass to make the right kind of friends in Shady Grove and the last thing he needed was to be caught socializing with someone like Gracie. She was too big of a dork with her weird clothes and misfit friends.

Too different.

She wasn't exactly a *complete* loser. She just wasn't in the same league as Luke and Kennedy and their friends.

Andrew's friends now.

Heavy panting sounded behind him. A moment later, her dog nudged his thigh. Andrew jumped, then coughed to cover what had sounded too much like a squeak of surprise. No matter how fast Andrew walked, the dog kept pace. He glared at Gracie. "You following me?"

"Seeing as how I was heading this way when I interrupted your little temper tantrum," she said, not sounding upset by his bitchy tone, "I'd say the answer to that is no. Besides, in case it's skipped your attention, I live next to you. I'm heading home. If it'll make you feel better, safer, Sauron and I can walk on the other side of the street."

And have her telling everyone he was afraid of her dumb dog? No thanks.

Though, in truth, he wouldn't mind if the animal were on the other side of the street. The other side of town would be even better. Andrew stopped, his hands fisted. "I told you," he ground out the words from between his teeth, "I'm not scared of him."

She kept walking as if she didn't care whether he was next to her or not.

Like she was the one who didn't want to be seen with *him*.

Fine with him, he thought, moving again. He'd wanted to be alone. Not be bothered by his chatty next-door neighbor. Or worse, listen to her lecture him on the proper way to handle his frustration, on how to deal with his anger.

He snorted. What did she know? She'd never had cancer. She hadn't been forced to move across the country. She didn't have to live with his mother.

He had real problems. Ones Gracie could never understand.

The dog paused to sniff a street sign. Andrew kept walking, his long legs closing the distance between them. Gracie didn't even glance his way. Good. He didn't want her attention. He'd just keep going. Pass her and not look back.

He would have, too, except when he got close,

he heard her humming "Rivers and Roads" by The Head and the Heart.

One of his favorite bands.

That surprise caused him to sort of stop and stare at her until she raised her eyebrows. Only then did he realize he was acting like an idiot.

"Your dog's name is Sauron?" he asked.

At the sound of it, the dog looked at Andrew. Wagged his tail.

"Yes," Gracie said, her curly hair lifting in the breeze. "It's from *Lord of the Rings*."

"I know." He wasn't a moron. "Sauron's the villain," he pointed out.

Her lips twitched as if holding back a smile. Or a secret. "He's too big to be named after a Hobbit. Even one as cool as Frodo. Plus, my mom gave him to me so it seemed only fitting to name him after the bad guy." She tugged the leash and she and the dog started walking again. Andrew went with them. "There were books before the movies."

His mouth tightened at her condescending tone. "I know that, too. I read them."

He'd read a lot when he was sick. It was his escape.

"What was your favorite one?" she asked.

"I guess *The Fellowship of the Ring*."

She nodded. "That was a good one, but my fave is *The Return of the King*."

He wanted to ask why but she might think it a dumb question. They walked in silence for another block, but it wasn't as weird or awkward as he would have thought. He glanced at her. She wasn't ugly—though the brown-and-orange dress she wore qualified—it was more that she didn't seem to care what she looked like. Each morning she must close her eyes, reach into her closet and put on the first thing she happened to grab.

Today's outfit was a perfect example. Brown tights, fur-topped boots that made an annoying clopping sound on the sidewalk, and that dress with its long, billowy sleeves. Plus, it ballooned around her stomach.

Like she wanted to look fat.

Her light brown hair reached her waist. There was so much of it, all these tight curls, one on top of the other, it was a wonder she could even hold her head up. But, he supposed, she could qualify as cute. If you weren't too picky.

They were in a couple classes together—AP history and trig. Even though he didn't put in much effort in his schoolwork any longer, he still managed to get good grades. But so did Luke and Kennedy, so he didn't feel like a dork about being smart.

More than once, he'd caught Gracie looking at him, only to drop her gaze when he turned her way. Maybe she had a thing for him.

The idea didn't totally suck. It wasn't inconceivable, either. Over the past year, girls had started noticing him more and more, thanks to his growing a few inches and finally putting on some muscle. It was cool, being checked out. Wanted.

Even if it was by someone like Gracie.

He didn't know her that well, despite their being neighbors. He'd been busy with football, work and his new friends all summer, but once or twice he'd seen her in her yard, either alone or with a few of the many younger brothers she had. In school, he didn't notice her much except for those few times in class when he'd feel her gaze on him.

It bugged him that she thought he was afraid of her dog. For some reason, it bugged him even more that she'd seen him acting like a brat.

"I wasn't having a temper tantrum," he blurted. "Back there. At the recycling bin."

"I have five little brothers with one more on the way. Believe me, I know a temper tantrum when I see it. And yours was top-notch."

Damn it, would his face ever cool down again? "I was pissed. I got carried away. That's all."

"What happened?"

"It doesn't matter."

She gave a half shrug that made her boobs rise in a way he couldn't help but notice and kept walking.

"My mom's making me quit the football team," he said, lengthening his stride. "She says it's too dangerous, which is bullshit."

"It doesn't matter if she's right or not when she has the power to make the decision about whether or not you play. Maybe instead of kicking harmless recycling containers and being grumpy to me, you could look into other options in order to keep playing."

"I'm not grumpy," he muttered. Little kids and old men were grumpy. "And there are no other options. I told you, she won't let me play. Nothing I do or say will get her to change her mind. I know her. You don't."

His mom didn't change her mind.

"You don't need her to change her mind," Gracie said.

He stared at her. Maybe she wasn't as bright as he'd thought. "If I don't have parental permission to play, I can't be on the team."

"You have two parents?"

"Duh, but—" Realization dawned and his eyes narrowed. "You think I could play with my dad's permission?"

"I'm not sure, but I do know that before my parents got divorced, any time my dad wouldn't let me do something or if I got into trouble, I'd go to my mom and she'd say yes or yell at my dad for being too hard on me and he'd let me off the hook."

"What do you mean divorced? Isn't that lady with the blond hair your mom?" He'd seen the mom out in the yard plenty of times.

"That's my stepmom, Molly. She and Dad got married when I was nine. My real mom left us when I was six."

He didn't know what to say. She sounded so matter-of-fact, as if it didn't bother her. "Sorry," he muttered, feeling like an idiot for even wanting to offer that lame attempt at sympathy.

Another shrug. "All I'm saying is that sometimes, the threat of going to someone else is enough to get parents to back down or give in. Do you need your mom's permission or just parental permission to play football?"

"I'm not sure," he admitted, but he'd look into it as soon as he got home.

"And you shouldn't feel bad about pitting your parents against each other," she said as they stopped in front of her house. She unhooked the dog's leash and he ran into the yard. "I mean, yeah, it's manipulative, but they don't get what it's like to be a teenager, you know? Besides, they're the ones who split in the first place, right?"

She was right. He hadn't wanted his parents to get divorced. They hadn't even fought. There had been no yelling, no slamming doors or threats or anything. Just...*we don't want to be married anymore so we're going to rip your life apart and oh, yeah, you have to move across the country because your mom doesn't want to be in the same town as your father so say goodbye to your life.*

It sucked.

But Gracie had a point. A good one. And standing this close to her, he started to think maybe she was cuter than he'd originally thought.

Plus, she smelled good. Really good, like vanilla.

He glanced at his house. He'd have to go back there eventually. But not yet.

"Want to sit on the porch for a few minutes?" He held his breath, hoping she wouldn't blow him off, telling himself it didn't matter if she did because she was just his goofy neighbor.

"Sure." She smiled.

He smiled back. Yeah. She was definitely cute. If they sat on her porch, there on the corner swing, no one would see them. And if they happened to become friends, that was okay.

Because no one would ever have to know.

"COACH? CAN I talk to you for a minute?"

Leo slowed as he made his way to the practice field and glanced at Drew. He was pissed at the kid, sure, but he didn't hold grudges. Besides, he liked Drew. "You've got as long as it takes me to reach the field," he said. "And then you need to be off that property since you're not a part of the team."

Okay, so maybe he was more than a little pissed. The kid had lied to him, after all.

Mainly, though, Leo was disappointed.

Drew caught up. "If I got permission to play, could I get back on the team?"

Leo stopped, frowned at him. "Your mom's going to let you play?"

He found that hard to believe given the way she'd reacted yesterday.

The kid shifted. "My dad will let me. If I get him to sign the papers—"

"Sorry. No can do."

And he started walking again.

Drew hurried past him, then turned to walk backward. "Why not? Look, the only reason I lied and forged my mom's name was because I knew she wouldn't let me play."

"You already gave your reasons yesterday," Leo said, nodding at one of his fullbacks as the kid jogged to the field. Being late meant extra laps. "But that doesn't excuse what you did. Now, you plan on using your dad to get what you want, to pit him against your mom? Trust me, that won't go over well."

"I read the rules," Drew muttered, all sullen and resentful. "It only says I need a guardian to sign the papers. Even though I live with my mom, my parents share custody of me, legally, so my dad can sign."

Leo stopped and removed his sunglasses. "You think you can trick the system again? I guarantee you it won't work. And even if it did, even if the superintendent or the athletic director allowed it, I still wouldn't let you on the team."

The kid looked ready to cry, his face pale. "What? Why not?"

Seriously? He didn't get it? Teenagers. Logic and reason often skipped right over their heads. They only saw and believed what they wanted, what would work for them.

"Because you lied to me and your teammates. You put the entire team in jeopardy. You were selfish and manipulative."

Red blotches appeared on Drew's cheeks. "But I told you why—"

"Doesn't matter why. You made the wrong choices and there are consequences for those actions."

"That's not fair," he cried.

Leo laid his hand on the kid's shoulder. "Hate to break the news to you, but life is often not fair."

It wasn't fair—not to her family, not to her friends and especially not to herself—that Samantha was killed in that accident over Labor Day weekend. The choice she had made to go too fast around that curve cost them everything, and it pissed Leo off that Drew didn't register that his decisions had consequences. Even something as seemingly small as forging a parent's consent had an impact on others. Leo didn't want him going through life thinking he could make mistakes and never have to pay for them or never suffer the outcome of the bad choices he made. In Leo's line of work, he too often saw those choices ruin a life or, worse, take one.

"Believe me, I know."

Leo was taken aback by the bitterness in Drew's tone, but put that aside to deliver a lesson about consequences.

"I could have been fired by allowing you to play without permission. More important, the team could have faced punishment or sanctions or been forced to forfeit wins if you'd played and it came out later that you were ineligible. You could have ruined your teammates' year, their chances of returning to the district playoffs, of getting scouted by college teams. You lied and you let your team down. I'm not about to forget that. So instead of trying to find a way around the rules, why don't you figure out a way to play without bending them or lying or manipulating the people around you? Growing up, acting like an adult, means taking responsibility for your actions and not taking the easy way out."

"But the rules say I can play," Drew insisted.

Leo pinched the bridge of his nose. Oh, to be so stubbornly clueless. He dropped his hand. "Doesn't matter. It's my team and I don't want you on it. Not this way."

Putting his sunglasses on, he walked away.

Only to be stopped again when Drew darted in front of him.

The kid put a whole new spin on the word *tenacious*.

Leo could almost admire him for it.

"What if my mom agrees to let me play?" Drew asked.

"Something tells me that's not about to happen." *Something* such as Penelope being even more stubborn than her son.

"But what if she did? Would you let me on the team then?"

Leo tipped his head back, blew out a heavy breath.

Since the heavens weren't providing any guidance, he rolled his shoulders and faced Drew. The kid looked so damned hopeful that, despite his intentions to teach him a lesson, Leo couldn't say no. "If your mother was fully on board, I'd consider taking you back."

Drew's face lit up like he'd just been handed his very own Playboy Bunny. "That's all I'm asking for, Coach. Could you…could you come to my house tonight? Around seven? Please," he added when Leo hesitated. "Please. It'd mean a lot to me."

Christ, but he was turning into a grade-A sap. "I'll give you fifteen minutes, not a second more."

Drew grabbed Leo's hand and shook it hard enough to make Leo's teeth rattle. "Thanks, Coach. Thanks. You won't regret it."

He already did.

# CHAPTER TEN

"WHAT ARE YOU doing here?"

Penelope winced, her hand squeezing her front door handle. That had been awfully rude. In her defense, the last person she'd expected to find on her porch was Leo Montesano of the broad shoulders and sexily rumpled hair.

"Drew invited me," Leo said, not the least bit perturbed by her lack of welcome. Must be nice to remain so consistently unruffled. "He didn't tell you?"

"For that to happen, he'd have to be speaking to me."

She'd waited for Andrew to return last night for almost thirty minutes before grabbing her keys, determined to track him down if need be and bring him home. But when she'd reached her car, she'd heard his voice next door. Ducking behind the hedge separating her driveway from the Weavers', she'd spied him on the neighbors' wide porch.

With Gracie.

Not quite what Penelope had expected, but at least she'd known he was safe. She'd slunk into her house like some inept stalker, then busied herself with dinner and laundry until he'd finally returned an hour later.

At which point her beloved son had grabbed the plate she'd fixed him, grunted in her general direction, then locked himself in his room. She'd let him go, had wanted him to have time to cool off before discussing his punishment. When she'd gone up at nine, she told him he was grounded for two weeks and took his phone.

This morning he hadn't even looked at her, just left for school. And when she got home from work over an hour ago, he'd refused to come out of his room.

Leo angled his body forward. "How much time do you think you're going to need?" he asked in a slow drawl that elicited gooseflesh on her arms.

The man was potent. Potent and an expert at working women, seducing them with that face and body into giving him whatever he wanted.

She'd do best to remember that. "For what, exactly?"

"To decide whether or not to let me in."

"No time needed there at all. I'm not interested in hearing anything you have to say."

A muscle contracted in his jaw. He straightened. "You made that perfectly clear yesterday."

Her stomach grew queasy with embarrassment. Sure. Throw her horrible behavior in her face. Honestly, how many times could one woman make a fool of herself in front of a man? There had to be a limit.

"Did I also make it clear that there's nothing you can do or say to convince me to let Andrew play football? That no amount of charm is going to work on me?"

He stepped closer, but this time, his expression was dark. Determined.

Dangerous.

Her mouth dried and she shifted behind the door, shutting it more, but he wedged his foot between it and the frame.

"Now, that," he said, his voice low and husky, his gaze dropping to her mouth for one long, nerve-racking moment, "sounds like a challenge."

The blood rushed in her ears. She locked her knees. All the reasons she'd given him for rejecting his date invitation held true, but this, this right here, had been a big part of it. She couldn't handle him. Was so far out of her element, she might as well be on a separate planet.

"It...it wasn't."

"That's probably for the best." Leaning forward, his chest pressing against her shoulder, he spoke close to her ear. "If I decide to charm you, I wouldn't want it to be about anything or anyone other than you and me."

Her lips parted on a soundless *oh*.

"Mom?"

With a small shriek, Penelope jumped and whirled around, her heart racing. "I... You..."

Andrew frowned, his gaze going from her to the barely open door. "What are you doing?"

She shook her head. "Nothing. I mean…" She eased away from the door. "Someone's here to see you."

Andrew nodded at Leo. "Coach," he said, his voice sounding deeper than it had a second ago. "Thank you for coming." And then her son stepped forward and offered Leo his hand. "Please, come on in."

Penelope gaped at Andrew. Polite manners and not a sneer in sight?

It was a miracle.

And extremely suspicious.

She shut the door and followed them into the living room. "Andrew, you didn't mention Leo was coming over." She hated surprises. Better to know what was coming so you could be prepared for it. "What's this about?"

"Sit down. Please," he added almost as an afterthought.

She perched on the edge of a chair while Leo sat in the middle of the couch. Andrew remained standing. Looked nervous. He paced the length of the room, then stopped and inhaled deeply. "I'm sorry. For everything."

Penelope blinked. Not at his words—though they were ones she heard rarely—but because he seemed sincere.

"Care to be more specific?" Leo asked.

Andrew nodded as if accepting that he had to step up and do this the right way. "I'm sorry I lied about where I was," he told Penelope. "And that I forged your name on those papers."

She sighed. She could see where this was headed. "I appreciate your apology, but it doesn't change how I feel about you playing."

"I know it doesn't. That's why I asked Coach to come here. So I could explain to you both why I did what I did." He faced Leo. "I'm sorry I lied to the team and risked getting them into trouble. I just... I know it was wrong, but I really wanted to play, to be a part of the team." Swallowing, he wiped his palms down the front of his jeans. "You see when I was little I was...I was sick."

Penelope stopped breathing. Andrew didn't like to talk about what he'd gone through. He'd kept it inside, not sharing his thoughts or feelings about his illness with her or his father. As far as she knew, he didn't talk to anyone about his illness.

"It was pretty bad," Andrew continued. "Bad enough that I spent a long time in the hospital. Even longer on bed rest, so I missed a lot of the things that my friends did. Sports and field trips and band practice. Stuff like that. Normal stuff, you know? Which is how I feel when I play football. Like a normal kid."

"Oh, Andrew," Penelope said quietly, her heart breaking for him.

Their eyes met and she was sure he was remembering, as she was, the long days in the hospital, the treatments and the fear that it was all for nothing. That no matter how much medicine they pumped into his body, they'd lose the battle.

They'd lose him.

But they hadn't. He was alive. Whole and healthy and standing before her wanting to put himself in danger.

How could she permit that?

Andrew shoved his hands into his pockets. "I was really mad at you yesterday," he told Penelope.

"I think that was fairly obvious," she said drily.

"I was so mad I called Dad about staying with him."

She felt as if the air had been knocked from her lungs. "What?"

"He didn't answer. He didn't even call me back."

She wanted to make excuses for Todd. Not for her ex-husband's sake, but for her child's. "You know how busy he is at work."

Andrew snorted. "Yeah. He's always busy." He shook his head. "It doesn't matter, because even if he told me I couldn't live with him, I came up with the idea of asking him to sign the papers and give me permission to be on the football team. But Coach said the only way he'll consider letting me play is if *you* give me permission. Even then it's not a done deal so I wanted to talk to you both, let you know how important playing is to me and how sorry I am. Really. I'll work extra hard and keep my grades up and I won't lie or anything if you'll just let me play. Both of you."

Penelope was still reeling from his attempting to go behind her back by asking his father. Thank God Todd hadn't answered Andrew's call. She didn't want her ex-husband to hurt their son. And he would.

Because if Andrew asked to live with him, Todd would say no. He'd reject their son the same way he'd rejected her.

"I don't understand why this is so important to you," she admitted. "There are so many other sports you could play, nonviolent sports where the risk of you getting hurt is significantly lower."

"I know," Andrew said. "But I'm not afraid of getting hurt."

"I'm afraid of you getting hurt," she said quietly. It was her greatest fear.

"Yeah, I get that and I understand, but I'm good at football and I like being good at something."

She leaned back in the chair. "Honey, you're good at a lot of things."

He rolled his eyes. Looked at Leo. "She means I'm good at school."

Was that something to be ashamed of? She straightened. "There's nothing wrong with being smart."

"Why can't I be smart and good at a sport? Look, I'm not afraid of getting hurt because after everything I've been through, there's no fear about stuff like bruises or broken bones or anything. When I play…" He pressed his lips together and seemed to think his next words through. When he spoke, his voice was quiet, sincere and earnest. "When I'm on the field, when I catch a pass and start running, it's like no one can catch me. Like nothing can touch me. I'm free. For the first time in forever, I feel free. Light. Like I don't have to be so scared all the time," he ended in a whisper.

Penelope's throat tightened. She understood what her son was telling her. The fear that he'd had, that they'd all had when he'd been so sick, would always be with them. Except he'd found a way to forget about it, if only for a few minutes.

She almost envied him.

Every day, every moment, she still lived under that fear, that weight. The constant worry and stress, afraid of tomorrow because she wasn't sure what it would bring. Clinging to today because for that moment, for those precious hours, her son was with her.

"Tell her, Coach," Andrew begged, obviously sensing her hesitation.

Leo crossed his ankle over his knee. "What would you like me to say?"

"Tell her all that stuff you told us at our first practice. How football isn't just a sport about hitting each other and who's bigger or stronger or faster. How it's about playing as a unit and learning how to put your ego aside for the betterment of the team. How you can learn plays and the rules, but to play you have to have the heart and the will to be your best. How you want us all to take those lessons off the field into our daily lives. And to work toward thinking of each other as a family and always being mindful of the needs of others."

When he was done, he was out of breath and almost sweating. Penelope couldn't remember the last time she'd seen her son so passionate, so eloquent.

Leo grinned. "Seems to me you just told her."

Apparently handsome Leo had a strong influence on her son. She wasn't sure whether or not to be happy about that. At the moment, though, she had bigger problems—like figuring out how to refuse Andrew's plea.

"I just don't feel comfortable letting you play football," she said.

Andrew nodded. "I know, but how about this? You let me stay on the team—that is—" he glanced at Leo "—if I'm allowed back on. For a month. I'll keep my grades up and will lose the attitude and you can come to all the practices and games so you understand what's going on, the rules and everything about football. And then, if I'm still in one piece, we'll discuss letting me stay on the team permanently."

She wanted to say no. She wanted to encase him in Bubble Wrap to protect him, but that was extreme, even for her. And she knew it.

"Please, Mom," Andrew begged, looking and sounding unlike she'd ever seen him. This was important to him. Very important. "Please. I want to be a normal teenager. Just for once."

He *was* normal. Perfectly normal. Weren't most teens sullen and rude from time to time? And even that was a fairly recent development. Up until she and Todd separated, Andrew had been the way she was as a teenager.

Quiet. Polite. Focused on academics.

But when she thought about her high-school days, she wasn't sure being like her was a good thing or not. She'd put her schoolwork first, had excelled in her studies.

And hadn't had any friends.

She hadn't known what to say to her classmates. Hadn't seemed to share any of the same interests as the other girls, so hadn't known how to make friends. As a result, she'd spent most weekends at home by herself. Though her parents had assured her she was smart to focus on her studies, she had felt twinges of loneliness. Had wondered if she was missing out on something by not having girlfriends and sleepovers and crushes on boys.

Had wondered if there was something wrong with her.

That didn't have to be her son's life. He could have courage and go after what he wanted. For years, Andrew had fought his illness. Now he was fighting to regain his childhood. She couldn't change the past. Couldn't change the time he'd spent weak and throwing up, his hair gone, his body racked with pain. They couldn't go back. But he could move forward—even if she couldn't.

"You can play," she said, having to force the words out because she was so afraid of him getting hurt. "But you have to keep your end of the bargain."

"Really?" he asked, his eyes wide, a huge grin splitting his face. "You mean it?"

No. "Yes."

"And you'll come to practices, learn the game so you don't just say I have to quit after a month?"

How bright was her child? She had considered doing that very thing. "I won't come to every practice." She did have a job, after all. "But I will learn all I can about football, and I will come to your games."

He gave a whoop and rushed over to her, pulled her to her feet and wrapped her in a hard hug. "Thank you," he said. "Thank you."

She hugged him back, not wanting to let go, but knowing she had to. She leaned away. Smiled. "You still have to convince your coach to let you on the team."

They both turned to look at Leo.

How THE HELL was Leo supposed to say no when Penelope and Drew were staring at him—Penelope warily, Drew with hope in his eyes.

"Can I come back, Coach?" Drew asked.

Leo tapped his fingers on his knee. "You lied to me. To the team."

The kid nodded. "Yes, sir. I'm really sorry."

"Being sorry is great, but it's only a start. If you want to play for me, you need to be respectful of your mother and obey her rules. No sliding by with the grades, either." All athletes needed to maintain a C average to be eligible to play. "If you're capable of As, you'd better get As, is that clear?"

Drew nodded, his Adam's apple bobbing as he swallowed.

"No more lies, no getting into trouble anywhere, not at home or at school. There are no three strikes with me. You get two, and only two, chances. You've already used up one." He fixed a long, hard stare on Drew, wanting the kid to realize exactly how serious he was about this two-strikes rule. "First thing you need to do when you get to practice tomorrow is apologize to the rest of the team and the other coaches. Then you need to spend the next month proving you're willing to work hard to make it up to them, and to me, and to prove to your mother you deserve this chance."

"So I can play? I'm on the team?"

Leo wasn't sure this wasn't a huge mistake, but the kid had obviously already been through a lot.

Besides, everyone deserved a second chance.

He nodded and stood. "I'll see about clearing things with the athletic director, but yeah, you're back on the team."

Drew stuck out his hand. "Thank you, Coach. You won't regret it."

Leo shook the kid's hand. "Make sure I don't."

Drew turned to Penelope. "Can I get my phone? Call Luke and tell him?"

"Sure." She still looked shell-shocked as she retrieved the cell phone and handed it to Drew.

"Thanks. I'll do the dishes when I'm done."

And he was gone, showing some of that impressive speed of his by disappearing before either Leo or Penelope could comment.

"I don't know whether to be angry at you for getting him so excited about football," Penelope said, "or grateful. That boy has never, not once in his life, volunteered to help with the dishes."

Leo stuck his hands in his pockets. "My mom always said kids may not be excited about helping out but they need to do so just the same. She didn't wait for us to volunteer. She simply told us what to do and expected it to get done."

"Unfortunately," Penelope said, sounding snooty and superior, "that doesn't work with every child."

He didn't point out that she wouldn't know if she didn't try—it wasn't his business whether Drew did chores around the house and helped his mother.

"I'll walk you out," she continued.

He followed her to the door, stopped when she opened it. "You okay?" he asked.

"No. I'm terrified something's going to happen to him."

"You can't protect him from everything." If parents could do that, he wouldn't have seen as many accidents as he had, wouldn't have had to see the grief and unmentionable loss on Samantha's parents' faces the night she died. "Football isn't without risk and it is a very rough sport. Then again, life isn't without risk."

She laughed, though the sound held no humor. "Yes, I'm well versed in that truth."

He remembered what Drew had said about being sick. Saw how overprotective Penelope was. There must have been something bigger in their past than Leo realized. "Do you mind me asking? About Drew's illness?"

Her lips thinned. "Leukemia."

Leo's head snapped back as if he'd been slapped. That explained Drew's response when Leo had said life wasn't fair. Christ, the poor kid. "I'm sorry."

She nodded and crossed her arms. "He got through it. He wasn't supposed to. At first, the doctors gave him only a thirty percent chance of surviving five years. Yet he somehow pulled through and proved them all wrong." She leaned against the doorjamb looking tired and vulnerable. "He was first diagnosed when he was eight. We went through three years of treatments and fears."

"That when you and your husband started having problems?"

"No, we were on decent footing until Andrew was thirteen. In the end, it was too much for us both. My husband…my *ex*-husband…has a demanding job and wasn't around the way he could have been until it all got to be too much. Though we separated, we tried working things out for over a year. Until Todd told me he'd found someone else and wanted a divorce. After that, he began to spend less and less time with Andrew. When the divorce was final, it seemed like a good time for Andrew and me to make a new start."

She paused, staring sightlessly at the floor, as though caught in memory. "I thought he'd outgrow the anger and resentment he has for me. He blames me for the divorce, for tearing him away from his life in California. I thought things were getting better because I'd stuck the course," she said quietly, finally lifting her gaze to his. "Now I guess any improvement is all thanks to you and some sport where boys run full speed into each other and try to break as many of their opponents' bones as possible."

"I didn't do anything," Leo said. "Maybe what he needed, what he *needs,* is something constructive to do with his time. He is really good at football and he has pride in the sport and his ability. And I promise, I'll do my best to keep him safe."

It wasn't a promise he made lightly, because he knew how difficult promises like that were to keep.

"I appreciate it," she said sincerely, although there was something in her expression that said she knew there was only so much Leo could control. And other than keeping Drew on the bench all the time, he couldn't guarantee anything.

She sighed and brushed back a loose strand of

hair. His fingers twitched to do it for her. He curled them into his palm.

"You can't protect him," she said.

"Neither can you."

She snorted. "I know. He resents that I try. I don't understand. When he was little, he always turned to me to make things right."

"He's not a little kid anymore. He's a teenager quickly growing into an adult. He's already been through so much. You both have. Maybe you need to give yourselves some credit."

"I like to think I do."

"You want him to respect you? It's a two-way street, and part of that is respecting his choices, his thoughts and feelings, his wants and what he needs, even when you don't agree with them."

"That's the problem," she whispered. "I don't know what he wants or needs. Not anymore. And if I don't know, how can I make sure he gets it?"

"I'm not a parent so I might be way off base, but it seems to me it's not your job to make sure he gets everything he wants. Instead, you help him cope when he doesn't. Help him figure out what's best for him. I know you're worried about him playing football, and I get why. His idea about you coming to practices is a good one. You're welcome anytime, and if you have any questions or concerns whatsoever, let me know."

He stepped forward, partly because he wanted to be near enough to get a whiff of her subtle floral scent and partly because he liked how nervous she got when he got too close. "You're a good mom. Maybe you need to worry less about things that are out of your control. Seems to me both you and Drew could use something to focus on other than his illness and worrying he'll get sick again."

She smiled, and it was as if he'd been smacked upside the head. "That's a great idea," she said, and he loved her dry tone. "I'll take up crocheting and I'm sure all my worries will disappear."

He grinned. "Actually, I was thinking of something else."

"Cross-stitch?"

He was intrigued by Penelope more so now than ever. She was obviously a devoted mother and an intelligent, capable woman, but it was the glimpses of fire and passion that she'd shown that really got to him. The way she had laid into him yesterday at the field was not what he'd expect from such a normally cool customer.

"Go out with me," he heard himself say and immediately wished the words back. She'd already shot him down, and he wasn't a glutton for punishment. But he needed to ask one more time. "We'll have dinner, maybe a drink or two. We'll talk and enjoy each other's company and maybe, just maybe, you'll find yourself going a few hours without those worries."

# CHAPTER ELEVEN

PENELOPE WAS TEMPTED—more tempted than any woman in her right mind should be. Then again, she *was* a woman and Leo was leaning toward her, his eyes dark and intense, his mouth curved up. It was impossible to act indifferent. To pretend her hormones weren't screaming at her to take a walk outside her comfort zone. Yet she'd never been ruled by her body or by her heart.

She used her head.

"As flattering as it is that you're still interested in dating me," she said, gripping the door tightly, "I don't think it's wise. Especially now that Andrew is playing football for you."

It was better to keep personal and professional relationships separate, and Leo was now firmly in the professional category—at least where her son was concerned.

His grin widened, and she had absolutely no idea what she'd said or done that was so amusing. "Anyone ever tell you that you think too much?"

She blinked. "No."

There was no such thing as thinking too much for

her parents. Intellectuals, they prided themselves on their intelligence. On their children's intelligence. Todd had often said he'd been attracted to her mind, to how organized she was. How focused.

Until he'd decided she hadn't been focused enough on him, that all she ever thought about, cared about was their son.

All Andrew ever said was that she worried too much. Nagged too much. Hovered too much.

To the point that some days she felt she couldn't do anything right.

"Maybe," Leo said, "it would help if you had something to take your mind off your problems and all those thoughts zinging around in your head."

His voice was low and husky, his eyes heavy-lidded. Her blood heated; her throat dried. With the dusk behind him, the only light illuminating his features was from the porch, which cast his face in shadows, making the angles appear sharper, his expression somehow predatory and dangerous.

A tingle of awareness climbed her spine, telling her she needed to retreat. Push him away. That this—being close to him with her son upstairs, with the twilight somehow making it seem as though they were the only two people in the world—was a mistake.

She stepped back. "My thoughts are just fine, thank you."

He chuckled, and Penelope knew he was undeterred. She wasn't sure whether to be flattered, excited or terrified when he moved closer, forcing her to press against the door, her back against the solid wood. "I don't want you to stop thinking," he murmured, his gaze dropping to her mouth for one heart-stopping second. "Just maybe...focus on something else besides Drew and your worries." She watched, mesmerized, as Leo lifted a strand of hair at her temple and rubbed it between his fingers, his eyes on the motion. "Isn't it about time you focused on yourself? On your wants? Your needs?"

Oh. My.

She told herself she was going inside, this very minute, to end this madness before it went completely out of control. Then he lowered his head and she froze. Stopped blinking, stopped breathing. Her eyes wide, her body ready, she waited, helpless, for his kiss. Only to have him shift direction and brush his lips against her cheek.

She jerked. Barely refrained from pressing her fingertips to her cheek where it still felt warm from his mouth. That chaste kiss had definitely made her lose focus—the brush of his lips on her skin had been electric. His fault. It had to be. She'd never responded to a man in such a way before.

"Have coffee with me," he murmured, his tone husky. "Just as friends."

That brought her out of her reverie. "Friends?"

He straightened, gave her that lethal grin. "You look like you could use a friend."

God, was she that pathetic? That easy to read?

"I don't have friends," she blurted, feeling inept and silly.

His eyebrows shot up. "Everyone has friends."

"I mean…of course I've had friends." The rare, cherished companionship of another woman. Never a man. And she sounded like a complete idiot. "But not since I got married. Not since I had Andrew."

Not since he'd become sick. All of her attention and energy went into his well-being, into getting him healthy.

Leo straightened. "Then I'd say it's time you changed that. Come to practice Thursday and after, we'll grab a bite to eat. Drew can join us."

She didn't know what to say. She knew what she should say. She should thank him politely and refuse his offer. But she could use a friend, and she was often on her own. She was lonely. And here a gorgeous, charming man wanted to spend time with her.

In this, at least, she could say yes to him. She could be his friend. She smiled and realized it felt odd, as if she hadn't done it in much too long. "Okay. Yes. That sounds fun."

He winked and headed down the porch stairs. "See you then."

She was already looking forward to it.

ANDREW QUIETLY SHUT the back door. Not that his mom would hear him or care that he was outside. She might wonder what he was doing on the deck when it was this late and so cold out. If she asked, he'd just tell her he'd needed some fresh air. He'd bring up his time in the hospital, remind her of how desperate he used to get to be outside, if even only for a few minutes.

She'd back off then, stop asking him so many questions.

He wasn't mad about it. For once, he didn't feel pissed. He'd gotten his way, after all, was back on the team and his mom was on board. For now. That could change, he knew, but he'd do everything he could to make sure she let him play football.

A light went on in the house next door, in one of the upper rooms, and his breath caught in his lungs. A shadow went by. Was it Gracie? Not that he cared, he assured himself. She was too nerdy for him. She wasn't even close to being as pretty as Kennedy or Estelle.

The shadow walked by the window again and stopped, and the curtain opened. He quickly grabbed his guitar and bent his head over it like he was concentrating on the chords when, in truth, he knew them all by heart and rarely had to look at his hands. He stopped strumming, his heart racing, then chanced a glance up again.

Gracie. She waved. He nodded and began to play, messed up a set of chords, and started over.

When he looked up again, she was gone. His shoulders lowered in disappointment. Not that he wanted to see her or anything. He'd come out here for the air and to play guitar, even though his strumming sounded harsh and discordant.

He looked at the window again. Dark. His room was on the other side of the house so he couldn't see her room from it. Not that he wanted to spy on her or anything creepy like that. Though in all the movies and TV shows the neighbors—if they were boy/girl—always had bedrooms facing each other. They would come and go into each other's houses, usually through their bedroom windows.

Weird.

He played, his fingers clumsy and cold. He hadn't picked up his guitar in months, had stopped when he'd started playing football, started being friends with Luke and Kennedy. Yet for some reason, he felt like playing tonight. He'd missed it.

His phone buzzed. A message from Kennedy, a friendly, chatty one, nothing flirtatious. Nothing suggesting she wanted to be anything other than friends.

"I didn't know you played."

He froze and glanced at Gracie. Her hair was pulled back and she wore tight bright blue yoga pants and a huge tie-dye T-shirt that made her chest look even bigger.

He set the phone aside. Cleared his throat. "A little."

"Cool." She sat on the deck step, tucked her feet under her and smiled at him. "It's nice. Hearing you play. Much better than my brother banging on his drums. I told Molly it was a mistake to get him a drum set. She should have made him stick with the trumpet. At least it was small enough I could hide it. He'd look for days before he'd find it."

"You hid your brother's trumpet? Did you get in trouble?"

"Not really. My parents don't believe in punishing us unless it's for something major like grand theft auto or murder."

He couldn't imagine not getting into trouble. Yeah, it was a relatively new thing—when he had been a kid, he'd never gotten yelled at or grounded. Probably because he'd been such a kiss-ass, always trying to keep his parents happy, to make up for worrying them by getting sick, taking up so much of their time and attention.

Though he liked to believe it was his mom's fault for leaving his dad, Andrew knew *he* was the real reason they had gotten divorced.

He strummed a series of chords. "Must be nice," he said. "Not having to worry about getting into trouble for anything."

She laughed, a surprisingly deep, husky sound, so different from the high-pitched giggles of most of the girls their age. "Believe me, there's plenty about being their daughter that makes up for not getting into trouble."

"Yeah? Like what?"

"Like them popping out a kid—and in the case of the twins, two of them—every two years like clockwork. Or Molly making a scene in the grocery store because they don't carry organic kale…or making us kale chips and thinking it's some sort of treat."

"Your family is so weird."

He hadn't meant to say that, but she didn't look offended. "I guess. Though I prefer to think of us as unique. We don't follow the crowd and I like that. Sometimes being different doesn't mean you're weird or a freak. Sometimes it just means you're different."

"I heard your brother practicing his drums," Andrew said, wanting to change the subject. "You're right. He sucks."

She shivered and hugged her arms around herself. "It doesn't matter. He'll eventually get bored and move on to something new. Hopefully something that doesn't make the dogs freak out so much."

"You have more than Sauron?"

"We have three. Sauron, Mickey and Bear—who's actually the smallest."

"They don't like music?"

"They're scared of loud noises, especially Sauron. The drums, fireworks, things like that."

He strummed some more, then set down the pick and began plucking out a song with his fingers. "My mom says dogs are too much work."

"She's right, but they're, like, part of our family so I can't imagine not having them. I mean, the kids are a lot of work, too, but that doesn't stop my parents from having more."

Maybe that's why his parents hadn't had any more kids. Because he was too much work, especially after he got sick. He played a song, a popular dance tune.

Gracie grinned. "I like that song better your way. Makes it sound less frantic than the original version."

Pleasure suffused him, but he pushed it aside. It didn't matter to him what she thought or what she liked. Still, he found himself playing another song, enjoying sitting out in the cool night with her. She did look chilled and he should offer her his sweatshirt, but he didn't want to give her the wrong idea, didn't want her to think he was into her or anything, though he was pretty sure she had a thing for him.

It made him feel good, knowing a girl had a crush on him, even if it was dorky Gracie from next door.

"My mom is letting me stay on the football team," he told her, wanting to celebrate with someone, telling himself it was because she was available even though he could easily tell Kennedy. But for some reason, he didn't feel like texting Kennedy tonight. Didn't want to have some stupid, useless conversation about nothing. Or, worse, about how Luke had promised once he'd quit the hockey team last year that they'd spend more time together but now he was all into football and back to ignoring her.

It was so much work, trying to think of things of say, topics to discuss that didn't make him sound like a loser. He worried about every word, how she would take it, how it made him look.

He didn't have those worries with Gracie. Probably because he didn't want to sleep with her.

"Yeah?" Gracie asked. "That's nice."

"Nice? I thought you'd be more excited."

"I don't understand your fascination with the sport, to be honest. It seems like a bunch of guys running and bumping into each other, trying to get some ball. And is it even a ball? I mean, it's not round. Think about it."

He did, then realized he actually was thinking about whether a football qualified as a ball and shook his head to clear it. "There's more to it than just running into the other team. There's skill in calling and running the plays. There's athleticism in avoiding a tackle. And there's being smart about the game. Take Peyton Manning, for instance. He's always studying the strategy, always learning and improving. It's as much mental as it is physical."

She was staring at him, and his face warmed. He sounded like an idiot. "Wow," she said. "It's cool that you're so into it. I didn't mean any disrespect or anything. I'm all for everyone having their own thing, marching to the beat of their own drum, you know?"

He nodded, relieved that she got it. "Anyway, I like playing. It's fun."

"Then that should be a good enough reason to keep doing it, don't you think? Most people don't concern themselves with what's fun or what feels good to them. They're too worried about how they come across, what other people think of them."

"Is that how you feel?" he heard himself ask. "Like others are judging you?"

She laughed. "I know they are. I get it all the time. People comment on how I dress, how my family lives."

"You could always, you know, pick out different clothes."

"I could," she said slowly. "But why should I? I'm not trying to prove anything or be different for the sake of being different. I'm being myself. People are either going to like you or not. You can't spend too much time worrying about which one it's going to be. Besides, I know plenty of people who dress the so-called right way, act how they think they should, say and do what others are saying and doing, and they still aren't accepted, not really."

That was his fear. That his friends would see behind his facade and he'd no longer be accepted.

"I think life's a little easier when you're part of the group," he said. "I've been on the outside, been different, and being accepted, normal, is much better."

"As long as you're being true to yourself, it shouldn't matter what other people think. I do believe, though, there are plenty of people who are part of the group because being *normal*—to use your term for it—is just who they are. They're not

pretending to be something or someone they're not."
She stood and stretched, causing her shirt to rise,
giving him a glimpse of her stomach. It wasn't completely flat like Kennedy's, but his mouth went dry
seeing that flash of pale skin, the slight slope of her
belly. "I'd better get home. I still have to finish reading for English."

He didn't want her to go, but wasn't sure how to
get her to stay without sounding pathetic. "What
are you reading?"

"*To Kill a Mockingbird.* Have you read it?"

He nodded. "Two years ago. It's pretty good."

"Yeah, I'm enjoying it, though *Lord of the Flies*
is still my favorite assigned-for-school book."

He didn't know any girls who liked *Lord of the
Flies.* Then again, when he'd read it in middle
school, he'd only been to class half the time and
hadn't had the nerve to talk to a lot of girls. "Have
you read *Animal Farm?*" She shook her head. "It's
pretty good," he said, trying to sound nonchalant.
"It's about how these animals take over their farm
and how the power changes them."

"I'll have to get it," she said. "By the way, I like
your song."

He stopped playing. "What do you mean?"

She nodded toward his guitar. "The song you were
just playing. It's one of yours, isn't it? I've heard you
practicing out here before when you first moved in
and I recognized it."

How had she known it was his? He ducked his head. "It's just something I've been fooling around with."

"It's good. Really good." She leaned close to him and his heart about stopped. "Don't worry," she whispered. "I won't tell anyone the newest jock is a songwriter."

She straightened and gave a little wave, the bright, full moon casting a golden glow over her hair. He watched her walk all the way to her house, told himself it was to make sure she got there safely, but really it was because he liked looking at her. Liked talking to her. Liked listening to her.

And when he lay in bed that night, he didn't think of Kennedy and her confusing texts, didn't remember Estelle and what it had been like to kiss her.

He thought about Gracie and how her hair looked in the moonlight.

PENELOPE SIMPLY DID not get it.

At football practice Thursday afternoon, she watched her son and the other members of the team out on the field. She had a hard time following what they were doing, which mostly seemed like running into each other, though at times, a tall boy with the number 12 on his helmet would throw the ball.

More often than not, the throw would make its way to Andrew. He caught almost every one, diving or sliding on the ground or leaping into the air if need be. He did whatever it took, it seemed, to catch that ball, then he'd run like mad toward the end of the field.

He was having a good time, and she supposed if catching the ball and running fast meant he was good at the sport, then he must be excellent.

"Mind if I join you?"

Shading her eyes, she looked up to see the same elderly gentleman who'd been outside Leo's office Monday when she'd first discovered Andrew was playing football. "Of course not."

She shifted over and he sat on the hard metal bleacher. Held out his hand. "Leo Montesano."

She blinked, shook his hand. "There's another one?"

Her face warmed. Well, she hadn't meant to say that. Must be something in the air in Shady Grove that had her blurting out whatever thought came to mind. She didn't used to be that way. She would say only what she should, what was necessary and polite. After she'd thought it through carefully, of course.

He grinned and yes, she could definitely see Leo in the sparkle in his dark eyes, the charming smile. "The original one." He winked and she could easily imagine Leo at this man's age, except she hoped he trimmed his eyebrows. "The other Leo is my grandson. You can call me Big Leo or Pops."

She didn't point out that *Big Leo* didn't really suit him as he was a good six inches shorter than his grandson. But she imagined when his family had named Leo after him, he'd seemed big compared to his grandson. "It's so nice to meet you, Mr. Montesano."

Because there was a certain way of doing things and there was no reason to change that or to be anything less than perfectly polite and respectful.

And because she could never call him, or anyone, Pops.

"That'll do, too," he said, not offended in the least. He nodded toward the field where the boys were in two separate circles. They clapped once, then lined up against each other. "Your boy's a natural."

"That's what I've been told," she murmured. "I know nothing about football so I'm afraid I can't judge his abilities."

"It's a pretty simple game once you get the hang of it. Each team has the ball for a series of downs or tries. That's when they're on offense. During those four tries they have to move the ball at least ten yards. So when the first try starts, it's first and ten. Each successive down you take away how many yards they gained." A chubby boy in the center tossed the ball under his legs to number 12 who caught it and ran a few yards. "See that? He got three yards so now it's second and seven. Second down—or try—and seven yards to go. Once you reach ten yards, your tries restart and you're back to four tries."

It was still a bit confusing, but she thought she

could follow it better now. "That makes sense." In a weird, two steps forward, three steps back way. Men. Why couldn't they invent games that were simple and logical? "Thank you."

"There's plenty more to it than that, but if you start with those basics, you'll catch on pretty quickly. And if you have any questions, you let me or that grandson of mine know."

She smiled at him, feeling comfortable in his easy presence. "I appreciate the help." Andrew got tackled and she tensed, her fingers curling into her thighs.

"He's okay," Mr. Montesano murmured, patting her hand. "See?"

He was right. Her son wasn't broken and bleeding on the ground. He sprang to his feet, hit the kid who'd knocked him down on the side of the helmet, though not in an aggressive way.

"I'm nervous," she admitted, then laughed. "But you already know that."

"Leo mentioned you might be, so he asked me to come sit with you, see how you were holding up."

He had? She sought him out, saw him on the sidelines, once again wearing a ball cap, his broad shoulders stretching the material of his sweatshirt. "That was…thoughtful of him."

Thoughtful. Kind. He *was* kind, she realized. Behind that devil-may-care grin and that charming glint in his eyes was a very caring soul.

"He's a good boy," Mr. Montesano said. "Takes after his grandfather."

She laughed. "It's nice you two are coaching the team together."

Mr. Montesano leaned forward, his elbows on his knees. "He's just being nice to an old man, letting me hang around, giving my two cents when they aren't wanted or needed. Doesn't stop me from giving them, though. It's fun, being around him and the kids. They're a great group of boys. Do you know many of them?"

She shook her head. "Only Luke Sapko. And I believe I've met that one—" she pointed to the boy kicking the ball "—once."

"That's Josh. He's a decent kid, but gets cocky when you criticize him. Kids these days can't take constructive criticism."

"I thought that was only my son."

"Andrew? He's one of the few who stays respectful and doesn't get all prickly about it. He just listens and then actually does what you suggest. You're doing a good job with him."

She flushed pleasantly. She was? "Thank you. There are times when I'm not sure."

"Kids often push away those closest to them because they know they'll always be there, that they won't push back."

If only it were so easy. "Sometimes I wonder if that's all there is to it." She smiled. "I worry about him too much—I know that—but he's…he's all I have."

And admitting that was hard. Admitting her entire life revolved around her son, around keeping him safe, made her seem like less of her own person.

"I've been there," Mr. Montesano said. "I have only one child. Believe me, I understand your concern about keeping Andrew safe. When my boy was little, his mother used to fret over every scrape he got into, every sniffle. But he got through them, got married and had himself four kids for me to spoil. Now I have three great-grandchildren and I still worry about all of them. You never stop."

"Wonderful," she said weakly, feeling suddenly overwhelmed. "I was actually hoping there'd be a cutoff date at some point."

He laughed. "Afraid not. But you learn that worrying does neither you nor them any good. It's better to teach them, to help them see what's worth risking and what's not. How to be careful and make smart choices, but also how to live. It's a tough job, parenthood. But it's the best one out there."

She used to think so, too. And then Andrew got sick and she was constantly stressed. Yet even during that horrible time, she was so incredibly grateful to be his mother. To have him in her life. "I'm not sure any risks are worth taking."

"Oh, I think you're more of a risk taker than you realize." Before she could assure him she wasn't, he nodded toward the field again. "Looks like Leo's finishing up practice."

The boys were crowded around him, all kneeling

on one knee, their helmets off, their undivided attention on their coach. "He's good with them," she said.

It was clear he related to the boys on a different level than a parent or teacher, but he wasn't trying to be their buddy or friend.

*You could use a friend,* he'd told her, and she thought he'd be a good one. And why couldn't she be friends with a sexy, handsome, charming man? No, it hadn't ever happened to her before in her life, but there was a first time for everything.

"He connects with them," Mr. Montesano said. "For Leo it's not about wins and losses so much as it's about helping them grow and learn. He knows it's important to be a mentor, to help them in all aspects of their lives. He has clear standards of what he expects from them, of their behavior on and off the field. He pushes them to work hard, is honest with them, and always finds something to compliment them on each day without laying it on too thick."

"You're very proud of him."

"I'm proud of all my grandkids—though my great-grandkids are my greatest joys."

With a wink reminiscent of his grandson, he stood and walked away.

Penelope's nerves jumped to see Leo staring at her. The boys had taken off toward the school and Leo stood in the middle of the field. He raised his hands to indicate ten minutes.

Ten minutes until their coffee date.

Not a date, she corrected. A…friendly meeting.

Just two people getting to know each other over coffee—possibly even chaperoned by her son. She nodded to let him know she'd wait, then settled in, anxious to get it over with.

More anxious to be with him.

## CHAPTER TWELVE

LEO APPROACHED PENELOPE. He liked seeing her sitting in the bleachers, the wind picking up loose strands of hair. "You look real pretty with the sun on your face," he told her.

She blushed. He liked that, too, how she got flustered from an honest compliment. She cleared her throat. "Thank you."

He leaned against the rail. "What did you think of practice?"

"It was…interesting."

He grinned. How could he not when she was so careful in everything she said and did? "Is that good or bad?"

"Interesting is just…interesting," she said. "Actually, your grandfather explained a few things to me, which helped quite a bit."

"Pops is a great teacher. If there's something you don't know or understand, you ask him and he'll explain it."

"He's very proud of you," she said, and he found himself caught in her intent stare. He wasn't sure how he felt about that, her studying him so closely.

He was the one who studied other people, who read them. He didn't like or want anyone doing that to him. "And you obviously respect him a great deal to allow him to help you out. Most people tend to ignore the elderly in their family."

Ignore Pops? That would be like cutting off his right arm. "He's the best," Leo said simply. "He's part of our family and, despite his age, he's still the head of it. What should we do? Put him adrift on an ice floe?"

"I'm only saying that it's nice. Your family is obviously close."

She sounded sad. Wistful. "Yours isn't?"

"My parents were...are...very focused on their careers."

"And your brother?"

"He's quite a bit older than I am and was out of the house for most of my childhood."

Leo touched her hand, glad when she didn't flinch or pull away. "I'm sorry."

"It's fine. It wasn't horrible. And I have Andrew. He's my family."

"I can't get away from family," Leo said, because he hated her looking so sad and trying to act as if it didn't bother her.

"Yes, your grandfather mentioned you have several siblings."

"Two older brothers and a younger sister. They all work for my dad's contracting company."

The breeze picked up and she brushed strands of hair back. "Do you feel left out?"

"Out of the business? Yes, and that's how I wanted it. I worked for my dad from the time I was old enough to haul scraps, put in my time during summers and after school. And while I can appreciate what they do and the craftsmanship that goes into building something, into building homes, it was never what I wanted."

"You always wanted to be a firefighter?"

He laughed. "I wanted to be a jet fighter, but I blame that on my parents letting us watch *Top Gun* when we were little. I also, at various moments in my life, wanted to be a cop, a cowboy, a deep-sea diver and a firefighter. That last one stuck after I spent a few weeks shadowing a friend of my father's who was the captain at the fire station."

"You like it."

"I love it." There was nothing else he could imagine doing. Nothing else he wanted to do.

"Even when it's hard?" she asked hesitantly. "When it's dangerous or when you lose someone like that young girl over Labor Day?"

He tensed, but forced himself to relax. People in town were still talking about Sam and the accident. Most, like Penelope, were simply curious. Though Penelope's curiosity was more about him than the gory details. Which was fine.

She couldn't get more from him than he was willing to give.

"I don't like those moments. What about you?" he asked, turning so their bodies were closer. She didn't back away. "Did you dream of being an accountant as a little girl?"

He expected her to say no. What little girl dreams of being an accountant?

"Yes. It was all I've ever thought about for a career."

He shook his head. "You're kidding."

Her mouth thinned. "Why would I joke about something like that?"

"It's just that most kids have different dreams. Didn't you ever want to be a movie star or ballerina or artist?"

"My parents encouraged me to pick a career that was both stable and one where I was guaranteed to succeed." She crossed her arms. "I like my job."

Shit. He'd pissed her off. Again. He'd never had so much trouble reading a woman. "I'm sure you do, and I bet you're great at it."

She unbent enough to give him a shy smile. "I manage quite well. I like when things add up, when everything's in a neat row, all lined up in orderly fashion."

"It suits you," he murmured, seeing how her eyes lit. She actually got excited talking about numbers. It was fascinating.

"Hey," Drew said as he joined them, his duffel bag slung over his shoulder. His gaze bounced between them, and Penelope quickly stepped away.

"Luke and some of the guys are going out for pizza and want me to come. Can I?"

"Actually," Penelope said, sending Leo a nervous glance. "Leo and I were going to go out for coffee and I thought you could join us."

Drew's jaw dropped and he stared at Leo. "What? You're going out with my mom?" He looked and sounded shocked. "Why?"

"Ouch," Penelope muttered, giving her son a narrow-eyed glare.

"Are you two going to talk about me?" the kid went on, having no idea it was past time for him to shut up. "Is she trying to convince you to kick me off the team?" He rounded on his mother. "You promised you'd give me a shot."

"I am giving you a shot," she said, sounding resigned and weary. Then again, if the kid argued with her all the time like this, Leo would be weary, too. And way more pissed than Penelope seemed to be. "Coach…Leo and I are…we're…"

"We're going out on a coffee date," Leo interjected smoothly. "I asked your mother out because I'm interested in getting to know her better. The only reason we invited you to join us was to be nice and considerate of your feelings. But since you obviously don't care about doing the same for your mother, we rescind our offer."

Drew seemed confused. "You want to date my mom?" he asked in a whisper, glancing around as if afraid someone would overhear.

"Yep."

"That is so weird," he said.

"Adults are a weird bunch," Leo told him solemnly. "You'll get used to it and join our ranks one day. Now, do you need dropped off anywhere?"

"Nah, I'm riding with Luke." He looked at his mom. "If that's okay."

"Of course. I'll see you when I get home. I won't be long."

Now Drew grinned. "Dude, you have your work cut out for you."

"No kidding," Leo muttered. They hadn't even left yet and already Penelope was ready to end the date. Talk about an ego crusher. "You ready?" he asked her as Drew walked away.

"I can meet you at the coffee shop since I have my car here."

"I'd rather ride with you. Pops brought me." He'd figured she'd want to drive separate and was afraid if she preferred to meet him somewhere, she might not show up at all.

"Oh. Of course." They walked across the parking lot in silence. She jiggled the keys and glanced at him over the top of her car. "Do you think Andrew was upset? About us going out. As friends," she added.

"I think if you let your sixteen-year-old son make all the decisions and let him control how you feel and what you do, you're never going to have his respect or his obedience."

"It's just…I haven't dated," she blurted. "Since the divorce. And to be honest, I didn't date all that much before I was married."

How could he stay upset with her when she was so honest, even when it was hard on her? Yes, she gave her son too much power over her, but Leo could understand why. "That's okay. It's a lot easier than you think. We'll have some coffee, maybe a sandwich because I'm starving, and we'll talk. I'll ask you questions, you'll ask me some, and at the end, if one of us decides you were right and we really don't have anything in common, we'll go our separate ways."

He really hoped they didn't go their separate ways.

THREE HOURS LATER, Penelope stopped in front of Leo's place. It was a cute, small house, one story with a wide porch and big windows that made it look warm and welcoming.

Three hours. She couldn't believe they'd spent so much time at the coffee shop. Couldn't believe she'd enjoyed herself so much. She could understand why Andrew looked up to Leo. He was smart, charming and funny.

He'd told her about growing up in Shady Grove. About his family—his brothers and sister and their significant others, his nephew and preteen niece and the little girl of the woman his brother Eddie was seeing whom they all considered family already. Leo amused her with stories of life at the station where the firefighters seemed more like a brother-hood than coworkers.

He'd even persuaded her to open up a bit about living in California and growing up in so many different places. How she'd been so different from her classmates, how she'd considered it a badge of honor to be herself and how she worried about Andrew not feeling the same way.

She liked Leo. It was a surprising fact to acknowledge. And daunting. She wasn't in the same league as him when it came to looks or dating experience. There were still plenty of reasons for them to be apart, plenty she'd been right about, such as their age difference and her having a son. But they'd also had several things in common—their taste in music, for example, though his favorite movies tended to be action thrillers while she preferred more cerebral films.

She was flattered he'd been so persistent in pursuing her. And there was a definite spark between them, one she'd never experienced before. She'd always dismissed sexual or physical attraction as a fleeting thing, thinking that once the burning desire was satiated, the flame would simply die out. And then what would you have?

No, her marriage had been based on common ground, interests and goals.

Too bad it hadn't worked out. It had looked so good on paper.

"Admit it," Leo teased, playing with her hair. "You had a good time."

She couldn't deny it when she'd voluntarily spent three hours with the man, but she still wasn't used to his charm, how he was so comfortable touching her casually, his fingers brushing her hand or trailing her neck. The way he laid his palm on the small of her back to let her precede him.

"It wasn't as torturous as I'd imagined," she told him.

He grinned, quick and honest. "I knew that sense of humor was in there somewhere."

She liked that she could tease him. "Well, I suppose I can admit, in this instance, you were right." She paused, unsure of what to say, then decided to say what was on her mind, in her heart. "I had fun. Thank you."

Before she could change her mind, she leaned forward and brushed her mouth against his cheek, as he had kissed her the other night. His skin was warm and he smelled wonderful, like fresh air and sunshine mixed with the spicy scent of his aftershave.

She leaned back and their eyes locked. The interior of the car seemed to shrink. Heated. His eyes narrowed slightly and his hand curved around her neck, tugging her against him.

She pressed both hands to his chest. "Wha—what are you doing?"

"I'm going to kiss you."

His words, the tone of his voice, sent a shiver

through her from head to toe. She'd never had a man look at her so heatedly, with so much intent. "You said we were going to be friends," she reminded him, but her voice sounded weak.

"Friends can kiss," he told her, still bringing her closer, slowly, so slowly she had every opportunity to break free, to push him away.

She didn't move.

His eyes open and on hers, he closed the distance between them and gently brushed his mouth against hers. "See?" he murmured.

Her eyes widened. That was it? Disappointment and a deep, crushing panic filled her. That was all she got? All he was going to take?

And she realized he wouldn't take. Not more than she was ready to give. Not more than she offered freely. And she had hardly done that, had she? She had no idea how to flirt with him, or seduce him into kissing her again. "I don't want us to be friends," she blurted.

He raised his eyebrows. "You don't?"

She shook her head. "I don't think it's the wisest course of action."

Disappointment settled over his features and he eased back. Leaned his head against the seat. "I see." His grin masked, but didn't hide, his frustration. "Can't blame a guy for trying." He reached for the door handle.

Oh, no, he was leaving.

"No." She grabbed his arm. "You don't understand."

He glanced at her hand, then at her face. "I guess I don't. Why don't you explain it to me?"

"I'm not sure I can."

He patted her hand. "You can," he told her, sounding emphatic, as if he believed in her, in her ability to do this even though it was difficult and went against every instinct she possessed.

She believed it, too, if only to prove him right. To show him his faith in her was appreciated.

"I don't want to be your friend," she whispered, swallowing the fear and self-doubts crowding her throat, trying to stop her words. "I want..."

"Tell me," he said softly after a few moments.

She could do this. In her car on the dark street, it felt safe. She felt safe with him. In this instance, she could take a risk. Could be brave.

If only once.

"I want you."

His eyes flashed, but she didn't wait for him to refuse her or to take the lead. She yanked him forward and kissed him, hard. He jolted in surprise but then he groaned. His tongue swept into her mouth and his hands caressed her from shoulder to waist and up again. She had no idea how long they stayed that way, hands clutching, mouths fused, but when they finally separated and stared at each other, both were breathing hard, the windows of the car fogging up.

"I want to ask you to come inside," he said. "I want to take you to bed, Penelope."

Wow. *Wow, wow, wow.* It was flattering and

frightening. Too much too fast. "I can't. Not yet. You need to know, maybe not ever."

He nodded. "Yeah, that's what I figured." Still, he leaned forward and gave her a sweet, warm kiss. "Too soon. That's okay, I'm a patient guy. I can wait for you."

He climbed out, then turned and leaned into the car. "You're worth waiting for, Penelope."

He shut the door and walked to his house. She sat there stunned, watching until he went inside.

*You're worth waiting for.*

No one had ever thought so before.

FRIDAY NIGHT, PENELOPE made her way through the crowd to the stands at the football field. She'd dressed in jeans and a heavy sweater, and prayed the weather held. She had no idea how long a football game lasted or how cold it would get.

"Penelope!"

Frowning—who on earth would be calling her name?—she glanced around, then smiled to see Mr. Montesano waving at her, a grin on his face. "Hello," she said when she joined him. "It's nice to see you again."

To her shock, he gave her a quick, hard hug. "You, too. Are you excited about the game?"

She glanced at the field where the teams were warming up. Excited wasn't exactly how she'd put it. "I'm…happy that Andrew's so excited," she finally said. And her son was that indeed. He'd practically bounced off the walls at breakfast, bugging her to make sure he had all his gear, checking and rechecking his bag, only to call her midway through the day asking her to drop off his spikes after school. "He's really looking forward to playing."

"Remember how Leo would get before a game?" Mr. Montesano asked the middle-aged gentleman next to him.

The other man chuckled. "Like a cat in a room filled with rocking chairs. That boy always did have too much energy."

"Penelope," Mr. Montesano said, "this is my son, Frank. And his wife, Rose—your Leo's parents."

*"Your Leo?"* a gorgeous brunette said, then gave Rose a nudge. "Did you hear that?"

Rose smiled. "There's nothing wrong with my hearing, Madelyn."

Madelyn. Penelope's eyes widened and she looked at the group, quickly surmising that this was Leo's family.

"It's nice to meet you," Leo's mother said, taking Penelope's hand. "These are my older sons, James and Eddie." James was as tall as Leo, though not as broad. Eddie, shorter than both his brothers, was wider, his eyes hazel instead of brown. "James's wife, Sadie, Eddie's girlfriend, Harper, and Harper's daughter, Cassidy."

Penelope tried to smile, hoped it looked less forced than it felt. "Nice to meet you all."

Sadie had long, flyaway blond hair and had

poured herself into a pair of tight bright pink jeans that no one over the age of eighteen should wear. Harper was just as pretty, her hair a darker honey-blond that swung to just above her shoulders. Her daughter was adorable in an oversize sports jersey.

"And I'm Maddie," the brunette said, not even bothering to hide how she was sizing up Penelope. "Leo's very favorite sister."

Penelope frowned. Wasn't Madelyn his only sister? Penelope abandoned that thought as she again surveyed the group. Goodness gracious. And Mr. Montesano had called Leo hers.

"He's not mine," she told Madelyn, but the words came out a squeak and that would not do. When she was nervous or around strangers, she often felt inadequate and unsure, but right now she wanted to show even a touch of confidence. "We're…friends."

*I don't want to be your friend. I want you.*

Horrified, Penelope glanced at Rose as if Leo's mother could read her thoughts, could somehow tell what she was thinking. Or, worse, see some of the heated and very non-platonic dreams Penelope had had about Leo.

"Right. Friends," Mr. Montesano said. "That's what I meant."

His expression seemed innocent enough, but she wasn't buying it. She shifted her blanket to her other arm. "Well, I hope you all enjoy the game."

"Won't you join us?" Rose asked. She was an attractive woman, her dark, chin-length hair sprinkled with gray. "Unless you're meeting someone? Or have plans to sit with some of the other mothers?"

"Actually, I haven't met too many of them yet." She supposed she should do that, should make more of an effort when it came to her son's social network. Should know the parents of the boys Andrew was spending so much time with. But the thought of doing it tonight, of sitting with strangers who didn't share her worries, who would probably think she was foolish to be concerned over her son's well-being, was too much for her.

"Come on," Madelyn said, scooting over so Penelope could sit between her and Rose. "Sit with us. I promise we don't bite."

"Don't believe her," James said. "I still have the scar from when she chomped on me."

"I was three and you were pissing me off," Madelyn said sweetly.

"She's right," Rose said. "You deserved it for teasing her."

"It still hurts," he murmured, giving his mother a hangdog look.

Madelyn jabbed her elbow into his leg. "You big baby."

James leaned forward and told Penelope, "Just a friendly warning. You always need to watch your back around Maddie."

Maddie rolled her eyes. "Yes, yes, I'm extremely dangerous, blah, blah, blah." She grinned at Penelope. "Come on. We'd love to get know Leo's latest... friend better."

Penelope sat. "Why do I get the feeling there's more to that statement than I'd be comfortable knowing?"

"Because you're obviously a very wise woman filled with good sense—though that begs the question of why you're friends with my idiot brother," Maddie said as the marching band came onto the field.

"I thought I was your idiot brother," Eddie said.

"Just one of many, my friend," Maddie said, patting his knee. "One of many."

Penelope didn't know how to act or react. She was sitting between Leo's sister and mother and feeling very uncomfortable about it all considering that the last time she saw Leo she'd kissed him.

She wrinkled her nose. Kissed? They'd made out in her car like a couple of teenagers. She slid a side-long glance at Rose. Oh, dear Lord, Penelope hoped his mother didn't know what they'd been doing. As a mother herself, she was pretty certain she could live forever without Andrew ever having sex.

"How long have you and Leo known each other?" Rose asked, but not in a suspicious way that made Penelope uneasy.

"A couple of weeks."

"From your son playing football?"

Penelope's face warmed. "Actually," she said, unable to meet the other woman's eyes, "we met on

Labor Day when Leo came to my house. I had a slight…accident with my gas grill that day."

"Gas grills are death traps," Sadie said, leaning forward to look at Penelope. Her expression serious, she nodded once. "Death traps."

Penelope had to agree. "Leo was very…capable."

"He's a regular Boy Scout," Maddie said, not sounding too happy about it. "Except when it comes to dealing with my boyfriend."

"No need to be mean," Rose said. "Whatever issues Leo has with Neil—and vice versa—they'll work out on their own."

Maddie crossed her arms. "Yeah, in the meantime I have to be the one in the middle."

Rose reached in front of Penelope and touched Maddie's arm. "If you don't like where you're standing—"

"I know, I know." Maddie sighed. "Move."

"Right."

"Who's Neil?" Penelope couldn't help but ask. Leo hadn't mentioned anyone named Neil.

"Maddie's boyfriend," Leo's mother said.

"I hate that," Maddie grumbled. "I'm a thirty-year-old woman. Aren't I too old to have a boyfriend?"

"Never. Besides, that'll change when Neil becomes your fiancé. And when will that be?"

"Oh, hold on," Maddie said, standing. "I think I hear my daughter calling."

"Bree's on the other side of the field," Rose pointed out.

Maddie still shrugged on her jacket. "Coming, Bree."

And she walked away.

Leo's family certainly was…unique. A voice boomed out of the loudspeaker and announced the teams' lineups, then a sweet-voiced girl sang the national anthem. By the time for kickoff, Penelope was a nervous wreck.

"Are you all right?" Rose asked.

"Fine," Penelope lied.

Rose gently pried Penelope's fingers from the program she was crushing. "Is this the first year your son has played?"

"Yes." Penelope couldn't take her eyes off the field where Andrew was lined up, ready to receive the kick from the other team. "This is the first game I've ever been to."

"Ever? You never went to a high-school football game?"

Penelope shook her head. "I never understood the game so I didn't bother." Had always considered sports to be a waste of time. "I studied up on the game this week. Mr. Montesano…that is…Big Leo—" and she felt incredibly silly calling him that "—explained the basics to me during practice the other day, but I was still confused so I looked up a few things online."

"That's smart. And shows that even though you

may not be one hundred percent behind your son playing, you're willing to find out more about the game and show an interest in it and him."

Penelope was proud Rose thought so and wondered if Andrew would agree with the other woman's assessment. The game started, and by the third quarter, she was more relaxed. Maddie had returned, and Penelope had figured out that whatever animosity existed between Leo and her boyfriend dated back years. She was curious enough that she planned on asking him about it, as he was so easygoing. She couldn't imagine him feeling hostility toward anyone.

The entire game was almost enjoyable. Almost. If she wasn't so worried about Andrew, didn't flinch and gasp each time he got tackled or bumped or hit, she might have enjoyed it more. The Montesanos were a loud, chatty bunch except for Eddie and, it seemed, his young son, Max, who stopped playing with his friends on the other side of the field long enough to come ask for money.

But she was definitely out of place with them. They were lighthearted, and there was constant teasing and what she hoped was good-natured ribbing. She felt stiff, rigid and humorless.

It was the middle of the fourth quarter when Andrew got hit. Hard. Penelope jumped to her feet when her son didn't get up. "It's okay," Rose told her, holding her arm. "Leo will take good care of him."

But she didn't want Leo to take care of him. She

should be down there. When she made to move forward, Maddie stopped her. "I understand you're worried, but give him a minute before you rush onto the field."

Penelope realized she was right. She'd look foolish racing down there, insisting she take him to the E.R. to get checked out. The wait until he finally got to his feet and limped off the field was agonizingly long.

"I should take him to the hospital," she said to no one in particular.

"It's a tough sport to watch," Rose said soothingly, rubbing Penelope's arm. "My own boys played. James was always careful, rarely got hurt. Eddie quietly went about his business, but Leo? That boy gave me a heart attack every Friday night."

"How did you deal with it then? And how do you deal with it now knowing that if there's danger, while most people are running away from it, he's running toward it?"

"It's not easy, believe me, but I couldn't ask him to give any of that up. It's a part of him. He loves helping people. He loves the thrill of it, too. As parents, sometimes the best thing we can do for our children is let them go. Encouraging them to take chances is the hardest thing we do because when they hurt, we hurt." Rose squeezed Penelope's hand. "Look."

Penelope followed Rose's gaze to see Andrew run onto the field from the sidelines. "He's okay," she breathed.

"He probably had the wind knocked out of him."

The minutes ticked away and Andrew's team was behind by six. To win they needed more points than a field goal would give them, so only a touchdown would do. Third down and long, Andrew raced down the field, cut left and lost his defender. The quarterback threw the ball—high and to the right of Andrew, but he somehow managed to leap in the air, catch it with one hand and evade two tackles to get into the end zone.

The crowd went wild. Even Penelope found herself on her feet cheering and yelling. They kicked the extra point and less than a minute later, the game was over, the defense having held their opponents to the middle of the field.

After the teams shook hands, Andrew ran up to the bleachers and gave Penelope a big hug. Tears stung her eyes. He was so happy. So proud.

Maybe this was one of those times when it was worth taking a risk.

# CHAPTER THIRTEEN

ANDREW COULDN'T STOP SMILING.

He felt like a dork but hey, he had caught the pass and run in for the winning touchdown. Maybe it was okay that he was standing there, getting slapped on the back by his teammates and enjoying the shit out of being the hero.

"Andrew!"

He looked over as Kennedy came running toward him, her hair floating behind her, a huge smile on her face, her breasts bouncing in a way that was hard to look away from.

"You were awesome!" she squealed when she reached him. Then she leaped into his arms.

He shut his eyes and held on tight. Yeah, being the hero was definitely the best thing ever. Kennedy did a little shimmy thing that had his body tightening. He knew he should let go, but she felt so good in his arms, all curvy and soft, and she smelled great, like sugar cookies, totally sweet and tempting.

While he probably was pretty rank, but she kept hugging him and making that squealing sound so he didn't think she minded.

Finally, she leaned back. "I was so excited when you caught that pass. Oh, my God, we were all going crazy. You're, like, the hero of the game!"

His thoughts exactly.

"Hey," Luke said, coming up behind Andrew and giving him a slap on the shoulder. Andrew tensed, worried Luke would be pissed his girlfriend had hugged Andrew—was still technically hugging him—but when he glanced over, Luke was grinning. "Great job, dude."

"Thanks," he said.

"That's what I was just saying," Kennedy said. She gave him another squeeze, then hopped over to hug Luke.

Envy ate at Andrew. Why couldn't she look at him like that? What did he have to do to make that happen? "You had a good game, too," he said, realizing he should say something to Luke instead of standing there staring at the other guy's girlfriend like a pathetic loser. "That block you made in the third quarter stopped them from getting the first down."

Luke shrugged. Slung his arm around Kennedy's shoulder. She wore Luke's other jersey, the one for the away games, and had tied the hem of the oversize shirt so it clung to her curves the way her jeans did. Andrew wanted to see her wearing *his* jersey with *his* number.

"I just did my job." Luke glanced at Kennedy. "I'm going to shower then we'll get something to eat." He faced Andrew. "You want to come?" He wiggled his eyebrows. "Jess said she'd go, too."

At that moment Jessica joined them. "Congratulations, Andrew!" She, too, hugged him. Hell, he'd never been hugged by two hot girls in one night before. He'd never been hugged by two girls *period* in one night.

Jess wasn't Kennedy, but she was pretty. Still, when Kennedy left to say goodbye to her parents, he didn't know what to say to Jess. He shifted. "You… uh…want to get something to eat with us?"

He winced because, duh, hadn't Luke already said she did? But Jess just smiled. Rubbed his arm. "Sure. I'll wait with Kennedy while you get cleaned up."

He nodded and headed toward the locker room.

"Drew," Coach called. "Wait up."

Andrew stopped to see the coach jogging toward him. He wasn't sure how he felt about his mom going out for coffee with him. He thought maybe it wasn't too bad. Coach was cool, though, so why he'd be interested in dating Andrew's mom was beyond him. She wasn't exactly fun. Yeah, he guessed she was pretty enough—for someone who was old. Still, he didn't really like the idea of her dating. Not that he thought his folks had a chance of getting back together—he wasn't an idiot. That dream had died when his dad remarried.

Even so, the idea of his mom dating, being single

and going out with men… It was too weird. She was his *mom*. Not a woman.

"Here," Coach said, holding out the game football. "You deserve this."

Andrew took it. "Thanks." Having the game ball was almost as cool as having two hot girls hug him. He knew exactly where he was going to put the football in his room, could already picture it on his shelf.

"I know I already told you this, but you did a great job out there. And not just with that last catch, but the whole game. I'm proud of you."

Warmth suffused Andrew and he dropped his gaze. It was cool that someone like the coach was proud of him, but there was still something Andrew had to know…

"Are you and my mom going to go out again?" he asked.

Coach raised his eyebrows. "I'm not sure. Why?"

Andrew shrugged. Tossed the ball from hand to hand. "It's a little weird for me, that's all."

"In what way?"

"You're my coach and she's my mom." *Duh.* How could he not get that?

Coach studied him as if he could see the real reasons Andrew didn't want them dating, didn't want his mom dating anyone at all. It was just wrong. "I am your coach and I'm sorry if it's awkward for you, but I enjoy spending time with your mother and if she's agreeable to it, I'd like to take her out again."

Even if Andrew didn't want him to? That didn't

seem fair. "Yeah. Okay. Whatever," he muttered and walked away.

Some days he hated being a kid. He didn't get to have an opinion or a say in things, even in his own life. He decided he really didn't want his mom dating his coach. If they cared about him or respected him, you'd think they could deal with that.

He hadn't wanted to move here in the first place but he'd been forced to because he was just a kid. His mom hadn't asked him where *he* wanted to live or even what he wanted. Neither of his parents had when they'd decided to get a divorce. They'd just told him at dinner one night—over pork chops, his favorite—that they were splitting up and oh, yeah, his dad would be moving out and Andrew would be staying with his mom. Whether he liked it or not.

It wasn't fair.

"Andrew. Andrew?"

He turned, frowned at Gracie walking toward him. God, did she have to dress so weird? Yeah, she had on jeans, but she wore a freaking tent thing—a poncho or whatever—over them and some sort of knit scarf covered her hair. "What?"

She stopped as if she'd hit a wall, and he saw the flash of hurt in her eyes. Guilt nudged him but he shoved it aside.

"I just wanted to tell you congratulations," she said, sounding unsure, yet still lifting her chin. "Great game."

"Yeah," he muttered, shuffling his feet. "Thanks."

She stepped closer, frowned at him. "Are you all right?"

"Why wouldn't I be?"

"Because you're scowling and you sound like someone stole your puppy."

"I'm fine. I'm just..." He didn't know what. He was pissed off all the time, and no matter how hard he tried not to be, he couldn't seem to stop. Even tonight, which should have been one of the greatest nights of his life, he was feeling unsure and confused. Seeing Gracie didn't help. He glanced around. Lots of people were still there, people who could see him talking to her. He stepped back. "I have to go."

"Oh. Okay." She looked disappointed and puzzled. "Sure. I guess I'll see you later."

She made it sound like a question. He couldn't respond, didn't want her to think he planned on hanging out with her, not when he had a date tonight with Jess. "Yeah. Maybe."

At the edge of the field, he met up with Kennedy. She hugged him again. Over her shoulder, he saw Gracie watching them. He bent his head and hugged Kennedy back, like he should. When he looked up again, Gracie was gone.

He wished he could call her back. Wished he could go home and sit on the deck with her. Not because he liked her, not in the way he liked Kennedy, but because he could talk to her. He could tell her about his mom dating the coach and why it bugged him. She'd understand.

Instead, he went inside to shower and wished he'd been nicer to Gracie even while he hoped no one had seen them talking.

LEO JOGGED ACROSS the dark parking lot to catch up to Penelope before she took off. His steps slowed when he realized she was talking to someone. He almost stumbled and stopped dead when he saw who she was talking to.

Maddie.

Determined to intervene before any damage was done, he hurried over to them. "Penelope," he called as she opened her car door. She turned and he was struck by how pretty she was, how much he'd missed her even though they'd seen each other yesterday.

Christ, he was losing it. He needed to figure this thing out, decipher these strange feelings he had for her, before they took over his life and he ended up like some chump pining after a woman who wanted very little to do with him.

"Leo. Hello." Then she smiled as if she was really glad to see him. Maybe she did want to be with him.

"Yes," Maddie drawled, sounding way too smug for his liking. "Hello, Leo."

He shot her a quick, hard glance, one that clearly told her to watch her step and not to blow this for him. She grinned. Obviously, she was as good as always at reading his mind, knowing what he wanted from her and then doing the exact opposite just to piss him off.

Little sisters were nothing but a pain in the ass.

"Maddie," he said. Then, because he couldn't be mad at her longer than ten minutes—his cross to bear—he hugged her.

She squeezed him back. "Good game, Coach. Though I would have run a different play on that third down conversion in the second quarter. You could have gotten a first down if you had."

"Too bad you don't have the whistle or the jacket that says *coach,*" he said, pretending to be sympathetic. "Then again, girls don't often coach football."

Her eyes narrowed. "You know I hate it when you call me a girl."

He grinned. "Why do you think I do it?"

Penelope cleared her throat, her wide-eyed gaze bouncing between him and Maddie. "I'm afraid I'm lost. You two do like each other, don't you?"

Maddie laughed. "How could I not like Leo? He's so pretty. The prettiest of us all."

"True," he agreed. "So true."

"What brings you out into the parking lot?" Maddie asked, glancing at Bree, who waited in the truck. "Were you looking for me?" she asked, acting as innocent as a nun at Mass. "Oh, that's right. You were calling for Penelope. Well, here she is."

Penelope still seemed confused by their relationship. "Yes. Was there something you wanted?"

Maddie batted her eyelashes. "Yes, Leo, was there something you wanted from the pretty Penelope? Do tell."

He jerked his thumb in the direction of her truck. "Your kid's waiting for you."

"She's fine," Maddie said with a wave. "She's texting. As long as her phone doesn't run out of battery life, she's good in there for hours."

"What are you even doing here?" he asked with a sigh.

"Here as in this life? Here as in this parking lot?"

"Here as in talking to Penelope."

Maddie linked her arm through Penelope's, leaving Penelope to look bemused and shyly pleased. "Penelope and I bonded during the game. She sat with us and—"

"Us? Not the whole family."

Please, God, don't have let her sit with his entire family. She was already skittish, and they could send the most confident person over the edge.

"Every last one," Maddie said so cheerfully he wanted to strangle her. "She especially enjoyed Mom's stories about how long it took to potty train you."

Leo's neck heated and he could barely make eye contact with Penelope. "She didn't."

Penelope nodded. "Don't worry. A lot of men weren't potty trained until they were six—"

"Seven," Maddie corrected helpfully.

"Seven," Penelope repeated, her lips twitching.

"I was fully potty trained before I went to kindergarten," he assured her.

"Oh, now, Leo, don't be embarrassed," Maddie

said, stepping away from Penelope to squeeze his arm. "It's not as if we told her all your secrets. We saved some for Sunday."

He almost didn't want to know. "What's Sunday?"

"Why, Mom invited Penelope and Andrew over for dinner. Isn't that great?"

Yeah, great. He nudged Maddie away. "Your kid's trying to get your attention."

She turned, saw Bree waving madly, then sighed and hugged Penelope, who looked shell-shocked. Maddie tended to have that effect on people. "It was so nice meeting you, Penelope. I'm looking forward to dinner Sunday."

"Me, too."

They watched Maddie walk away, then get into her truck. He waved to Bree before turning to Penelope. "You don't have to come Sunday."

"You don't want me to?"

Why did she have to sound so disappointed, so worried about it?

"No, no, it's not that. I just don't want you to feel pressured or uncomfortable."

He wasn't used to having a woman he was seeing invited to a family meal. But so far things with Penelope hadn't exactly gone according to plan, so why should this be any different?

"Like I said," Penelope told him. "I'm looking forward to it. I enjoyed your family tonight."

"My family and the game?"

She smiled, and he didn't think he'd ever get tired

of seeing her do that. "I'll admit I enjoyed your family a lot more than the game."

"Drew did well," he said, leaning against her car. "And he had fun."

"I know. It's just hard. Hard for me to let go, I guess."

He could only imagine. "Hey, have you eaten?"

"Only a quick bite when I stopped home after work to change."

"Great. Why don't you come over to my place? I'll cook a celebratory dinner. Do you like pasta?"

"You want to cook for me?" she asked, as if he'd suggested he give her his liver, so she'd have an extra on hand in case she ever needed one. "I mean, I didn't know you could cook."

"Come on over and find out for yourself." She hesitated so long he felt like shuffling his feet, felt like the teenager he'd been at this very school fifteen years ago asking a pretty cheerleader out, hoping against hope she'd let him get to second base. "You worried about Drew being home alone?"

"No, he's going to Luke's to spend the night there. I had grounded him for joining the team without permission, but he was so excited about winning the game, I couldn't say no."

Better and better. Though it wouldn't hurt Drew to face some consequences for his actions. Still, Leo wasn't going to complain. Not if it meant Penelope was free. "Great. We'll have some dinner, a glass of wine."

She bit her lower lip. "Why?"

"Well, I usually have beer, but if I'm making pasta, I go for red wine."

"No, I mean, why are you inviting me?"

He brushed her hand with his. "I thought we'd been over this. I find you interesting and I'm attracted to you. And, unless I completely misread the way you kissed me in your car, you're attracted to me, too."

"That's it? You're attracted to me? So you just want to sleep with me."

Wincing, he glanced around to make sure no one overheard her. "If that was all," he said, angry at her for not giving herself much credit, angry at himself for stumbling over his words like some adolescent, "I would have moved on long ago. Believe me, I've never had a problem finding someone to sleep with me. You're different. I like you, Penelope. I like being with you. I thought you liked being with me, too."

"I do." She rested her hand on his arm. He froze. She rarely made the first move, rarely touched him at all. Which was why her kiss last night had thrown him for such a loop. "I'm sorry. I'm always saying the wrong thing or embarrassing myself."

"You've done nothing to be embarrassed about and you haven't said the wrong thing. Just say what's on your mind and we'll be fine."

She nodded. Inhaled deeply. "Okay. Want me to bring the wine?"

He realized that meant she was accepting his invitation. He glanced at his phone. "That'd be great. By the time you get to my place, I should have dinner ready, but take your time, I need to stop at the store and pick up a few things first."

"Oh, don't go to any trouble for me."

He winked. "It's okay. You're worth it."

*YOU'RE WORTH IT.*

It was the second time Leo had said that, and Penelope found herself wanting to believe it. To believe him. Why shouldn't she? He'd been honest with her so far. He'd told her what he wanted from her. Yes, he liked her, but he was also attracted to her, which meant he wanted to have sex with her. A physical release, a few hours of pleasure and then... well...she had no idea. She'd never had a relationship based solely on sex, on physical attraction.

She was starting to wonder if now was the time to change that. If she had the courage for a physical relationship that couldn't possibly go anywhere.

Looked as if she might soon find out.

She wiped her free hand down the side of her jeans, then rang Leo's doorbell. A moment later, he opened the door. His feet were bare and he'd changed into a Montesano Construction sweatshirt. His hair was mussed, and her fingers itched to smooth the silky strands.

"Right on time," he said with a grin as he stepped aside to let her in. He took her jacket, then kissed her cheek. She was still trying to get used to how casually affectionate he was. It always took her by surprise. "Come on in."

She followed him down a short hallway into a large, bright kitchen. "Wow," she said, turning in a slow circle. Stainless-steel appliances and white cupboards gave it a modern feel. The counters were wide marble, the floor hardwood. A huge center island dominated the space with an eating area at the end framed by three futuristic stools that looked as if they belonged on a space ship. "I repeat—wow."

He went to the stove where something delicious-smelling bubbled in a pot and added pasta to a pot of boiling water. "Yeah, it's pretty great. I told James what I wanted and he designed it for me. Even let me pitch in with the remodel so I'd have a sense of ownership. As if my name on the mortgage wasn't ownership enough."

She sat on a high-backed stool. There was a loaf of bread on a cutting board, grapes and cheese on a cheese board. "You really can cook," she said as she helped herself to a grape.

"Almost as good as my mom. And if you tell her I said that, I'll deny it and call you a bald-faced liar."

"I wouldn't want that," she told him solemnly. "Did she teach you?"

"A few things. I wasn't really interested in cooking when I lived at home." He winked at her. "Too busy chasing pretty girls to worry about how to feed myself. She taught all of us the basics, and Pops has a few recipes from his grandmother that are family secrets, which we all know now, like Nona's ragù sauce. But mostly I learned when I joined the fire department."

"So firefighters really do cook for the entire station and eat together?"

"We do, although not every day and not all the guys cook nor would we want them to. But I enjoy it so I tend to throw together a couple of meals every week. What about you? I know you grill, but do you cook?"

Surprisingly, she wasn't that embarrassed to be teased about her grill incident. At least, not much. "I'm fairly sufficient," she said, taking his question seriously and giving it deliberate thought. "I can make the basics—roast chicken, pork chops, that sort of thing. And I can throw together a lasagna—"

He held up his wooden spoon. "No one throws together lasagna. You're killing me."

She grinned. "Sorry." He opened the wine she'd brought and poured her a glass. She took a sip. "I'd rather bake than cook," she admitted. "I like the precision of baking, of knowing that you need to add exact amounts of certain ingredients to get the desired results. It's like playing with a chemistry set except you get to eat your experiment when you're done."

"Next time, then, I'll make dinner and you can handle dessert."

*Next time.* She wasn't sure there should be a this

time, but she was here and she liked being with him so maybe, just maybe, she could relax and enjoy it without worrying about what would happen next.

"That's a deal," she told him, and he smiled at her, pleased. She wondered if he knew how difficult it was for her to even agree to that.

"I wasn't going to bring this up," he said slowly as if still hesitant to do so, "but Drew was less than thrilled when I told him I wanted to see you again."

She about choked on her wine. *"What?"*

"He asked if we were going out again and I told him I hoped so. I'm not going to lie to him or to you about what I want, Penelope. I enjoy being with you. You know I'm attracted to you—"

"Yes, but my son doesn't need to know that." Goodness, that would make things between her and Andrew even more awkward. "What did he say?"

Leo checked a piece of pasta for doneness, then turned off the flame below the pot. "More or less that you were his mom and shouldn't be dating."

Leo was now watching her carefully as if trying to read her reaction, to see her thoughts. "I am his mother," she said, sounding defensive and agitated. Well, why shouldn't she? She'd been having a perfectly lovely time when he'd tossed this little verbal hand grenade into their evening. "He comes first."

"As he should," Leo said smoothly and so sincerely, she believed him. "But that doesn't mean you let him run your life or make the decisions for you."

She bristled. "No one runs my life but me," she

insisted, though a little voice inside of her wondered if that was true.

He smiled and crossed to her. Took her hands in his. "Good. Because I want to keep seeing you and I don't want it to be hard on you. I don't want you to feel caught in the middle of something that doesn't have to be there."

She inhaled and told him the truth. "I want to keep seeing you, too."

He leaned down and kissed her, then pressed his forehead against hers.

She shut her eyes, her head already so full of him, she had to will herself not to fall for him completely.

No, that wouldn't happen. She wouldn't allow it to happen. This was…well…she wasn't exactly sure. But it wasn't forever.

She eased back, picked up her wineglass and took a sip, both because her throat was dry and to put some distance between them. "Is there anything I can do to help get dinner on the table?"

Instead of calling her on her extremely inept attempt at changing the subject, Leo nodded. "There's a salad in the fridge. I hope you don't mind eating at the island. The next step in the renovation process is to knock out that wall to open up more space in here."

"This is fine," she assured him. She crossed to the fridge as his phone buzzed.

"Excuse me," he said, after checking the number. "I have to take this. Hello?" he said, tucking the phone between his ear and shoulder while he drained the pasta.

Penelope put the already dressed salad on the table then wandered around the room. It was as neat and tidy as her own kitchen with no unnecessary items cluttering the counters, no bursts of color to take away from the sleek lines.

It was a far cry from what she had expected.

*He* was turning out to be a far cry from what she'd expected.

"Sorry about that," he said, shoving his phone into his pocket. "Ready to eat?"

She studied him. His tone was as easy as always but his smile was strained. His eyes sad. "Is everything all right?"

As if by magic, his expression lightened. His grin turned cocky and he winked. "I'm about to have dinner with a gorgeous woman. Things couldn't be better."

She frowned. She didn't believe him. Oh, he was very good, exceptional at pretending he was fine, but she knew, with an inner certainty she'd never had before, that he was lying.

He pulled out her stool and she murmured her thanks. He obviously didn't want to talk about whatever was bothering him. Obviously didn't wish to talk at all seeing as how he dished up her plate in silence then began eating.

She took a small bite of pasta, wiped her mouth with a napkin. "This is delicious."

When he didn't respond, she glanced at him, saw him scowling at his plate.

"Leo?"

He lifted his head. "Hmm?"

"Are you sure you're all right?"

He turned so that he faced her fully. "Sorry. I guess I am a bit distracted."

Usually, she'd mind her own business and give him the space he needed, but what if…what if he needed her to push him, just a bit?

What if he needed her to listen?

"You do seem upset," she said. "Do you… Would it help if you talked about it?"

He laughed harshly. "I doubt it."

She shrank back at his sharp tone.

"Shit," he muttered. He rubbed his forehead. "I'm sorry. It's just… It's not something I want to talk about."

Blushing, feeling like an idiot, she stared at her plate. "Of course. I apologize," she said, unable to stop from sounding so stiff. So hurt. "I shouldn't have pried."

He certainly didn't owe her anything. Not an explanation of his mood or who had called, what they'd said to upset him.

She twirled her fork in the pasta—around and around and around. This would teach her to keep her mouth shut. She knew better than to push for more than someone was willing to give. Better than to reach out to someone.

Reaching out meant there was the chance of your hand being slapped.

"Hey," Leo said softly, giving her free hand a gentle squeeze. "You weren't prying. And I appreciate your concern."

"You appreciate it, but don't want it. Have I got that right?"

He winced—either at the bite in her tone or her assessment. "I'm being an ass, I know. But could… could we maybe table this discussion, at least for now? Talk about the weather or some new tax law?"

He looked so hopeful, what other choice did she have? Well, she could say no. Could make her excuses, gather her things and leave.

Go to her empty house where she could spend the rest of the night alone.

Or she could set aside her injured feelings, embarrassment and her assumption that she was lacking in some way that made him resistant to open up to her.

She could stay. She could be here for him.

She twirled pasta onto her fork. "I'm sure you'll find the new estate law I read about this afternoon fascinating."

His grin was so relieved, she knew she'd made the right decision. He may not trust her enough to open up to her, but he needed her. Whether he realized it or not.

For now, that would be enough.

# CHAPTER FOURTEEN

ANDREW'S PALMS WERE sweating so he wiped them down the sides of his jeans. He wasn't nervous. That would be stupid. Besides, what would he be nervous about? Nothing, he assured himself as he crossed his backyard. He was just going to see if Gracie was home and if she was, cool. If she wasn't, no big deal.

She could be out, he supposed. She had friends— he'd seen her with them last night at the game. Not that he'd been looking for her or anything. He'd just happened to glance at the stands and had spotted her with a small group.

What if she wasn't home? He'd look like an idiot, coming over like this.

Shit.

He turned to head down the porch steps then whirled around and knocked on the door before he could change his mind. Inside, it sounded like chaos. The dogs started barking and kids were yelling. Gracie's brother banged on his drums.

Andrew winced. Someone should burn that kid's drumsticks. Who ever thought it was a good idea to give a seven-year-old drums?

Finally, the door opened. "Hello," Gracie's step-mom said, her very pregnant stomach stretching her shirt to its limits. "Andrew, right?"

He nodded, then cleared his throat. "Uh…right. Hi. Is, uh…is Gracie home?"

"Far as I know," she said, ushering him inside before a cat could escape. He stepped into the bright kitchen. It was an explosion of color, like the Mexican restaurant he used to go to with his mom and dad in California, all bright reds, oranges and the occasional splash of yellow. "Make yourself at home and I'll see if I can find her."

He should tell her that wasn't necessary. He didn't need to actually see Gracie. He could just give his message to her stepmom and get going. He was hanging out with Kennedy and Luke later, anyway.

He wasn't looking forward to it in the least.

It sucked being the third wheel. And he hated how Kennedy hung all over Luke whenever they were together.

Sometimes Andrew wondered if she was trying to make him jealous.

Last night hadn't been much better. Yeah, Jess was nice and she was really pretty, but he hadn't known what to talk to her about. Plus, she had this super annoying laugh, a machine gun rapid heh-heh-heh that sounded like a horse on speed.

Gracie's stepmom left and a kid, a really little one, walked in and stared at Andrew, his thumb in his mouth, his light brown hair all crazy like he'd recently been electrocuted or something. "Uh…" Andrew glanced around, but it was just him and the kid. "Hey."

The kid, wearing only a shirt and a diaper, crossed the room and stared at Andrew. Then he lifted his arms. "Up."

Andrew's eyes about popped out of his head. *Up?* He'd been around little kids before, mainly in the hospital, but he'd never interacted with them much.

"Up," the kid repeated, sounding more demanding and urgent.

If he didn't pick up the kid, would he start bawling or screaming or something? Andrew lifted him under the arms, held him out away from his body as they studied each other, the kid's legs swinging.

"I'd tell you he won't bite, but that would be a lie."

Andrew glanced over to see Gracie walk in from what looked to be the living room. "He bites?"

How pissed would these people be if he dropped the kid?

"Only when he's frustrated and can't verbalize why."

"Doesn't seem like a good reason," Andrew muttered, eyeing the kid warily. He grinned, showing straight little teeth. Straight little *sharp* teeth.

"I think you'll be fine."

"I've never held a kid before," he heard himself admit.

She crossed to them and smiled. "It's not that difficult. Here." She gently pushed on the kid so that

Andrew's arms bent. "Set him on your side, right here." She touched him and he almost jumped out of his skin. "And then put one arm around his lower back."

He did and the kid settled in like he never wanted to leave. He was sort of cute up close, except for the purple mustache and what looked to be chocolate in his hair. "What's his name?"

"This," Gracie said, "is my youngest brother, Chandler."

Andrew frowned. "I thought the biggest one was Chandler."

"Nope. That's Conner. The twins are Christian and Colin. Caleb's the redhead." Gracie tilted her head. "What are you doing here?"

She didn't sound as if she was upset he was there, more…curious. The nerves he'd experienced a few minutes before disappeared. "I—"

He'd wanted to see her. Christ, how lame was that? And it would give her the wrong idea.

Luckily, her stepmom came into the room. She clapped her hands and smiled at Chandler. "Come on, kiddo. Time for your nap."

Chandler agreeably went with his mom, leaving Gracie and Andrew in the kitchen. Around them, though, chaos reigned. Kids ran in, screaming and chasing each other and the dogs. The twins—both older, taller versions of Chandler—pushed past Andrew then began kicking at each other. The redhead barreled up to them, crying about being left out, shouting he was going to tell on them. A cat zipped through, twined itself around Andrew's legs, then shot out of there when one of the kids screeched.

"Come on," Gracie said, "let's go somewhere quiet."

She took his hand and he let her, telling himself it was only so he didn't get lost—her house was really big and had lots of rooms and little alcoves and hallways. But he was honest enough to admit he didn't mind holding her hand. The feel of her palm against his was nice.

She led him up a set of stairs littered with toys and action figures. For a moment, the sound of those banging drums grew louder but then they turned and went down a hallway, took a right and stepped into a room. She shut the door behind them, the drums muted to a low, distant thrum.

It wasn't until she let go of his hand that he registered they were in her bedroom. It was huge, like, three times the size of his room, with an attached bathroom and even a small room where she had some sort of paint studio set up.

She sat on the double bed cross-legged. "There. No one will bug us. My room is off-limits."

He turned, took it all in. He'd never been in a girl's room before, wasn't allowed in his own room with a girl there—as evidenced when his mom humiliated him in front of Estelle last spring all because they'd been doing homework in his room with the door shut.

Gracie's room wasn't what he'd expected from her or the rest of the house. It was subtle in color and pretty neat. She had a huge bed covered in a deep purple bedspread. She scooted back so she was sitting against the wall. "You can sit if you want."

"You get three rooms?" he asked, sitting on the edge of the bed, his hands between his knees.

"Molly and Dad figured since I was outnumbered by boys I deserved a place of peace and tranquility away from all the testosterone, so they gave me these rooms."

It was cool how her parents took her needs seriously. He couldn't imagine his mom doing something like that. She just did what she wanted and he had to follow along.

"You want to watch a movie or something?" Gracie asked, leaning forward to retrieve a remote control from the bedside table.

"I can't stay long." His friends were waiting. But he wished he could stay. Taking a deep breath, he slid back so that he sat next to her. He'd like nothing more than to stay right there, maybe put his arm around her shoulder and watch a movie. Or make out. Both if he was lucky. No one would ever have to know. "I actually just wanted to drop this off."

He lifted his hips and pulled the book from his back pocket.

"Thanks," she said, seeming really pleased as she looked at his tattered copy of *Animal Farm*. "Is this like a first edition or something?"

"I don't think so. I found it in this really cool used bookstore back home." He frowned. "In California, I mean."

She watched him, her gaze searching. "You miss it, don't you? California?"

He lifted a shoulder. "Not as much as I used to."

"I'm glad." She smiled and touched his arm. "I'm glad you're here, that you and your mom moved to Shady Grove and bought the house next door. And that I ran into you that day when you were having your temper tantrum."

"I wasn't having—" He noted her teasing grin. Rolled his eyes. "Whatever."

"I'm just… I used to think you were like everyone else, all those stupid guys who only care about scoring—on and off the field. It was wrong of me to judge you without knowing you. And I'm sorry."

Shame filled him. He'd judged her, too. Had thought she was a freak with her weird clothes and odd family, with how she was usually alone. How she was comfortable being alone. Hell, he'd gotten mad and embarrassed when she talked to him after the game. "It's okay."

She slid closer, her hip pressing against his. "Andrew?"

Her voice was soft, a whisper of air, her breath washing across the nape of his neck. He swallowed. "Hmm?"

"Do you want to kiss me?"

He jerked his head to look at her. "What?"

She didn't seem embarrassed in the least. Just watched him serenely. "I asked if you want to kiss me. You can, you know."

He knew. He knew she had a crush on him. Had liked the idea of it. He'd never considered taking advantage of it, though.

*Liar,* his inner voice whispered.

He ignored it.

He turned slightly and, before he could overthink it, could talk himself out of it, brushed his mouth against hers. Her lips were warm and soft and full, and she placed her hands on his shoulders, so he kissed her again. And again. Slow, deep kisses. She didn't seem to mind that he wasn't experienced, couldn't seem to tell that he'd kissed only a few girls. She responded to his every move, her tongue touching his when he swept it into her mouth.

He kept kissing her, settled his hand on her side, his thumb centimeters from the side of her breast. Heat suffused him and he rubbed his thumb back and forth. Back and forth. She didn't stop him. Growing bolder, he slid his hand higher when a loud bang had him jerking upright.

Gracie smiled. "It's all right," she whispered. "It was just the boys messing around."

She leaned forward to kiss him again, but he slid away. "I have to go. I'm, uh…meeting Luke," he said, for some reason not wanting her to know Kennedy would be there, too.

"Oh." She looked disappointed. "Okay. I guess I'll see you later."

He pushed himself to the edge of the bed and stood, wishing he still had the book so he could hold it, cover his hard-on. Praying she didn't notice it. "Maybe I could come over later?" he asked, his heart in his throat. "When I get home?"

"What time will that be?"

"Around eleven." His mom hadn't extended his curfew yet. He held his breath, hoping Gracie would say yes. "Unless that's too late," he added quickly.

She nibbled her lower lip and he grew harder thinking of her mouth on him. "I guess that'll be all right. My parents will be asleep, but there's a trellis you can climb up to the window. Just text me before you come over and I'll make sure it's unlocked."

Triumph and relief flowed through him. It was just like all those stupid movies and TV shows. And they usually ended with the neighbors hooking up. "Yeah. Okay. See you later."

He left, more excited about getting his time with his friends over with so he could see Gracie again.

"What's the matter?" James asked Leo with a hard slap on the back. "You're looking a little pale."

Leo's mouth flattened. "Shut it."

James followed Leo's stare then laughed and slung his arm around Leo's shoulders. "That's a pretty picture, isn't it?" he asked, nodding to where their mother and Penelope stood by the living room window, deep in discussion, their heads close together. "Mom and your girlfriend—"

"She's not my girlfriend," Leo muttered. He wasn't sure what Penelope was, but they'd gone out only twice—and that was including dinner at his house two nights ago.

"No?" James asked. "Could have fooled me. And everyone else. Not that it matters what label you give her. Here she is, having survived her first Sunday family dinner, having a friendly chat with Mom." He sighed. "Ah, look at them. Bonding the way females do."

*Bonding.* Leo was sure he could feel the blood leaving his face. He didn't want them to bond. It hadn't bothered him that his mom had invited Penelope and Andrew to Sunday dinner. At least, not much. When he'd asked Rose why she'd felt the need to ask a woman she'd only just met to a family function, his mom had told him she thought Penelope could use some friends.

Which was what she and Leo were. Friends. Possibly becoming more.

And things had gone smoothly tonight. Better than he'd imagined when he'd picked up a nervous Penelope and a sullen Drew two hours ago—the kid obviously still didn't want his mom seeing Leo. But his family had been on their best behavior so far and, as the evening progressed, Leo could see Penelope relaxing and enjoying herself.

Even Drew was having fun.

Then again, he'd perked up quite a bit when he'd met Maddie, Sadie and Harper. He was, at this moment, sitting on the sofa laughing at some story Sadie was telling him. Nothing like the attention of a beautiful woman—or three—to make a teenaged boy happy.

Cassidy climbed onto Drew's lap and gazed at him adoringly.

Three women and one very enamored three-year-old.

So, yeah, things had gone pretty well.

Except his mom and Penelope had been huddled together going on fifteen minutes. That had to mean something. But what?

Finally, his mom laughed, patted Penelope's arm then walked toward the kitchen. Leo shrugged off James's arm and hurried after her.

"What were you talking about?" he asked as he stepped into the room.

Rose frowned. "Excuse me?"

"You and Penelope. What were you talking about?"

Rose filled the coffeepot with water. "What do you think two intelligent, interesting adult women were discussing? You, of course."

His head snapped back as if she'd tossed the water in his face. "What?"

His mother—his middle-aged, way-too-old-to-be-rolling-her-eyes mother—did just that. "No other topic of conversation could possibly compare to the wonder that is you. It's just lucky that we both find your life so fascinating or Lord only knows what we would have to discuss."

He shook his head. Grinned sheepishly. "I'm an idiot."

"You'll get no argument from me on that one." Rose patted his cheek. "But you're one of my very favorite idiots."

"It's okay," he told her, giving her a quick hug. "We both know I'm your number one favorite. Don't worry I won't tell the others." He got down the coffee, measured out enough for the pot. "Penelope was just so nervous about coming here—she's not as comfortable as we are in social situations."

"You were looking out for her."

He lifted a shoulder, feeling like the idiot he claimed to be. "Something like that."

"Because you care about her."

Something in his mom's too-casual tone alerted him he needed to watch his step. And his words. "I like her," he said slowly. "Yes."

Rose flipped on the coffeemaker. "I like her, too. And Andrew."

"There's no higher compliment," he assured her.

She snorted softly. "Flatterer. Now, you watch the coffee while I go in there and start planning your and Penelope's wedding."

He could only stare. She was kidding. Right?

He took a step to follow her when Penelope entered carrying dirty dessert plates.

"Everything okay?" he asked.

She smiled. He rubbed a hand over his suddenly aching heart.

"You have to stop asking that. What did you think your family was going to do to us? String us up over a fire and have us as the main course?"

"You never know," he muttered, taking the dishes from her and setting them in the sink. "This could all be an elaborate trap and they're luring you in with jokes and kindness and my mom's roasted chicken. Then, when you least expect it, they'll turn on you." He narrowed his eyes at the good-natured shout from the dining room. "They're sneaky."

She laughed and he grinned in response. She'd done a lot of that since arriving at his parents' home. Laughed. Smiled. Seemed at ease. "The only thing I'm afraid of is Andrew asking them to adopt him. And to think, he hadn't even wanted to attend, had claimed he'd be bored and would feel stupid not knowing anyone or having any kids his own age there. Funny how those complaints stopped soon after we got here. I'm not sure if it was Sadie teasing him or the food that won him over."

"I just want to make sure they weren't too pushy. Or nosy. And half those stories they told you about me were bald-faced lies," Leo said. "I never, not once, dated twins. At least, not at the same time."

"They've been wonderful," she said. "Growing

up, my family's dinners were stiff, awkward affairs. I was always so unsure of myself, afraid to speak my mind lest I say the wrong thing. But your family welcomed Andrew and me—virtual strangers—made us feel a part of your family, if only for a few hours." She began filling the sink with water. "Where does your mother keep the dish soap?"

"Hey, now," Leo said, coming up behind her. "None of that. You're a guest."

She opened the door under the sink, found the soap there. "I don't mind."

He gently pulled her away, shut off the water. "Are you kidding? Mom would kick my ass if she knew I let you wash the dishes."

"But it's the least I can do after everything she's done for me and Andrew."

"She roasted a chicken and mashed some potatoes. Believe me, she can do that in her sleep. And I'm sure she was happy to include you."

"No, it's more than that. You don't understand because you're so accustomed to it."

He wrapped one arm around her waist, lifted her chin with his other hand. "Accustomed to what?"

"To this," she burst out, waving her hand and almost hitting him in the chin. "Sunday dinners and your brothers and sister teasing you and you teasing them right back. To your grandfather sitting at the head of the table and your parents holding hands and your nieces and nephew chatting away. To the noise and the laughter and yes, even the occasional argument. You're used to being a part of it."

"A part of the insanity?"

"A part of a family," she whispered. "I guess I never realized what I'd been missing. Not really. Thank you. Thank you for sharing yours with me. With us."

She humbled him. He kissed her, a quick brush of his mouth over hers. Straightened. "Thank you."

She looked dazed. "What for?"

"For reminding me how lucky I am."

"Glad I could help." She eased away, turned on the faucet. "Now you can repay me by helping with these dishes. I'll wash. You dry."

Shit. He hated doing dishes. "I'm telling you it's not necessary. If we wait a few minutes, Sadie will volunteer."

"She already did," Penelope said, squirting soap into the sink. "I told her we'd take care of it."

He sighed. Damn. He guessed it wasn't such a bad way to spend a little bit of time. The scent of coffee filled the air, his stomach was full and he stood close to Penelope. Plus, his siblings would avoid the kitchen for at least twenty minutes. None of them would want to take the chance of being roped into helping.

"I think Andrew was a little disappointed that Maddie's boyfriend wasn't here," Penelope said, handing Leo a bowl. "He's never met a professional athlete before."

"Believe me, he's not missing much."

Penelope frowned at him. "You really don't like Neil, do you? I thought maybe Maddie had exaggerated."

"She didn't."

"Want to tell me why you dislike him so much?"

"It's a long story."

She gestured to the pile of dishes that hadn't fit into the dishwasher. "I have plenty of time."

True. But he didn't want to spend any amount of time talking about Neil Pettit. Bad enough he had to deal with him at most holidays. Had to live with the knowledge that the man would likely become his brother-in-law. "It's not important."

"Why do you do that?" she asked quietly.

"Do what?"

"Brush me off when I ask you a question."

He stilled. "I don't do that."

She nodded slowly, her eyes sad. "Yes. You do. You have no problem quizzing me about my life, asking me about my marriage, discussing my son and his illness. But when the conversation gets too personal for you, too uncomfortable, you shut down. Shut me down. Friday night, I wanted to help you with whatever was bothering you but you wouldn't let me. You don't trust me enough to open up to me."

"Hey," he said, reaching for her only to drop his arms back to his side when she stepped back, her chin lifting. "It's not like that."

"No?" She crossed her arms. "Then what is it like?"

He'd pissed her off. Worse than that, he'd hurt her. "I dislike Neil because he hurt Maddie."

"What do you mean, hurt?"

"Not physically. He broke her heart." Leo stabbed his hand through his hair remembering how distraught Maddie had been when Neil had left. "He got her pregnant when she was sixteen then took off to become a hotshot hockey player."

"But they're together now," Penelope said, looking confused. "She obviously forgave him."

Leo whipped the towel onto his shoulder. "What if he does it again? What if he leaves her again?"

"I can understand why you'd be worried for your sister, but Maddie seems quite capable of taking care of herself."

"I should have taken care of her." He ground out the words from between his teeth. "I should have protected her. I was the one closest in age to her, the one still at home when Neil started sniffing around her. I never should have let him near her. Never should have let him hurt her that way." He flung the towel onto the island. "I knew what Neil was capable of. I should have said something, done something when he first took an interest in Maddie."

"What could you have possibly done?"

"I could have warned her that he was dangerous. That he'd use her. Take advantage of her feelings for him."

Penelope laid her palm against his cheek. "You can't save everyone."

Her words blew through him. Chilled him. "You think I don't know that?" he asked, his voice ragged, his tone sharp. He grabbed Penelope's upper arms and dragged her onto her toes, ignoring her gasp, how her eyes widened. "I know that better than anyone. While you're sitting behind your tidy desk I'm responding to accidents and heart attacks and strokes and overdoses. While you're adding up numbers I'm trying to put people back together."

"Leo," she said softly. Gently. "You're hurting me."

He yanked his hands away, curled his trembling fingers into his palms. Shit. *Shit!* What the hell was wrong with him? He rarely lost his cool. His control. "I'm sorry." His voice was reedy and thin. He cleared his throat. "Penelope, I…I apologize. I never meant to hurt you."

"I know." She stepped closer. Shocked him by taking his fisted hands in hers. "Tell me. Trust me."

He shut his eyes. Tipped his head back and blew out a heavy breath. He didn't want to. He wanted to make a joke, to use his wit and charm to steer the conversation in a different direction.

*Tell me. Trust me.*

He needed to do both. For himself, yes. For the hope of gaining some measure of peace, of closure. But for Penelope as well. To prove how much he was starting to care for her. That he did trust her.

"You were right," he admitted, straightening his fingers and linking them with hers. Liking how the feel of her palms against his centered him. Grounded him. "That phone call the other night did upset me. It was one of Samantha Coles' sorority sisters. Samantha was the young woman who died in the car accident over Labor Day weekend."

"Yes," Penelope murmured. "I remember."

"Her sorority is putting on a fund-raiser to help the Coles with funeral costs. They wanted me to attend as the guest of honor." His mouth twisted. "Samantha's dead and they want to honor me for not doing enough to save her."

"You tried," Penelope said. "I'm sure you did your best."

"It wasn't enough. Sometimes I hate it. I hate that no matter what we do, no matter how hard we try to help someone, to save them, it isn't enough. I told Sam she'd be all right," he whispered. "That I was going to take care of her. That I'd save her."

Penelope's eyes glistened with tears. For him. It ate away at him. "Oh, Leo." She rose onto her toes and hugged him. "It wasn't your fault. It wasn't your fault at all."

Burying his face in the crook of her neck, he wound his arms around her slim waist and held on tight. Took comfort from her words, her presence there. And in that moment, found his peace.

LEO WALKED PENELOPE to her door. They'd gone out again, this time into Pittsburgh for dinner, then to

the art museum. The third weekend they'd spent together in as many weeks. Penelope fished around
for her keys, not sure how she felt about this connection she was creating with Leo, this need for him
that was growing inside of her. He never spoke of
the future, never hinted that he wanted to continue
seeing her, but the way he treated her, how he continued to want to spend time with her, told her he
cared for her.

She unlocked the door and turned to face him.
"Thanks again."

He grinned, ducked his head and kissed her.
"You're welcome." He kissed her again. "Next time,
though, I pick the venue."

She laughed. "Please, I saw you studying those
abstract paintings. You enjoyed yourself, admit it."

"I was trying to figure out what the hell they
were," he said. "But it wasn't bad."

She couldn't believe he'd grown up so close to
Pittsburgh and had never gone to any of the muse-
ums except for one on a field trip in grade school.
She tipped her head back and grinned at him. "Next
time I'm thinking we should check out the ballet."

His wince was small but noticeable. She laughed.
"Kidding. You do get the next pick."

"Great. We'll take in a hockey game, then hit Pri-
manti Bros. for a sandwich." He set his hands on her
waist and pulled her toward him. Nuzzled her neck.
"By the end of the night, you'll be wanting French

fries on all your sandwiches and rooting for the Penguins to win the Stanley Cup."

She had no idea why penguins would want a cup or who Stanley was, but whatever Leo was doing to her neck felt really nice so she didn't ask. Just tilted her head as he moved his mouth along the side of her neck.

"Well," she gasped, not stopping him when his hands slid to her back and brought her flush against his body. "I'd better get inside."

"Uh-huh," he murmured, his lips moving against her skin. His fingers dug into the slope of her rear. "It is late."

It was. Past midnight. "I'm not very tired," she heard herself say.

He hesitated a moment, then continued his exploration of her neck. "Me, either. I could come in. Have a drink."

He raised his head, his eyes glittering in the porch light. A drink. That wasn't what he wanted, wasn't what she wanted, either, she realized. "You could…" She licked her lips and watched his gaze narrow as it followed the movement. "All I have is some white wine, though."

"I love wine." He moved to guide her inside, then paused. "Do you think Drew is still up?"

"Probably," she said as casually as she could. "He's spending the night at Luke's, and I don't think they go to sleep until the wee hours of the morning."

Leo went so still, Penelope worried he'd stopped breathing. "He's not here."

He made it sound like a statement, but she took it as a question. "No."

"He's not coming home tonight."

She shook her head. "Not until tomorrow. He usually rolls in around noon." He would grunt at her, then head up into his room, shut the door and sleep the rest of the afternoon.

Her mouth tightened and she forced herself to relax. She wasn't going to think of her son. Not tonight. She wanted to focus on Leo, on their relationship. For once, she wanted to focus on herself.

"We have the house to ourselves." She felt emboldened by the way he looked at her, how he touched her. Emboldened and empowered. She was wanted. This handsome, kind, funny man wanted her.

And she wanted him.

The past few weeks had shown her she didn't need promises for the future. She didn't even need to know where they'd be tomorrow. She knew where she stood now, right here and now, with him. That was all she would ask for. Tonight, she would accept what was in front of her and not look for anything else.

But, in case Leo didn't understand, she wanted to be clear with him. "I want you to spend the night," she said. "I want you to stay with me."

"Penelope," Leo said, his voice incredibly kind

and gentle. He touched the ends of her hair. "Are you sure?"

She was scared and nervous and excited. And very, very sure. "I'm positive."

And she was. She wanted this, wanted him more than she could ever remember wanting to be with a man. More than was wise, certainly. But for tonight, just this once, she was going to follow her instincts and go after what she desired.

She prayed she felt the same way, that she had no regrets, when the morning came.

Still, she smiled tremulously at him, linked her hand with his and tugged him inside her house. Heart racing, she shut the door. She had no idea what to expect. Would he ravish her against the front door? She almost wished he would, wished he would kiss her, touch her, and take away all her doubts and fears. Let the desire he brought out in her so easily overwhelm everything else.

Instead, he smiled at her. "Will you take me to your bedroom?" he asked in his husky, sexy voice.

All she could do was nod. She shut off the lights and led him through the house to the kitchen and up the stairs. In her room, she let go of his hand and turned on the lamp on the bedside table, stood next to her bed.

He crossed to her, his gaze intent, and set his hands on her shoulders.

She about jumped out of her shoes.

He searched her eyes. "Nervous?"

She opened her mouth to deny it, but what was the use when the truth was crystal clear? "Yes. I—I haven't been with anyone in a long time."

"Since your divorce."

She nodded. "I was married for fifteen years and there was only one man before my ex-husband so…"

She didn't have much experience. Didn't have nearly as much as Leo did, she was sure. But she wouldn't think about that. Wouldn't consider the other women he'd been with before he met her, refused to think about the women he'd be with once they went their separate ways.

Penelope had tonight, and she needed to make the most of it. She knew, better than most, how precious those moments could be, how fleeting.

"Pretty Penelope," he murmured, tracing his fingertip down her cheek. "I won't hurt you."

He wouldn't mean to, she was sure. He wasn't cruel or heartless. But he might not be as careful with her heart, with her feelings, as she needed him to be. Still, it was a risk she was willing to take. She'd spent too much of her life being careful— always so careful—trying to make the right decision. No matter what, this felt right.

"I know," she said on a sigh. "I trust you. I want you, Leo. I want to be with you tonight."

His gaze heated and he kissed her, deep, hot kisses that weakened her knees, inflamed her blood. He walked her backward until the back of her knees hit the edge of her bed. He kept kissing her, his hands cupping her face, his fingers in her hair while she smoothed her hands over his broad shoulders, down his chest.

He was solid and warm, and she wondered what his skin would feel like, then realized she could find out. Slipping her hand under the hem of his shirt, she brushed her knuckles across his flat stomach, felt his muscles quiver and tighten. His skin was smooth, hotter than she'd thought.

He leaned back enough to strip his shirt over his head and bent to kiss her again, but she stopped him by placing her hands on his chest. She wanted to see him, and he obliged, dropping his arms to his sides. She touched him the way she'd been dreaming of touching him, her fingers tracing the hard planes of his chest and shoulders. The ridges of his stomach. She'd never seen anyone outside of a male model so perfect. That's what Leo was. Perfect.

And she was a thirty-eight-year-old woman who crunched numbers, not her abs.

"This might not have been a good idea," she said, dropping her hands and trying to put some space between them.

He looked concerned. "We can stop whenever you want."

"I don't want to stop," she blurted. "It's just… You're…you, and you look like…that—" she gestured to his body "—and I'm…" Now she swept her hand down to indicate her own body. "Believe me, what's under these clothes is nothing compared to that. Maybe we could try again in six months…no, a year or so? That should give me enough time in the gym to catch up with you."

He didn't smile, but she could see the humor lighting his eyes. "I think you're underestimating yourself. This is what you do to me." He gently took her hand and placed it on the zipper of his jeans. Under her palm, he was warm and hard. Extremely hard.

She swallowed and raised her gaze to his.

"That's what you do to me," he said softly. "That's what your touch, your kiss does to me."

It was a heady experience, knowing she made him that aroused, made him feel as weak as she felt around him. Holding his gaze, she slowly unbuttoned her top. Each time a button was freed, it was as if she lost another inhibition, another doubt. When she reached the bottom, she nibbled on her lower lip, inhaled deeply for courage and shrugged the shirt off, letting it fall to the floor in a puddle of silk.

His eyes heated; his expression turned hungry. For her. Giddiness swept through her, but it was pale in comparison to the heat suffusing her body as his gaze traveled over her, flickering on the slope of her breasts encased in a pink, silky bra, the indentation of her stomach.

He lifted his hand and she watched, mesmerized, as he dragged the tip of his forefinger along the curve of her breast over her heart. It beat frantically. He scraped the edge of his nail lightly across her nipple, which beaded, pressing against the fabric of her bra.

He bent his head, his expression fierce as he unsnapped the closure between her breasts, then used the back of his hands to push the cups aside.

"Penelope. God." He raised his head and in the depths of his eyes, she saw how much he wanted her. What he thought of her. "You're perfect."

She wasn't. Had tried so hard to be perfect at everything, at her job, at her marriage, but mostly to be the perfect mother. She'd failed so many times, had come up short too often. But now…here with Leo…she felt perfect. Perfect for him.

He cupped her breasts, and the feel of his rough palms against her sensitive skin was an enticing and arousing contrast. His thumbs brushed back and forth, coming closer and closer to her nipples until they finally touched them. He circled the peaks, drawing them into tight buds, then, lifting one breast higher, he lowered his head and took her into his mouth.

Her knees, already weak, threatened to dissolve completely. But it didn't matter if they did because he was there, one arm clamped around her waist while he feasted on her breast. She let her head fall back and let herself feel. Just…feel. No thoughts, no worries, no plans on what to do next.

He leaned her back and she lay on the bed, pulling him with her so he was on top of her. He kissed her again and her desire for him built. His hands moved over her as if he couldn't get enough. And when he rose so he could undo the snap of her pants, she did the same for him, her hands frantic and eager as she undid his jeans, shoved the material down his legs. He rolled over and tugged them off while she kicked off her own pants. He hooked his thumbs into the waistband of her underwear and yanked them down, tearing the fragile material.

She gasped in surprise, in excitement. Then he was kissing her again, his erection long and hard and smooth against her thigh.

"I want to make you come," he told her, his words, the dark tone of his voice, amping up her desire. "Do you want that, Penelope? Tell me you want me to make you come."

She couldn't. She'd never spoken words like that, had never had a man talk to her so blatantly. So honestly. He trailed his fingers along her body from her clavicle down to her core, stopping shy of the coarse hair there. She lifted her hips in entreaty.

He shook his head, continued his torturous exploration of her, now drawing circles on her inner thighs, keeping his touch light and seductive. Keeping his touch away from where she wanted it the most. "Tell me," he demanded softly. "Tell me what you want. Trust me enough to tell me."

How could she refuse?

"I want you, Leo," she said hoarsely. "I want you to make me come. I want to feel you inside of me."

A light in his eyes flared and he kissed her, hot

and hungrily, his hand seeking her most intimate place. The pressure inside of her built, her body heating as he worked her, harder and faster until finally, she broke apart, splintered into a million pieces of sensation and pleasure.

He rolled aside and she grabbed at his arm. "No. Please. I want you now. Now."

She didn't care if she sounded demanding or even desperate. This freedom to say what she wanted was empowering and she wasn't about to give it up, not now. Not yet. Not until she'd had him fully.

He came back to her, rolled a condom down his long length and braced himself on his elbows, his erection nudging her inner thighs. "Are you ready for me, Penelope?"

She wasn't sure. She wondered if there was some deeper, hidden message behind his words. But she was too far gone to worry about it. "I'm ready." To prove it, she reached between them and guided him to her entrance. "I'm more than ready for you."

# CHAPTER FIFTEEN

IT WAS TORTURE, being so close to Penelope's heat, but Leo held back. He wanted this moment to last. Wanted it to be more than the quick flash and burn of desire, though desire was currently running hot in his veins, making his good intentions hard to hold on to.

Penelope was more than he'd imagined. Naturally sensuous and giving, her body so responsive to him, she practically shot up in flames when he touched her. And with her small, soft hands on him, it was torture, yes, but it was the best kind of torture, the kind that meant pleasure would be following, an unimaginable release.

"Do you want me?" Penelope asked, obviously turning his earlier words against him.

He liked it.

"I want you," he told her.

She arched her back, brushing her curls against his erection. "Show me."

With a groan, he slid into her. She was so tight. So wet and ready for him. He threw his head back, clenched his jaw and shut his eyes as the pleasure of being surrounded by her, of being inside her, washed over him. She made this sound, an incredibly sexy little whimper deep in her throat, and he opened his eyes, held her gaze.

Gripping her hips, he lifted her higher and began to move. He'd never before had an experience like being with Penelope. Watching the emotions, the pleasure sweep over her face, the way a flush began at her breasts and rose into her cheeks, the stain of her desire for him. He worked to keep himself in check, not to go too hard, too fast, but she was so tight and her hands were tugging at him as if she couldn't get him close enough to her.

He lowered her, readjusted his grip and twined his legs with hers, kept moving, his hips pumping. She met him thrust for thrust, her hands skimming across his shoulders, down his back to his ass and up again as if seeking some sort of purchase, as if she couldn't get enough of him.

It was a heady experience, an arousing one, having her so out of control for him. Their bodies grew slick with sweat; the scent of their lovemaking filled his nostrils and he breathed in deeply. He grabbed her underneath her thighs and lifted her, pulling her legs higher.

She wrapped them around his waist and locked her ankles.

"Oh," she cried on a soft gasp as he quickened his pace. Her eyes were wide and she nodded. "Oh, there. I think I'm going to…I think…"

She came hard around him, tightening and convulsing, her head thrown back, her body bowed. Watching her, he tumbled over the edge himself, his orgasm shaking him to his very core.

THE NEXT MORNING, Leo awoke to the sound of a car driving by. He was alone, the sheets warm and soft against his skin. He was used to waking alone. He lived by himself, after all, and while he was a big fan of sex, he'd never had the urge to actually sleep with a woman, to hold her through the night.

Until Penelope.

But when he reached for her, she wasn't there. He wasn't sure which part of that equation bothered him more. He swung his feet over the side of the bed, padded naked down the hall to the bathroom, then, when he was done, returned to her room and pulled on his jeans. With a yawn, he went in search of her.

He found her in the dining room at the table, a cup of coffee in front of her, a blank look on her face as she stared into space. Even wearing her robe—tightly tied—she was all neat and tidy, her hair smooth, her face clean.

He wanted to mess her up. To run his fingers through her hair, to kiss her mouth until it was pink, to undo that sash and watch that robe pool around her feet.

"Good morning," he said as he stepped into her view.

She startled, almost knocking over her coffee.

"Oh. Yes." She cleared her throat, smiled, but it was strained and that did not make him a happy boy. "Good morning. Did you sleep well?"

She was nervous. Nervous he could handle. Nerves he could soothe. But regrets? He didn't want her to have any of those. Regrets meant there would be little chance of what had happened between them last night ever happening again.

And he wanted it to. Wanted her with a need that scared the hell out of him.

"I slept just fine," he said. "Though I wasn't too happy about waking up by myself." She flushed and he wanted to eat her up, to wrap her in his arms and kiss her, make love to her again. Never let her go.

"I'm sorry… I thought…" She gave a small shrug and a self-deprecating grin. "I don't know what I thought. I don't have much experience with this, as I told you last night, and I wasn't sure what the… protocol for it was."

"Protocol?"

Was it any wonder he was crazy about her?

She nodded, smoothed a hand over her hair, though not a strand was out of place. "The standard operating procedure for a one-night stand."

The warmth left him in a rush. "One-night stands usually don't occur between people who have been seeing each other, dating exclusively—at least on my part—"

"Mine, too," she said, sounding indignant as if

offended he'd suggested she was seeing someone on the side.

He hid a grin. "People who are dating and who are in a relationship." He raised his eyebrows. "Unless you want it to be only one time?"

Her color deepened and he almost felt sorry for her. Almost. But it was tough to work up sympathy when she'd left him in her bed and now looked and sounded unapproachable, as if she could barely face him.

"Okay, not a one-night stand," she conceded. He supposed that was as close to answering his question as he was likely to get. "A…" Her nose wrinkled while she searched for the right word. "A…casual, physical relationship. I'm not sure of the rules, or what's right and what's wrong."

He stepped farther into the room. "There are no rules except maybe we both agree to stick with that exclusivity agreement." He didn't like the idea of her seeing other men. Ever. And he had no desire to see other women. "But I was hoping to wake up next to you," he admitted honestly, letting his voice go husky. "I wanted to make love to you again this morning when we were both still sleepy, when you were all warm and flushed, your hair a mess, your eyes heavy-lidded."

Just thinking about it made him hard, and it took all his willpower not to throw her over his shoulder and march upstairs to her bed.

"I'm sorry," she said, "I'm just not sure what this…this is."

Panic tightened his spine. Was she trying to end things? Or was she angling for a big commitment before he'd had the chance to think everything through? "This is two people who enjoy being together taking their relationship to the next level. It's not complicated. Why do we need to define it?"

To put a name on it, or a title, when it was so easy right now?

Her smile was strained and sarcastic. She stood. "I'm sorry," she repeated and he wanted her to shove her apology. Damn it, he didn't want her apology, didn't want her to be sorry for anything that had happened between them. "Like I said," she continued, "this is all new to me. I've never had a casual affair before."

Irritation spiked. His fingers curled. Damn it, why did she keep saying what they had between them was casual? There was nothing casual about the way he felt about her, nothing easy about how much he wanted her.

"You're overthinking this," he said more harshly than he'd intended.

She held the edges of her robe closed, her knuckles white, her chin lifted. "It is *not* overthinking to ask for clarification on a subject one is unfamiliar with."

"You don't want clarification. You want to shove

what we shared last night into a neatly titled box. You want some sort of definition you can read and decipher."

She wanted, he realized with a sudden and swift clarity that took his breath, to push him away.

No way in hell he'd let that happen.

He crossed to her, grabbed her shoulders. "You want us to be like the numbers in your ledgers," he growled. "All added up and balanced. But the last thing I feel when I'm around you is balanced."

Her hands clutched his biceps, her nails digging into his skin. "Wha...what do you feel?"

At the moment? Out of control. Angry. Irrational. He should walk away. Give her some space.

Give himself some time to figure out how in the hell she'd managed to twist him into so many knots.

Yes, he thought as he slid his hand around to cup her neck, fisted it around her hair and gently tugged her head back. He should definitely walk away.

But not yet. Not today.

"I feel so much," he murmured, brushing his mouth over her mole, a whisper of a touch that wasn't nearly enough. "Too much."

PENELOPE WASN'T SURE it was possible to feel too much. And if it was possible, was that was a good or bad thing?

But then Leo kissed her as though he could never

get enough of her. As if trying to tell her exactly how much he cared for her.

Maybe it was a good thing, after all. A very good thing.

Doubt crept into her mind, however, when he continued to kiss her instead of expanding on his statement. Instead of explaining his thoughts, his words. His kiss deepened. Heated. His fingers gripping her hair in a way that stung pleasantly, his other hand strong on her waist, holding her against him.

"You drive me crazy," he muttered against her mouth, his words coming out heavy as if weighed down with hidden meaning.

Meaning she was unable to decipher. Afraid to.

Should she apologize? Assure him he did the same to her? But she realized how easy it would be to convince him of it without saying a word. Her body was already responding to him, craving his touch. It scared her how effortlessly she lost control around him, how quickly he made her forget anything and everything but him. But when he walked her backward, pushed her against the wall and pressed his body to hers, she couldn't stop a moan from escaping her mouth. Couldn't stop wanting more.

They were hidden from view of the French doors by the short wall, she knew. But even the idea of her neighbors spying her in such a position wasn't enough to stop her from grabbing hold of Leo's head and kissing him voraciously. He rubbed his pelvis against her, and her core heated and swelled.

He broke the kiss and quickly untied the sash at her waist and yanked the robe down her arms, trapping her arms against her sides. She wiggled, but he ignored her, simply slid his warm, rough hands up her outer thighs and under the cotton of her nightgown. He shoved the material out of his way, then dropped to his haunches in front of her.

Her breathing quickened, her eyes widened. He held her waist in his big hands, brought her closer to him and pressed his nose against the juncture of her thighs and breathed her in.

*Oh, my.* Her knees went weak and she would have collapsed into a boneless heap on the floor had he not held her up. With one hand, he dragged her panties down her leg, then once again leaned forward and pressed his mouth there.

She whimpered. She should stop him. She would stop him. In a minute. Or two. It was wrong…letting him do this to her, for her, in the middle of her dining room. Wrong and decadent and the most arousing thing she'd ever experienced. His tongue worked her and she couldn't help but watch him, the sight of his dark hair against her pale skin. Pleasure built and then ripped through her. She cried out, the sound loud and echoing in the empty room.

When she could think again, he was standing, holding her, soothing and comforting her. She didn't want to be soothed. Didn't want to be comforted. That had been the most intense experience of her life and she wanted to ride this wave of desire, didn't want to crash and burn or let it fade away.

"Please," she gasped, helping him undo his jeans. "Please, now."

Leo shoved down his pants, lifted her by her hips and entered her in one smooth motion. It felt wonderful. And when he started to move, his hips pumping into her at a quick, almost rough pace, she held on to his shoulders tight and let him take, take whatever he wanted, whatever he needed from her. She'd give him everything. Anything.

It was wild, their lovemaking, quite different from the night before, but felt just as powerful to be held in his strong arms, to have his body moving within hers. Her hair was caught, stuck between the back of her head and the wall. She didn't care, could only feel the sensations coursing through her body, the crazy pleasure and mindlessness of being taken against a wall.

Her body tightened, the beginning of her orgasm soaring through her. "Leo," she gasped, holding his gaze.

His eyes darkened and he pressed his face against her neck, groaning with his own release while she came around him.

Penelope wasn't sure how long it was before they both came back to their senses. Minutes…hours… who could tell? When her breathing finally settled and she was able to peel her eyelids open, Leo was still inside of her, his arms around her like a vise, their bodies coated in a fine sheen of sweat.

She brushed his hair back, loving the feel of it under her fingers. Loving that she had the right to touch him like this, that she could kiss him, run her hands over his face.

"I think I'm dead," he murmured against her neck.

She smiled. "That wasn't the act of a dead man."

He lifted his head. Grinned. "No, but if it's the last thing I do, I'll die a happy man."

Nodding, she whispered, "Me, too. Except for the man part."

He laughed, his chest vibrating against her, the sound wrapping around them, and she kissed him, let her feelings for him come through in the kiss, kept it warm and lingering.

He slowly lowered her until her feet touched the floor. He stepped back. "Shit," he breathed. He looked shaken. Scared. "I didn't use anything."

It took a moment for his comment to get through her sex-hazed brain. He hadn't used a condom. They'd just had sex, semi-rough, quick sex in her dining room like a couple of teenagers without any thought as to the repercussions.

Shit, indeed.

More upset and worried than she wanted him to know, she tugged down her nightgown. "It's okay."

"You're on the pill?" he asked hopefully.

"No, I—I can't have any more children." Had chosen not to after Andrew was diagnosed, hadn't wanted to bring another child into a home where so much focus was on one child already. She'd wanted Andrew to have her full attention and commitment.

"I'm sorry," Leo said.

She lifted her chin. "It was a choice I made." She felt sorry enough for herself, and she didn't need or want his sympathy.

"No." His voice was low and husky. "I mean, yeah, I'm sorry for that, too, because it's obvious you were born to be a mother. You're a good one. I'm sorry about... Christ, Penelope, I took you against the wall. I was rough."

"I didn't stop you." Hadn't even considered doing so, truth be told. It was flattering and amazing that she was able to make him lose that much control. And frightening he had the same power over her. "It was..."

"Amazing."

She couldn't help it. She smiled at him. "Yes."

"Listen," Leo said, buttoning his jeans. "Why don't we get cleaned up and dressed? I'll take you out—"

"Mom?" The kitchen door slammed shut. "Mom, you down here?"

Penelope's eyes widened, her stomach turned. Andrew. Dear Lord, what on earth was he doing home so early?

Frantic, she looked around, spotted her panties behind Leo. She made a mad dash for them, shoved them into the pocket of her robe as Andrew's voice grew louder.

"Mom? Is that Coach's car in the driveway?"

Panicked, sick with dread, she yanked her robe closed, but there was little she could do about her hair or Leo's state of undress. She scanned the doorway to the living room. Maybe they could sneak—

"What the hell are you doing here?"

Too late.

Trying for composed, Penelope faced her son. Tried to smile, but it died a slow and painful death at the glower on his face, at the way he stared at Leo.

"Honey." She swallowed but it still felt as if she had to throw up. "Leo and I were… We didn't…" She looked to Leo for help, but that only made things worse as he was as disheveled as she was, minus his shirt, his chest smooth and muscled. A clear reminder of how she'd lost her head.

A clear confession of what they'd been doing.

FOR ONE LONG, breathless moment, Andrew couldn't figure out what he was seeing. It didn't compute. Coach was in his dining room in nothing but a pair of jeans while his mom…he could hardly look at her because her hair was messy, her robe open, and under it, all she wore was a nightgown.

Bile rose in Andrew's throat. No. No, no, no. It was wrong. Wrong and disgusting. That was his mother, for God's sake, not some bimbo off the street.

What the hell?

"You son of a bitch," he growled and leaped at Coach, knocking him back a good two feet. It was like running into one of those 250-pound linebackers on the team. Still, Andrew didn't give up or give in. Coach had to pay. Andrew shoved him, hard, with two hands, pleased when Coach stepped back again.

"Andrew," his mom gasped, her tone horrified. Good, she should be horrified. She should be ashamed. "Stop that! Have you lost your mind?"

"I'll kill you," Andrew snarled. "I'll rip your head off, you bastard!"

He swung wildly, hoping to knock a few of Leo's teeth loose, but the coach ducked. "Don't do anything you'll regret," Leo said in that calm tone he used at practice when he was trying to get his point across. "Let's sit down and we can discuss—"

"Discuss what?" Andrew yelled. "Discuss that you're at my house at seven o'clock on a Sunday morning? That you obviously spent the night here? That you're screwing my mother?"

His mom made a sound, like he'd punched her in the stomach, but Andrew ignored it. She deserved it. She was the one always harping about responsibility and being careful not to sleep around with anyone, safe sex and all that entailed, about waiting for the right person. And now she was hooking up with the coach?

Un-freaking-believable.

"Watch your step," Leo said in a low, dark tone Andrew had never heard from him before. "And your mouth. Your mom deserves better than that. She deserves to be respected."

"Is that what you're doing?" Andrew spat. "Respecting her? Because from here, it looks like you're fu—"

Leo grabbed Andrew by the upper arms and shook him. Hard. Andrew's teeth snapped together and he tried to yank free but couldn't.

"Leo," Penelope cried, rushing over to try to break them up. "No."

But Coach wasn't listening to her. His eyes were on Andrew, his gaze hard and cold. "You don't speak about your mother that way," he said, his voice dangerously quiet. "You hear me? You don't speak about any woman that way."

Shame filled Andrew. Tears stung his eyes. He wasn't in the wrong here. They were. They were the ones sneaking around, acting like teenagers. They didn't care what he thought, what he wanted.

He lifted his hands, tried again to break Leo's hold. "Get off me."

His humiliation and frustration grew when Leo let go and Andrew realized he wouldn't have been able to get free unless Leo had wanted him to.

"Andrew," his mom said, her voice shaky, tears in her eyes. She should feel shaky. She should feel horrible. "I'm sorry. So sorry."

"You're sorry?" Leo asked, frowning at her. "He comes in here acting like a brat and you're apologizing?"

She shot him a hard glance. "Leo, please—"

"Forget it," Andrew said, stalking to the door. "I'm out of here."

"Andrew," his mom called, chasing after him. "Wait. Don't you walk away," she said as if she had any right to tell him what to do. "Andrew? Come back here."

He slammed the door behind him, then raced across the yard to Gracie's house. He couldn't bear seeing or talking to anyone in her family so he skirted the front door and climbed the trellis to her window. He'd done it many times over the past few weeks, always late at night when their parents were sleeping. They'd made out a few times, yeah, but they'd also talked. A lot. He'd even told her about when he'd been sick. He tapped on the glass. *Please be home,* he prayed. *Please.* He waited, then tapped again.

A moment later, she appeared, her hair messy, sleep marks on her face. She lifted the window. "Andrew? What…" She frowned as if noticing something was up. "Are you okay?"

He shook his head. "Can I…can I come in?"

"Of course."

She backed up and he climbed in and waited by her bed while she shut the window. She was in a tank top and yoga pants that clung to her curves. "Can I get you something?"

"No. Thanks. I just… Can I stay here? Just for a little while?" Until he figured out what his next step was, where he'd go, what he'd do.

Her expression was soft and sympathetic. "Of course. Come on," she added, sliding into bed. She opened her arms and he didn't hesitate. He sat with his back against the headboard and pulled her into his arms and just held her.

"WHERE ARE YOU GOING?"

Penelope whirled around to gape at Leo. "To find my son, of course."

He sighed, ran a hand through his hair. "You don't even know where he went."

Did he have to sound so reasonable? So calm? "He's probably heading to Luke's or with that girl he's been seeing…Jamie or Jodi or something."

"Honey, come sit down," Leo said, taking her arm and gently leading her to a chair. "You're upset."

"Yes, I'm upset. My son just walked in on me having sex." Her voice sounded shrill and overly dramatic—the complete opposite of Leo's. "Of course I'm upset!"

"He didn't walk in on us having sex."

"He could have." And she hadn't considered that possibility once. Hadn't thought, for one second, what would happen if her son were to arrive home early. She'd been too focused on her own needs, on being with Leo.

It was all too much. The emotional roller coaster she was on, the way her body responded to making love with Leo, how out of control she'd been with him not ten minutes ago. Her feelings for Leo, her attraction to him, pushed her into taking chances, stupid risks with her life, her heart and now her son.

Leo knelt in front of her. "You're in a nightgown and robe," he said. "You're not exactly dressed to scour the town for Andrew."

That he had a point—and that he gently took her car keys from her—only fueled her ire. He went to brush her hair back and she slapped his hand away. "How can you act so calm after what happened?"

"It's bad, yes. But it's not the end of the world."

"My son attacked you." She'd never forget the look in Andrew's eyes when he'd taken that swing at Leo, the way he'd glared at her as if she totally disgusted him. "He could have hurt you."

"He lashed out at me, at both of us, trying to hurt us because he's confused. And yes, angry. But we didn't do this to him on purpose—we had no idea he'd be home early." Leo paused and looked directly in her eyes—almost too directly. She wanted to look away. "He was wrong and acted badly. You need to stop taking responsibility for his choices. Stop feeling guilty for having your own life. Let him be responsible for his own actions and mistakes and especially for that shitty attitude. He had no right to talk to you like that. None."

And Leo had stood up for her. She could appreciate it. Would have appreciated it if she didn't suspect she'd deserved Andrew's ugly words.

She was also surprised by Leo's reaction. She'd never seen him be anything less than pleasant, patient and easygoing with anyone, yet within the space of five minutes, he'd manhandled her son and now sounded angry with her.

"We went too far," she said wearily. "I'm trying to teach Andrew to be a good man, a good person. How can I expect him to listen to me, to be decent and caring, to wait and not have sex, or to always have protected sex, when I jumped into bed with you? When we both got so carried away like we did this morning?"

"You didn't jump into bed with me," Leo growled. "That's your guilt talking."

"Maybe." Her head ached; her heart ached. "Or maybe it's the honest truth, the realization of what I have to do."

Leo's eyes narrowed. "Which is?"

"I can't hurt Andrew this way. I won't. He's been through enough." She inhaled deeply. "I can't… I don't think we should see each other anymore."

# CHAPTER SIXTEEN

FURY SWEPT THROUGH LEO. He was pissed at Andrew, yeah, but the kid had the excuse of being an idiot teenager. No, what really irritated him was Penelope being willing to indulge her son's rotten behavior.

"I can't believe you're caving to Andrew's tantrum," he said from between his teeth. He straightened, his hands fisting. "Jesus, Penelope, be in charge for once."

She flinched, but he wouldn't take back his words, not when she needed to hear the truth. Then her eyes flashed and she, too, stood. "Funny, but it didn't bother you when I caved over his desire to play football."

He waved that aside. "That was different."

"Really?" She crossed her arms, the look incredibly sexy with her mussed hair and gaping robe, the knowledge that her underwear was in her pocket. "How so?"

"Because that was something he wanted to do. Something that would help him focus and become a better person."

"So putting on tight pants and bashing into other boys is character building?"

Leo's jaw clenched at her snotty tone. "Damn right. With the right coach, the right teammates, it is. Youth athletics teach kids the importance of working together and putting in one hundred percent effort. They learn how to prioritize and manage their time. Giving in to Drew now only teaches him that he can push you around."

She sighed, as if the fight had gone out of her. "I'm sorry. I just... I can't. I can't fight with him, I can't stand to see him so upset. Not when I know there's something I can do to stop it. And I can't look him in the eye and tell him to respect the girls he goes out with when his own mother—who isn't in a committed, long-term relationship—is having unprotected sex against the dining-room wall."

"There's a difference between what happened between us and a couple of kids fumbling around in the backseat of a car." Unbelievable that she'd lump their experience, what just happened between them, in with teenagers experimenting and considering it all wrong, some sort of sin. "There's a difference between two single, consenting adults—emphasis on the *adults*—having a monogamous sexual relationship and a couple of teenagers blindly following their hormones."

"There's a difference, yes, you and I know that. But Andrew doesn't, and my first priority has to be my son."

"I would never ask you to put me first," Leo said, fearing he was close to losing something important, something he'd never have again if he let her push him out of her life. "I'm asking you to put yourself first. And maybe, just maybe, that you put us, as a couple, at least on equal footing with your son."

"Don't you see? I can't." Tears filled her eyes and it ripped him apart inside. "He's suffered enough. He's gone through what no child should have to, what no one should have to face, and he's come out on the other side. Now it's up to me to keep him safe. It's my responsibility to make sure he reaches his potential. I have to focus on him. I have to do what's best for him."

Leo paced the length of the kitchen, wishing like hell he'd at least brought his shirt down. He could use a bit of armor about now. Stabbed a hand through his hair. "Look, don't make any decisions now." Especially ones that would affect both of them, ones that meant his having to walk away. "You're upset. Andrew's upset. *I'm* upset. Let's just…take a step back. See how we feel about everything tomorrow."

She nibbled her lower lip. "I don't know…"

"I do. Please. I—I care about you. I want to see where this goes between us. I don't want it to end. Not now. Not like this."

He wasn't sure he ever wanted it to end, but he'd never had that thought before, had never seriously considered forever when it came to any of the women he'd dated. He wanted to explain to her how he felt, but his feelings for her were so new, so fragile, he wasn't sure what to say. How to tell her what was in his heart.

Especially when he was terrified she didn't feel the same way.

What he needed was time. Time to see if his feelings for her were real and deep enough to last—strong enough for them to make their relationship work for the long haul, like his parents and his brothers and Maddie.

Time for him to convince her to take a chance on him despite all those negatives she had stacked against him. That orderly list of hers that told her they wouldn't work, that they were too different, that she was Andrew's mom and nothing else.

"Please," he added quietly. "I'll leave now, we'll take a break for a few days, then we'll see how we feel."

She seemed unsure, so he did what he could to sway her to his way of thinking. He kissed her, kept the kiss gentle and warm until her mouth parted under his and she responded. His body reacted to the kiss, but he stepped away before he could take it deeper and hotter—mainly because he didn't want Andrew coming back unannounced and catching them in the middle of a heated lip-lock.

He smiled, putting all of his charm into it. "Come on, Penelope. Don't give up on us. Not yet. Not without a fight."

She exhaled heavily, her breath washing over his

chin. "A few days. You'll give me that much time to get through this with Andrew?"

"I'd rather help you," he said honestly, "but if you don't want it or need it, then yeah, I'll leave you be."

She eyed him warily as if she weren't sure whether or not to trust him. "You won't call me or stop by?"

"I'll wait for you to call me."

But if she didn't by the middle of the week, he was coming after her.


PENELOPE LOOKED UP when the door opened to see Andrew walk in, his face drawn. When he saw her, his shoulders stiffened. Leo had left hours ago and during that time, she'd done all she could to keep busy while waiting for her son to return home. She'd showered and washed her bedding—couldn't bear to sleep on her sheets when they still smelled like Leo. She'd cleaned the kitchen and done the laundry, paid bills, anything and everything in an effort to keep her mind occupied.

It hadn't worked. All she could see was Andrew's expression when he'd realized what she and Leo had been doing. All she could hear was his voice, ugly and accusing.

"Are you all right?" She refused to ask him where he'd been or why he'd been gone for so long, wasn't going to get into a fight over his leaving the house when she specifically told him to stay. This wasn't the time for any of that. What she needed to do now was to get her son to see her side, to reason with him.

"I walked in on my mom and my football coach screwing," he sneered. "What do you think?"

A chill ran through her. "I think," she said slowly and carefully, "you need to be careful of how to speak to me."

"Or what? You'll sic Leo on me, let him beat the shit out of me?"

"Leo would never hurt you." Though he had become physical with her son, something she couldn't forget. She cleared her throat. "Sit down. I want to talk to you."

"Not interested." He opened the refrigerator door, stuck his head inside.

"Andrew Mark, I told you to sit. Down. Now."

Her tone brooked no argument, but he was obviously still upset because he slammed the refrigerator door shut. "How could you? Was that why you left Dad? So you could hook up with other guys?"

"Of course not!" How could he even think such a thing? "You know your dad and I were having problems—"

"That's just it. I didn't. I thought things were fine. You guys never argued. You never fought. And then, bang, one day you tell me you're splitting up, like it's no big deal."

She fiddled with the centerpiece on the table. "Your father and I drifted apart. We didn't fight, no, but we didn't talk anymore, either. We didn't laugh. We both deserved better than that."

Andrew's hands fisted and he looked so much like a man, but also so much still like her little boy. "Are you going to marry Coach?"

She jerked in surprise. "We've only been seeing each other a few weeks."

"That didn't stop you from sleeping with him."

"No," she said slowly. "But while I'll be honest with you, I refuse to discuss my personal life in that detail. Suffice it to say, I care for Leo. What happened between us wasn't wrong." She truly believed that. What they'd shared was special and she wasn't going to apologize for it. "But that doesn't mean I want you to think you should be having sex."

He laughed harshly. "Right. Talk about a double standard."

"Maybe it is, but I'm going to give you my thoughts, anyway. Sex is a big responsibility and shouldn't be taken lightly. You need to always respect the girls you take out."

"I'm not an animal. I know no means no."

"I'm glad to hear it. But if you do decide to have sex, you need to make sure you use protection, both for your own health and well-being and for hers."

He tipped his head back. "I'm in hell," he muttered. "This day has been nothing but total hell and now I'm discussing my nonexistent sex life with my mother, which is only slightly worse than my knowing, for a fact now, that my mother's sex life is very much existent."

She rolled her eyes. Honestly, sometimes dealing with her son frayed her last nerve. "I realize you know everything there is to know about sex and how to act like a gentleman, but I'm still your mother and it's still my job to reiterate my beliefs and expectations of you. Now, I realize that once you leave my sight, once you walk out that door, you're going to do what you want without any thought or care as to what I'd like you to do. But I can't, in good conscience, not express my hopes for you and the values that are important to me."

"Yeah, whatever." He opened the fridge again, grabbed a bottle of juice, shut the door and stomped up the stairs.

Penelope slumped in her seat. That had gone... not quite as horribly as she'd expected. Not great, but not the worst conversation she'd had with her son.

What that said about him—not to mention about her as a parent—she wasn't sure she wanted to know.

*You need to put yourself first.*

Leo's words echoed in her head. Put herself first. She was a mother. She had to put her child first. Had to focus on him. But a part of her, a small, resentful part, wished she didn't have to. Wished she could focus on herself, on her own happiness, instead of trying, always trying, to make Andrew happy.

Especially when it never seemed to work.

Leo wasn't sure what to expect Monday at football practice, but after the way things had ended with Penelope yesterday, and then a long shift at work, he was in no mood to put up with any bullshit.

Too bad Drew seemed to have bullshit to spare.

"Hustle up," Leo called when Drew lagged behind getting to the team huddle. During the entire practice Drew had been sulky and sullen and a grade-A idiot. Leo didn't know how Penelope put up with it. Wasn't sure he would be able to much longer, and what did that say about any hope he had of continuing a relationship with her? He wasn't the kid's dad, wasn't sure he wanted or was up to the responsibility of being part of a couple that included making sure a teenager reached adulthood as a compassionate, hardworking individual.

"Let's run Omaha," Leo said of the next play he wanted them to practice. "Ready?"

The boys lined up and Leo blew his whistle. The ball was snapped, the quarterback dropped back and sent a beauty of a pass to Drew.

Who didn't even try to catch it.

"Drew, put some effort into it." Leo blew his whistle again. "Let's try it again, gentlemen."

They ran the play four more times. Four. More. Times. And each time Drew's lack of effort was eclipsed only by the glower and sulky expression on his face.

"Okay, let's move on to something different," Leo said.

"Can we try a reverse?" Luke asked.

"Sure. Knock yourselves out. Except you," Leo told Drew when he tried to join the huddle. "You can hit the showers. Gakowski?" he called to the second string receiver. "You're in for Freeman."

"What?" Drew asked, his face red. "Why?"

"Because you obviously have better things to do than be here," Leo said, keeping his cool. "You're not even trying and you're making it that much harder for everyone else, so hit the showers and we'll see you tomorrow. If you can have a better attitude."

Leo walked away from him toward the rest of the team.

"This is bullshit!"

He sighed. Noted the wide-eyed expressions on the other kids' faces at Drew's outburst before he turned to the kid. "You think so?"

Drew lifted his chin, his helmet in his hands. "Yeah. I do."

Leo nodded. "That's your prerogative. Too bad it doesn't matter what you think. What matters, here, on my football field, is what I think. You get me?" His words were all the more serious and dangerous for their quiet tone. "Now get out of my sight before I lose my temper."

But Drew, stubborn, defiant Drew, stepped closer, the physical threat in his body language clear. Leo raised his eyebrows and sent him a look that said, *Boy, you wouldn't be stupid enough to make the same mistake twice, would you*?

The kid backed down. Maybe he was smarter than he acted.

"You're just pissed at me because of yesterday," Drew said with a sneer.

Now it was Leo who closed the distance between them, lowered his voice and spoke directly into Drew's ear. "Don't go there."

"You run this team like a dictator," Drew said as he backed up and raised his voice. "It doesn't matter what we say or what we do. All that matters is what you say."

"You want to have your say?" Leo asked, still in that same quiet tone. "We'll discuss this later. After practice."

He turned once again.

"Later?" Drew called. "I want to discuss it now."

"Dude," Luke said in a loud whisper. "Shut up."

"Go home," Leo told him without even turning around.

"Screw you!" Drew spat. "Oh, wait. That's my mother's job, isn't it?"

Everything went still and quiet. Leo didn't so much as glance at the faces of the team or his assistant coaches, even knowing Pops was there and witnessing this didn't matter. Furious, he stormed over to Drew, saw the flash of fear in the kid's eyes, but got no satisfaction from it.

"Leo."

Pops, saying his name, bringing him down from the ledge. Good thing or else he would have made a huge mistake and he couldn't let this snot-nosed kid do that to him. "My office," he told Drew. "Either you walk there on your own, or I drag you there by the scruff of your neck. You have two seconds to decide. One."

Drew snorted and crossed his arms as if it would take a bulldozer to move him.

"Two."

Leo had barely gotten the word out when Drew started walking. Leo turned to the people watching, handed his whistle to Pops. "Could you run the practice until I get back?"

Pops nodded. "Keep your head."

He would. He wouldn't let Drew push him into doing something he'd later regret. He found the kid inside his office, standing as rigidly as a statue, his hair mussed, his pants dirty.

Leo shut the door and went behind his desk. Sat down. "You have a problem with me? That's fine. But you also have a responsibility to your teammates not to act like an idiot while on the field. I let you back on the team because you begged to be on and now I'm regretting that decision."

Drew just smirked.

Leo leaned back. "You think you have a right to act that way?"

"I've got a right to my feelings."

"Damn right you do. You can be pissed and unhappy, but that's no excuse to have such a shitty attitude. Then again, that's your thing, isn't it? Giving your mother grief all the time, acting like an asshole. Yeah, you got a shitty deal when you were younger. It wasn't fair you were so sick, and it's not fair you could get sick again, but you can't hide behind it forever."

Drew flushed angrily. "I'm not hiding from anything. And this has nothing to do with my being sick. I want to get past all that, but Mom won't let me."

"Bullshit," Leo said mildly. "You hide behind that illness, let Penelope take care of you like she always has, and then you act like a spoiled, selfish, resentful brat. You can't have it both ways. You can't take and take and take from someone and never give back. Look, there's no shame in being afraid—"

"I'm not afraid," Drew said quickly. But his lower lip trembled.

"But there is shame in using people and being selfish."

"What's this, Coach?" he asked, saying the word *coach* the way most people say *rat-fink bastard*. "Playing daddy?"

"I'm not your dad and don't want to be," he told him honestly. "But I was hoping we could, eventually, be friends. To tell you the truth, I'm not so sure that's such a good idea now. I'm not so sure I want a friend like you."

Drew flinched, but the kid still had more resentment inside of him, because he stepped forward. "You're nothing but a hypocrite. You tell me I'm using people, that I'm taking advantage of my mom? Right. What are you doing? I'm not the one using her. You are."

Anger simmered in Leo's veins and he slowly got to his feet, kept his gaze on Drew's, his voice low. "Your mom is a wonderful, bright, beautiful, caring woman. If you can't see that, if you can't appreciate her for the person she is and don't understand why I enjoy being with her and appreciate her as well, then you're an even bigger idiot than I thought." Leo pressed his mouth together, knew what he had to do next even if he hated it. "Clean out your locker."

The kid's head whipped up. "What?"

"Your locker. Clean it out. Anything you don't take will be thrown away at the end of practice."

"Why?" Drew cried, his face white.

"You're off the team."

The kid's eyes about popped out of his head. "You can't kick me off the team!"

"Want to bet? I can do whatever I feel is necessary for the benefit of the team as a whole. And I think it's better, for all of us, not to have you as a member. So pack up your stuff and go. And don't even think about coming back."

# CHAPTER SEVENTEEN

IT WASN'T FAIR.

Anger zipped through Andrew's body, making his blood hot, his heart beat too hard, too fast. He picked up his pace, his duffel bag bouncing against his back as he walked home. He was a block away from his house, hadn't wanted to call his mom to get him, could barely even look at her after what he'd walked in on yesterday.

Who the hell did Leo think he was, kicking him off the team? They needed him a hell of a lot more than he needed them, that was for sure. Asshole. And he wasn't the only one. You'd think Andrew's friends could have had his back, too, instead of standing there like sheep, blindly following orders.

He walked around the rear of his house, dug his key from his pocket and inserted it into the lock.

"Hey," Gracie said breathlessly as she crossed the yard. As if she'd noticed he was home and had rushed over. She smiled. "Done with practice already?"

"Yeah." He didn't usually hang out with Gracie in the afternoon, only at night when he snuck over to her room. Those visits were their little secret. He checked his phone. His mom wouldn't be home for almost two hours and he really didn't want to be alone. "You want to come in?"

Her smile brightened. "Sure."

He let her in first, then shut the door and tossed his bag on the floor. Stuck his hands in his pockets only to take them out again. Hell. He was nervous. Which was dumb. It was just Gracie. And this wasn't the first time he'd been alone with a girl in the house before. He and Estelle had hung out in his room for well over an hour. Almost as long as it had taken him to work up the nerve to kiss her.

He'd kissed her and she'd brushed him off. But this time was different. Gracie already let him kiss her. Whenever he wanted. And she'd let him do other things, too, had let him put his hand under her shirt, touch her boobs through her bra. Yeah, this time was different. Maybe because he already knew Gracie liked him. Maybe because he was so edgy and amped up. He didn't know.

Didn't care.

"Want a drink or something?" he asked.

"Sure. Whatever you have is fine."

"Except milk, right?" he asked.

She looked at him as if he was some sort of genius for remembering she was a vegan. "Right."

He grabbed two bottles of juice. Would have given one to her so he could hold her hand but his palms were sweating. "Come on."

She followed him up the stairs to his room. He winced. For the first time, he wished he'd listened to his mom's nagging about keeping it clean. He shoved clothes off his bed, then handed her a bottle. "I need to jump in the shower. You can watch TV or whatever."

"Oh. Okay."

He grabbed clean shorts from his drawer and crossed to the bathroom, his palms still damp, his heart pounding. He liked seeing Gracie on his bed, her colorful clothes a bright contrast to his dark bedspread. He wanted to see her lying on it, he realized, but when he imagined it, he got hard.

Shit.

He took a cold shower, but as he did, he wondered if this wasn't an opportunity in the making. He got out and dried off, and put on his shorts, but left his shirt off. Gracie liked him, he reminded himself. It was obvious in how happy she was every time she saw him. How she always seemed to be waiting for him to tap on her window.

He just hoped she liked him enough.

He went back into the room. Her eyes widened and her cheeks turned pink when she took in his bare chest. He'd worked hard to develop some muscle tone, and now had ridges and hard planes instead of a sunken chest and too-skinny arms.

He sat next to her, drank deeply from his bottle of juice, then set it down.

And kissed her before he lost his nerve.

She kissed him back, hesitantly at first, but then with more eagerness. He kissed her again and again until they were lying on his bed, side by side. He shoved her hair aside and kissed her neck, loving how soft her skin was. She tipped her head to the side and made a funny little sound, as if she liked what he was doing, her hands kneading his bare shoulders. Emboldened, he slid his hand under the hem of her shirt, skimmed his fingertips over the silky material of her bra, praying she couldn't tell how badly he was shaking.

She squirmed, started running her hands up and down his arms. It felt so good, having her touch him. Her letting him touch her. He reached behind her and unhooked her bra then cupped her breasts.

She grabbed his wrists and tugged his hands away. "Andrew—"

"It's okay," he whispered, his voice unsteady. He wanted, more than anything, to touch her there again. To brush aside the bra and maybe even kiss her there. Instead, he kissed her mouth, her chin. "I really like you, Gracie," he told her, trailing his fingers over the skin of her stomach. It was so soft. So smooth. "I like you a lot."

She sighed, her body softened. "I like you, too, Andrew."

Good, that was good. He went back to kissing her until she relaxed again, then he moved his hand up, up some more until he tugged and she let him pull her shirt off. She was beautiful. Her hair a riot of curls, her skin so pale and creamy. Excitement battled with reason inside of him, but there was a girl on his bed wearing only her jeans and an undone bra, and she was kissing him, so excitement won out.

They were both breathing hard, and she kept wiggling under him, but not like she wanted to get away from him. More like she really liked what he was doing, so he kept doing it. He gently rubbed his palms across the front of her bra and she made a sound in the back of her throat. It wasn't enough, though. He wanted to touch her, more of her, skin to skin, wanted to kiss her, all over, wanted to see her naked.

Mostly, he wanted to have sex with her.

"Andrew," she gasped, stopping him when he went to unbutton her jeans. "Wait."

"What's the matter?" he asked quietly. She was driving him crazy, her hands touching him all over his shoulders and back, down his chest. She was so soft and curvy and she smelled good, like mint. "Don't you want to?"

"I..." She licked her lips and he got even harder imagining her licking him. "I'm not sure..."

"It's okay," he assured her, talking fast, trying to sound convincing. "My mom won't be home for hours and I have condoms."

She swallowed visibly. "It's just I've never...you know."

He hadn't, either, but he didn't want her to know that. "We'll take it slow." Though his body urged him to hurry up. "We'll just…we'll keep doing this and if it doesn't feel good… Or if you…you really don't want to, you tell me and I'll stop. I just— I really, really like you, and I think about you all the time."

She stared at him, eyes wide. "You do?"

He nodded. He did. Yeah, he thought about other girls, too, but she was the one he liked the most. "We won't do anything you don't want to do. I promise."

She bit her lower lip. "You really like me?"

"Yeah," he said gruffly. "I think…I think I love you." He wasn't sure that was true, but it seemed like the right thing to say at this moment. Especially if it convinced her to go all the way. Really, he wasn't sure what love was or how you knew, for certain, when you were in it.

She sighed and then smiled up at him. He'd never seen anything as beautiful as her. "I love you, too."

And though he wasn't sure he'd meant it, not like he should have, she obviously did, because she kissed him sweetly, then let him do what he wanted. On that afternoon when his life was in the dumps, when he'd been kicked off the team and was pissed at the entire world, and wanted nothing to do with his mother, he lost his virginity with the girl next door in his bed.

Only after they were done and Gracie was cuddled up next to him did he realize he'd just made a huge mistake.

"CARE TO TELL me what that was all about out there?" Pops asked Leo after practice while they walked to Leo's car.

"Not particularly." He unlocked the doors, climbed in and waited for Pops to do the same. He felt like calling his brothers, having a beer with them, but they'd know something was wrong and would bug him until he spilled the details.

"I suppose an old man could guess," Pops said, buckling up. "You tell me if I'm close. You and Andrew's lovely mother have gotten closer and Andrew is less than thrilled with that turn of events."

"That sums it up." Leo pulled out of the parking lot. Tapped his fingers on the steering wheel. "Andrew has a hard time being told no and not getting his own way." Leo just hoped getting kicked off the team taught the kid a lesson.

Pops laughed. "Sounds like a typical teenager to me."

"Bree isn't like that."

"She's only twelve. Give her a few more years. Oh, I'm not saying she'll turn into some juvenile delinquent, but she will have moments where we'll barely recognize her or when we'll wonder what's gotten into her. And just as quickly those moments will be gone and she'll go back to being her usual self."

"Yeah, well, I never acted that bad."

"You had your own moments. Besides, we're talking about you and Penelope and your future with her."

"Actually, we were talking about Andrew."

"Now we've moved on. Keep up, boy."

Leo glanced at his grandfather. "Don't start reading into things. Penelope and I are seeing each other, casually, that's it."

Pops snorted. "Didn't seem so casual to her son. And by your reaction, to you, either."

"Yeah, well, that's Penelope's own definition of what's going on between us. Her definition. Her rules. I'm just trying to stay in the damned game," Leo muttered. "Though I'm starting to wonder if I'd be better off forfeiting."

"What's this? You're thinking of giving up? That doesn't sound like you."

Maybe not, but he also didn't fight battles he couldn't win. "Things between Penelope and I are complicated."

Pops snorted. "Complicated. Life is complicated. When you find someone you care about, you make it work."

"You shouldn't have to make it work," Leo said. "It's either right, or it's not. And maybe, in this case, it's not right. Penelope has a teenage son who isn't thrilled with me, and a lot going on in her life."

"You telling me you're going to walk away from a woman you obviously care a great deal for because her son is acting like a brat? You run into burning buildings and you can't face one sixteen-year-old kid?"

Leo strangled the steering wheel. Imagined, for a brief second, it was Pops's neck. "I never said I couldn't handle Drew. It's just, being a parent is a lot of work. I'm not ready to settle down."

Wasn't seriously considering settling down at any rate. Though the idea of doing so with Penelope didn't seem so bad. Seeing her every day, waking up with her, going to sleep with her. Kissing her when he wanted, making her laugh.

His throat tightened. No, that didn't seem like a bad thing at all.

"I haven't had feelings this strong for anyone before," Leo said. "I'm not sure how to handle it."

Pops clapped him on the shoulder, almost causing him to drive off the road. "The first step in getting what you want is figuring out what you want."

"I want Penelope in my life."

"Why?"

"Because…" His throat got tight.

"Don't overthink it, boy. Just spit it out."

Overthink? Leo almost laughed. Pops was accusing him of the same thing Leo had accused Penelope of doing. "Because I want to be with her." Because he thought of her all the time. Missed her when they weren't together. "But it won't work. It's already too difficult, too complicated. Relationships should be easy and fun and without conflict."

Pops laughed so hard, he ended up gasping for air.

"What's so funny?" Leo demanded, wondering if it would be considered elder abuse to drop off the old guy here and make him walk the mile and a half home.

"You sure have a skewed vision of what a relationship is like," Pops said, still chuckling. "No one ever said life was easy or fair. I know you weren't brought up to believe that, so why would you think you wanted a relationship that wasn't complicated? Complicated women are the most interesting, if you ask me."

Penelope certainly was complicated. And fascinating. "I'm not sure I'm up to being with a woman who already has a mostly grown son."

"Do you care for her?"

"Yeah." And admitting that wasn't so hard, after all.

"Do you care for Andrew?"

He sighed. Even when he was pissed at the kid, he still cared about him. He nodded.

"You've forgotten what your brothers and sister went through before they were able to work through their problems with their significant others," Pops said, counting off Leo's siblings with his fingers. "Maddie had to forgive Neil and accept her part in what happened between them. James had to convince Sadie to give him a chance as her lover and not just her friend. Eddie and Harper are still working through her grief and guilt over being with

Eddie after her husband's death. Life is constantly evolving. You go from being single to falling in love to getting married and maybe having kids. And every step of the way you have to figure out who you are as a husband or wife, a father or mother. You have to compromise and communicate, mesh your parenting styles, how you feel about spending money, where you want to live, values, beliefs, everything."

"That's what Penelope said," Leo told him, pulling into Pops's driveway. "She said couples need to be compatible in every sense."

"I'd say it's more important that they be willing to compromise and work through their issues. To care for each other enough to set aside preconceived notions and be willing to bend a little bit."

Pops climbed out of the car, then leaned down. "I asked your grandmother to marry me three times before she finally said yes. Those rejections hurt, bruised my heart and my pride but I didn't give up, thank God. It was worth it...*she* was worth it. The most important things in life are worth the effort. Besides, since when do you give up on something because it's hard? Because it might be difficult or take extra effort on your part?"

Pops was right. Leo didn't give up. Never had.

"I don't want to lose her," he heard himself say, and he realized he'd never meant anything more. "I don't ever want to give her up."

He wanted a future with Penelope. He even wanted to be a part of Drew's life.

Pops grinned. "Then go get her."

"LEO," PENELOPE SAID, and frowned at him. "What are you doing here?"

They had agreed just yesterday he would give her a few days, that he would wait for her to call him, yet here he was at her back door.

"Have you talked to Drew?" Leo asked, looking grim.

"I just got home and I don't think he's here," she said, stepping aside and letting him in. Simply because he hadn't upheld his part of their bargain was no reason for her to be rude. "Why? Did something happen at football practice?" she asked, her stomach falling.

Leo removed his hat and ran his hand through his hair. "We got into it a little bit and, long story short, I kicked him off the team."

Penelope blinked. "Wow, that must be some long story." Part of her was relieved Andrew was no longer playing such a dangerous sport, but part of her was sympathetic toward her son. "I—I don't know what to say."

"You don't have to say anything to me. I wanted to tell you, in person, my side of things. He was openly disrespectful and disobedient and refused to do anything I asked. I can't let one of my players act that way. I won't. It disrupts practice and his bad attitude makes it harder on the rest of the team."

Insulted on behalf of her son, she bristled and crossed to the refrigerator. Pulled out a package of chicken. "I'm sure Andrew didn't mean to be disrespectful. Weren't you the one who told me before he was a good kid?"

"He is a good kid, but he's not perfect."

Her head snapped back. "I never expected him to be."

"Didn't you?" Leo asked quietly.

"That's a ridiculous and hurtful thing to say." She slammed the chicken on the counter. She needed to get dinner ready for herself and her son, she didn't have time to argue with Leo. Didn't want to have to explain herself to him. "All I've ever wanted is for him to be healthy and happy."

"You've devoted your life to keeping him healthy, to making him happy. Except no one can make someone else happy. Your job as his mother is to keep him safe and raise him to be a good person, but even then there are no guarantees. People, kids, all human beings, have free will, and right now Drew is using that free will to be resentful and selfish." Leo leaned against the counter, looking tired and dusty from being at the practice field. "Look, I do think Drew is a good kid, but even good kids make mistakes."

"Thank you," she said drily. "For that expert parenting analysis."

"I may not be a parent, but that doesn't mean I don't care about Drew."

She felt ashamed for being so snide, but he'd just kicked her son off the team. The very same team he'd persuaded her to let Andrew join. It felt like manipulation, and she was so tired of being manipulated. "I'm not sure why you came here," she said, turning on the oven, then pulling out a bag of potatoes from a lower cupboard. "What were you hoping to accomplish? You've kicked Andrew off the team. Was there something else you needed? Permission from me to do so?"

"I came here because I wanted to tell you what happened and I thought, maybe, we could figure out a way to handle this. Together."

She sighed. She felt pressured by his showing up after he told her he'd give her space. And she was taking the resultant anxiety out on him. He hadn't even mentioned their relationship, so she needed to stop jumping to conclusions.

"I'm sorry. I guess I'm still upset about yesterday." She scrubbed potatoes, then put them into the oven. "I'll talk to Andrew. I'm sure he's upset about being off the team, but you were right not to let him disrespect you."

"I thought we could talk to him together."

She frowned. "Why? You mean, as his coach?"

"No. As his mother's…boyfriend."

*"Boyfriend?"* She laughed. "I'm not sure we're at that stage yet." Wasn't sure she wanted to be at

that stage. Besides, she was too old to have a boy-friend, wasn't she?

"I care about you and we slept together," Leo said, sounding calm enough, but his eyes flashed. "We spend time together and neither of us is seeing anyone else. Sounds to me like we're together. And being together means we're a team. My parents were a team when it came to raising me and my siblings and that's what I want for us."

A team? She wasn't on anyone's team. She was on her own. She'd always been on her own. "I appreciate the sentiment and the offer, but I'm not comfortable turning to anyone for help or relying on anyone for it."

"You and your ex didn't help each other when Drew was sick?"

He sounded shocked, but then, he had a very close family, a completely different experience from what she'd had growing up. And he'd never been the parent of a sick child. "We were both focused on keeping things as normal as possible, but I focused more on Andrew and his health while my ex worked."

She'd taken control of the situation, and her ex had let her.

"You don't have to do this alone," Leo said. "I'm here and I want to be by your side. All you have to do is reach for me."

Penelope's eyes stung, but she blinked the tears away. "I appreciate the offer. However, I'm used to standing on my own two feet. I've got things covered and I can handle raising my son just fine on my own."

His expression darkened. "You don't want me in your life."

"I didn't say that." Honestly, she didn't know what she wanted. She had no idea how to fix things with Andrew, how to fix him. How to make things between her and Leo better. Or if she even should. Her life was spiraling out of control, away from the well-ordered existence she preferred, and she had no idea how to stop it except to go back to the way things were.

If she didn't, she'd get caught up in the vortex and she was terrified of that free fall.

Leo closed the distance between them and took her arms, turned her to face him. "Penelope, I'm here. Right here. I'm not going anywhere. I want us to have a future together. I want to be a part of your life. A part of Drew's life."

She gaped at him, her stomach falling. "It's too much, too soon."

"It's not if it's right, and you and I are right."

He seemed so sincere, so earnest. But how could he be? They'd known each other only a month or so. They couldn't possibly commit to each other at this stage.

She broke free of his hold and crossed to the French doors. "Things are so out of control right now, my *life* is out of control. I can't even think about tomorrow, let alone make a commitment to you after such a short period of time. I have to focus on getting my life in order, in helping Andrew deal with the idea of me dating."

Leo frowned. "Your son needs to step up and deal with that on his own. He's two years shy of adulthood. It's time he stopped acting like a kid, blaming you for every little thing that doesn't go his way."

"He's a child. He's *my* child." She shook her head. "You couldn't possibly understand."

"Why not? Because I don't have kids? Because I've never been through anything like what you and Drew went through with his illness? You wear that like a badge of honor, a way to keep yourself above the rest of us mere mortals."

She gasped, felt her face lose color. "That's a horrible thing to say."

"It's the truth. You hold yourself above other parents who haven't been through it. What happened to you all was horrible, but you can't keep using it as an excuse to not fully live. You need to take chances."

"I need to take things slow. Things between you and I are moving too fast, can't you see that? I like a slow and steady pace."

He gripped her hands. "Slow and steady will get you there eventually, but wouldn't you rather take a risk? Jump off the cliff? You need to expand, to explore your other options and step out of your comfort zone."

Her mouth thinned and she tugged her hands free. "Why? Because that's what you do? I like being in my comfort zone. I like my pace. If you truly accepted me for who I am, you'd understand that and you wouldn't pressure me to change."

He looked stricken. "That's not what I'm doing."

"It is. You don't understand my fears. If you did, you wouldn't keep pushing me. I need to go slow, to be cautious, but you keep asking for more than I'm ready to give. I already failed at my marriage, and I'm not in a hurry to repeat that mistake."

"We are not a mistake."

Exhausted, emotionally and physically, she leaned against the door frame. "We're not exactly a good bet, either. There's too much between us," she said gently, though it felt as if her world were ripping apart. "We're too different. Yes, in the short term those differences don't matter. We can fool ourselves into thinking we can get past them, but if we tried to make this work between us long-term? It would be a disaster. I'm sorry you can't see that and I'm sorry you expected more from me than I can give, but I think it's best we don't see each other anymore."

## CHAPTER EIGHTEEN

THERE WAS A buzzing in Leo's ears, loud and insistent. But it couldn't drown out Penelope's words. How she looked at him with compassion, but not the slightest bit of regret or remorse, despite her words.

She was sorry?

Shit.

"You mean more than you're willing to give," he said.

She frowned at him. "I don't understand."

No, and that was a big part of the problem. "You said you were sorry I expected more from you than you could give, but really it's what you're willing to give. And that's not much, is it?" he asked quietly.

She flinched, dropped her gaze.

Good. She'd damn well better flinch. Christ, he'd raced over here after dropping off Pops to tell her how he felt about her, to tell her he wanted to commit to her, to being in her life, and what did she do? Tossed his words right back at him without batting an eye.

She was the first woman he'd cared enough about to declare himself to. But he hadn't, he realized. He hadn't told her what was in his heart. Maybe he had pushed her too hard, too fast. But he couldn't keep his feelings hidden any longer.

"I love you," he told her, practically spitting the words out. Not exactly the romantic declaration most women dreamed of, he assumed. He cleared his throat. Tried again. "Penelope, I'm in love with you, and I want us to be together. Don't push me out of your life because it might be difficult. We can get through this. Together."

He held his breath, and for a moment, he thought he had her, that she would leap into his arms.

Instead, she shook her head sadly, covered her mouth with a trembling hand. "Leo, I...I can't," she whispered. "I'm so sorry."

So was he. More than she would ever know.

His throat tight, he shoved his hands into his pockets. "I guess you were right. I guess we are too different. You want life to add up, to be neat and tidy. Life doesn't work that way. I would have thought you, more than anyone, would have realized that by now."

Then he did the hardest thing he'd ever done in his entire life. He walked away from the woman he loved. For the first time in his life, he gave up.

"DUDE," LUKE SAID to Andrew the next day before the first bell. "What the hell happened to you last night?"

Andrew jerked guiltily. "What do you mean?"

Luke frowned. "At practice. What the hell's going on?"

Practice. Right. Andrew breathed a sigh of relief. For a moment, he'd thought Luke was talking about what had happened between him and Gracie. Not that he could know anything about it. That was between him and Gracie, and he doubted she'd tell anyone they'd had sex.

He sure as hell wasn't about to.

Andrew shrugged and shut his locker. "I'd just… had enough of Coach's bullshit."

"Are you really off the team?"

"I guess so."

"That's harsh."

Andrew noticed Luke didn't offer to quit in an act of solidarity. Then again, if their positions had been reversed, Andrew wouldn't have quit the team, either.

"Is it true?" Kennedy asked as she and Jess joined them. "Did you really get kicked off the team?"

"It's true," Luke said before Andrew could answer.

"I'm sorry." Kennedy gave Andrew a hug. "That sucks. I didn't think Coach Montesano was that unfair."

"That's only because he's so hot," Jess said, sidling up next to Andrew. "I mean, no one wants to think he's an ass. That's like thinking Channing Tatum severs the heads of kittens or something."

Kennedy rolled her eyes. "Eww. Graphic, much?"

Jess shrugged. "What? I'm just saying…"

"Well, don't worry about it," Kennedy told Andrew. "I'm sure if you apologize, Coach will let you back on the team."

"Maybe." He wasn't interested in playing for Leo, though. Not anymore. And he really didn't want to listen to the girls go on about how hot they thought Leo was. Not when he knew what Coach had been doing with his mom.

It was so freaking disgusting. It wasn't right. She shouldn't be going out with Leo or anyone. She was the one who'd wanted the divorce, and Andrew had assumed it was so she could be single, since she'd gotten married sort of young. She couldn't change the rules on him now, couldn't decide she wanted to be one of those moms who went out all the time, hooking up with guys like she was still in her twenties.

Like one of those reality-show housewives.

A buzzer went off, three quick times, warning the students they had five minutes to get to their classes before first bell. "I have to go," Jess said. She and Luke both had homerooms on the third floor. "See you later?"

He nodded. He shut his locker and Kennedy, holding her books against her chest, smiled at him.

"Walk me to homeroom?" she asked, tipping her head and giving him a view of the long line of her neck.

"Sure."

"Freak alert," Kennedy said under her breath, glancing at something behind Andrew.

He turned. And met Gracie's eyes. She smiled. "Hi, Andrew." Still smiling, she turned to Kennedy. "Hi."

Kennedy's grin was this side of mean. "Hey, Gracie. Great skirt." She said it with such falseness, Andrew was sure Gracie wasn't fooled for a minute.

"Thank you," Gracie said, obviously not bothered in the least that Kennedy was being all *Mean Girls* on her. "Do you want to meet for lunch?" she asked Andrew.

From the corner of his eye, he saw Kennedy's shocked expression and the way she curled her lip at Gracie. "Uh…" He shifted. Cleared his throat. "I'm eating with Luke and Kennedy. Sorry."

Gracie looked confused, but her smile didn't dim. "Oh, okay, well, I could sit with you guys—"

"I don't think you'd have much fun at our table," Kennedy said, all fake sympathy. "We're not really into the same things. Plus, there's no room. Sorry."

Gracie kept her eyes on him as if waiting for him to stick up for her, or tell her that they'd make room or even offer to sit somewhere else so they could eat together. His throat felt tight, and his palms were sweating. "Yeah, uh…sorry."

"What about after school?" Gracie asked, her gaze steady, though her smile was long gone. "We could walk home together."

"Why would you want to do that?" Kennedy asked, linking her arm with his and pressing close to his side. "I hadn't realized you two even knew each other." She wrinkled her nose. "I mean, enough to actually speak to each other. And nobody walks when they can drive. But then, I guess walking is better than taking the bus."

Gracie raised her chin. "I take the bus."

"Oops." Kennedy smirked. "My bad."

"Actually, I have…things…to do after school," Andrew said. He looked at Kennedy. "Uh…Gracie and I live next to each other so I've been doing a lot of work around her house," he lied. "For her family and stuff. Yard work and some painting. Things like that." He held Gracie's gaze. "Is that what you want to talk to me about? Doing more work?"

*Please,* he begged her silently. *Please go along with this.*

She looked at him as if he was a piece of dog shit on her shoe. "Yes," she said, her cheeks red but her gaze steady and condemning. "Actually, I just wanted to let you know there's no reason for you to come over anymore."

"Guess there's no more work for you," Kennedy said. "Now that you're off the football team, that means we can spend more time together."

With one last disappointed look at him, Gracie turned and walked away.

"She is such a freak," Kennedy said in a loud whisper guaranteed to make Gracie hear her.

She didn't stumble, didn't look back, just kept going.

PENELOPE COULDN'T DENY IT. She missed Leo.

It had been five days since he walked out of her house—and out of her life. Five days since she'd sent him away.

*I'm in love with you.*

She couldn't get his words out of her head. He hadn't meant it. He couldn't have. They hadn't known each other long enough, didn't know each other well enough, to be in love. It was ridiculous and irresponsible to believe in that sort of connection. There was no such thing as love at first sight or even love after a few weeks. No, love—true, lasting love—took time to grow.

She moved the laundry from the washer to the dryer. She was behind, had taken it upon herself to bring Andrew's dirty clothes down to the laundry room since he hadn't cleaned his room in over a week.

It was a mindless task, one guaranteed to give her too much time to think. To mull. To brood.

And to wonder if she'd made a huge mistake in letting Leo go.

But she couldn't trust that his feelings were real. Couldn't trust that her own feelings were real. How could they be? There were steps that needed to be taken in a relationship. You couldn't...skip over them because you were in a hurry. Jumping into things, into any situation, without careful forethought was a recipe for disaster.

But her own marriage had failed, even though she'd taken those steps, had done everything right, her inner voice reminded her.

She was so confused. It had taken all her willpower not to call Leo to ask him for another chance. He wanted too much from her, though. More than she could give. So she would move on with her life. Get back to living it the way she had been, focusing on Andrew and her career.

Spending her nights alone while her son stayed closed up in his room, spending weekends doing housework and wondering if she was always going to be alone.

She sighed and picked up a pair of Andrew's dirty jeans, automatically checked his pockets and pulled out a small foil wrapper.

An empty condom wrapper.

She frowned at it, her mind refusing to compute what was right in front of her. Her son had an empty condom wrapper in his pocket. Empty. Not put there in the hopes of being used some magical day, but already used and discarded.

She went cold all over. The room spun. Her son was having sex. Had had sex. Or, at least, it appeared so.

Breathing deeply to fight off a wave of dizziness,

she leaned against the washing machine. It was okay. She could handle this. She'd talk to him, stay calm and cool, and keep the lines of communication between them open. She could do this, would handle it. On her own.

She wished Leo were here. Not because she needed him to take over or handle this for her, but because he would have her back. Because she wouldn't be alone.

Resolute, she marched up the stairs, and entered the kitchen to find Andrew drinking milk straight from the carton. She didn't say a word. She had bigger issues to discuss with him. "Andrew, please sit down. I need to talk to you."

He lowered the container, glared at her. Yes, that was her life this past week, him stomping around the house, sullen and miserable because he'd been kicked off the football team, because she had dared to go out with a man. "About what?"

"I guess you'll find out when you sit down."

"Can't it wait? I have homework."

Irritation spiked at this brooding man-child. She was seriously sick and tired of his attitude. "Sit. Down."

He wiped his mouth with the back of his hand, put the milk in the fridge, then slumped onto a seat.

"I found this—" she held up the used condom wrapper "—in your pocket."

His face went white, but then he gave an irritable shrug. "So?"

She raised her eyebrows. "So, I hadn't realized you were dating someone, and yet you're having sex." She sat across from him, kept her tone nonthreatening and nonjudgmental. "I just…I want to make sure you're being careful."

"I don't need another safe-sex talk," he said, standing. "Especially from you."

"You're not going to get one," she said, fighting to remain calm. It wasn't easy when she was so very tired of his attitude. "Do you have feelings for this girl?"

"For who?"

Her irritation grew. "The girl you're having sex with."

"I'm not having sex with anyone. It was one time, okay? And you had no right snooping around in my room!"

"I wasn't snooping. I picked up your dirty clothes. It's not like I went through your dresser drawers. Listen, let's not argue. I simply want you to know how important it is to always use protection and treat women with respect. If you don't care for this girl, you shouldn't be sleeping with her."

He sneered, set his hands on his hips. "Why not? You slept with Coach. You telling me you care about him?"

"Yes," she said slowly, realizing it was truer than she'd wanted to admit. "I do care about Leo. Very much."

And she'd pushed him away.

"Great. So now what? You're going to marry him and I'll be stuck with you two until I graduate."

It felt as if time slowed. Penelope stared at her son, and in that moment, with him glaring at her, his bad attitude and complete and total lack of respect out in the open for all to see, she suddenly had it with him. It didn't matter if he liked her or wanted to be with her. It didn't even matter if she lost him, because the way he was now, she didn't want to be with him.

"I'm tired of you blaming me for everything," she said slowly, softly. "The divorce. Having expectations of you about your grades, your behavior. I'm tired of being the scapegoat for your problems."

He snorted. "What are you talking about?"

"I'm talking about you and your horrible behavior and attitude. I'm not putting up with it anymore. I've spent so long trying to make it up to you that your father and I got divorced. Well, guess what? That wasn't all my fault. Your father wasn't happy, either. Maybe we handled it badly, not letting you know we were having problems, but we were trying to protect you, and honestly, I had thought we could work things out. Until the day your father told me he wanted a divorce. I couldn't stay married to him when we were both miserable. So maybe that was selfish of me, but I deserve to be happy."

"You could have stayed together," Andrew accused. "I went from being sick to moving. I didn't have a say in any of it."

"No, you didn't. That's what parents do. They

make decisions for their children. All your life, I've lived for you. Do you have any idea how terrifying it is to love someone that much? So much that you're willing to put their needs ahead of anything and everything else? Have you ever thought about how scared your father and I were when you were sick? It was all we could do to get through each day, hating that you were suffering, wishing it was us instead, and being unable to stop your pain." The memory of Todd abandoning her hit with unexpected force. Some of the anger she'd suppressed then came out.

"Your dad turned to work, hours and hours of work to keep his mind occupied. Me? I couldn't eat. I couldn't sleep. All I could think about was getting you well. All I could do was read about treatments and pray and pray and pray some more that you'd pull through. That helplessness is the worst feeling in the world, especially when it comes to your child. But it was out of my hands."

The truth of her words registered and she shut her eyes. "It was out of my hands," she repeated on a whisper.

For so long, she'd thought it was all up to her to save him, to keep him safe and healthy. But some things were beyond a person's control.

It was a frightening, and liberating, realization.

"Yes, I want you to be safe and healthy." She blinked away tears. "And I want you to be happy. But if you can't manage that last part on your own, if you don't choose happiness, there's nothing I can do or say to change that. So I'm going to stop."

He looked shaken. "Stop what?"

"Stop trying so damned hard all the time. I can't worry about you being happy. I'm going to focus on my own happiness instead of always worrying about yours. Because, you see," she continued, sniffing, "I can't make you happy. Only you can do that. It's taken me this long to realize that and to realize that maybe bringing you here was a mistake."

"We're moving again?"

She shook her head. Wiped the wetness from her face. "I'm staying. But if you can't or won't obey my rules, if you don't help out around the house and keep your grades up without me nagging you, if you refuse to treat me with respect—the respect I deserve—then you will no longer be welcome here."

His eyes widened. "You're kicking me out?"

"I'm giving you a choice. You can see about living with your dad or your grandparents, but you will no longer live here if you're going to continue to be the selfish, rude, disrespectful person you've been. You won't live here, because to be honest, I'm not crazy about this person you've become." Feeling empowered and well-deserving of everything she expected of him, of everything she wanted, she evenly met his shocked gaze. "You have until Sunday at dinner to let me know your decision. But know this, once you do decide, you'll follow through whatever that decision is."

She walked away, proud of herself for finally being the parent Andrew needed.

Wishing she could call Leo and tell him about it.

# CHAPTER NINETEEN

ANDREW'S HANDS WERE SHAKING.

He set his head in his hands. His mother was going to kick him out. How could she? Where would he go? It was obvious his dad didn't want him, and he didn't want to live with his grandparents. He'd just gotten used to living here. He finally had friends.

Shit.

His throat clogged. What had he done? He wanted to blame his mom. He really did. And he tried to convince himself this was all her fault for being too strict, too overbearing and controlling, but he couldn't lie to himself anymore.

But he really, really wanted to.

She'd cried. He wiped his palms down the front of his jeans. She'd handled the condom thing pretty well, but then she'd broken down and cried. He'd never seen her cry before. Never wanted to see it again. Even when he was sick, she'd been a rock, steady and always there for him to lean on.

He'd taken her for granted, and that shamed him.

A movement outside caught his eye, a flash of color. Gracie. His heart pounding, he raced out the door, not bothering to close it, just ran across the yard, his socks getting wet from the cold grass.

"Gracie," he called. He tripped, landed on his knees, but was up again in a flash. "Gracie, wait."

She didn't. He chased her, hoping he'd get to her before she reached the front door. At the steps to her house, he caught her arm, swung her around.

She immediately yanked free. Stepped back and crossed her arms.

"Gracie." That was it. All he could say, just her name. He hadn't seen her since that morning in school with Kennedy. She'd gone home early and hadn't returned all week.

"Andrew," she said, sounding distant and cool, which was not like her at all.

He swallowed. "How are you? I mean, I stopped by the other day and your mom—your stepmom said you were sick."

"I'm fine, thank you."

But she wasn't. She wasn't acting like herself. She wasn't looking at him like she used to, with warmth and love. Now she looked right through him.

His blood chilled. "I've been wanting to talk to you."

She lifted her chin. "About?"

"About, you know, what happened with Kennedy. I'm sorry we didn't have room for you to sit with us at lunch. I don't think you understood what I was saying."

"I understood quite clearly. You didn't want me

to sit with you at lunch. You don't want your friends to know you and I hooked up, or that we have hung out. You lied about our relationship because you're embarrassed by me."

He shook his head, chilled to the bone. "That's not—"

"You're ashamed to be seen with me because I'm not beautiful like Kennedy, because I don't dress like her and her friends, because I don't act like them. You told me you loved me so I'd have sex with you and now you think I'll have sex with you again because I'm so pathetic and needy. That I'm so in love with you I'll shove aside any small amount of pride I have, any self-respect, and open my legs for you whenever you want. And then you can ignore me or treat me horribly as soon as you've rolled off of me." Her voice was flat, her eyes cold. "Does that about cover it?"

He wanted to throw up. Wanted to tell her she was wrong, about all of it. That of course he thought she was beautiful. "I...I..."

The denial stuck in his throat, choking him.

She looked at him with pity. Shook her head. "You lied to me. You used me. And you humiliated me. I don't see what else there is for us to discuss."

She turned to go and he knew he should let her, knew she was right about everything, that he didn't deserve for her to hear him out, but the thought of her walking away made him feel as if he were breaking apart inside.

"Wait," he said, not daring to touch her again. He leaped in front of her, blocking her from going into her house. "Just…give me two minutes. Please."

"Two minutes." She smiled, a thin, mean smile that should never be a part of who she was. "Only because Chandler is watching us and I don't want him to get upset."

Andrew glanced behind him, saw the kid with his face pressed against the smudged window next to the door. He'd never been so glad to see anyone in his life. "Okay. Sure." But when he looked at her, he didn't know what to say, or what to do to make this better.

But he had to try.

"You're right, about a lot of things," he finally said. "But you're wrong, too. I did lie about us… hanging out. And I'm sorry. I'm sorry I treated you that way in front of Kennedy. I'm sorry I let her treat you that way and didn't say anything. But I really do like you."

Fury flashed in her eyes. "Don't." Her voice was sharp as a whip. "Don't lie to me again. We both know you got what you wanted. Any girl would have done. I just happened to be there. I made it so easy for you, didn't I? Fawning all over you. Eating up every word you said."

"No. It wasn't like that." Not completely. "I did like you. I do. It's just…I'm not even sure what love is. I mean, how am I supposed to know when I'm in love?"

"You're not," she said flatly. "Because if you were, you wouldn't have to ask that question. So please don't try to act as if you're confused or whatever because of your past problems. I used to feel sorry for you. That you had to go through so much. You must love that, huh? Now you can use it as an excuse for treating people like dirt."

He wanted to touch her. To take her hand and promise her he'd never hurt her again. He wanted to beg for her forgiveness. "Please, Gracie. I'm sorry. Just…give me another chance. A chance to make it up to you."

"You want another chance?" She shook her head, stood rigidly in front of him. "To what? Be my boyfriend? You going to tell your friends we're together? Hold my hand in the halls?"

He dropped his gaze. "It's complicated…"

"It's not. It's so very simple." She pushed past him and opened the door.

Chandler ran over, grinned at Andrew and held up his arms. "Up."

"Gracie, I…" Andrew swallowed. "I'm sorry. I'm really sorry."

She picked up Chandler and turned. Studied him then nodded slowly. "I believe you are. But I don't forgive you. You don't deserve my forgiveness. You used me. You knew I had feelings for you, and you used them to manipulate me. You made me feel stupid," she continued, her voice not as strong, not as sure, and it tore him up inside, especially when he saw tears in her eyes. "But most of all," she continued quietly, "you made me feel cheap. And I will never forgive you for that."

She shut the door, not with a resounding bang, but a soft, quiet click that echoed in his ears. His vision blurred and he sniffed. Shoved his hands into his pockets.

He realized his mother was right. He wasn't a good person. He hadn't been for a long time. He just hoped he could change.

SUNDAY NIGHT, PENELOPE carried the pan of lasagna to the table and set it down. She'd hesitated about making it, mainly because doing so reminded her of when Leo had cooked for her and he'd told her no one threw together a lasagna.

She hadn't. She'd asked Pops for his recipe. It had been nice speaking with him, seeing him, and now she had a new recipe. One that made enough for her and her son for at least eight meals.

Five if Andrew was really hungry.

He came in. Ever since their conversation a few days ago, he'd been quiet. Oh, him spending most of his time in his room was nothing new, but this was different. He'd been acting different, not sullen so much as…sad.

But she hadn't asked him about it, was not going to worry. She'd realized that every emotion, every problem her son had did not need to be her responsibility. She refused to get upset or to try to coax him out of his silence as she would have done in the past.

She had her own issues and problems to focus on. Such as how she was going to get over Leo.

"Need any help?"

She glanced at Andrew, who looked like a little boy with his head ducked, his hands in his pockets. "You can get the drinks and salad," she told him, not letting herself get overexcited about his lending a hand. "Thank you."

A few minutes later, they sat down to eat.

She served them both huge slices of lasagna. It smelled delicious and was wonderfully gooey and cheesy.

Andrew frowned at his. "Are there mushrooms in here?"

"Yes." She forked up a bite, blew on it then ate it. Fantastic.

"I don't like mushrooms."

She ate some more. "I know. Eat around them."

Before she never would have added mushrooms to anything he was eating. She'd even stopped getting mushrooms on her half of their pizza because he claimed the smell contaminated his half.

No more.

Yes, she could have added mushrooms to only half the mixture, baked his half of the lasagna without them, but she was making a point. To him and to herself.

They ate in silence. More time for her to think

of Leo. To miss him. Had she made a mistake in breaking things off with him? He must not be too upset seeing as how he hadn't tried to contact her since that day. Yes, yes, she'd told him they were through, but if he really loved her, wouldn't he have made more of an effort?

Maybe he'd been in it for the chase. Someone like Leo lived for adventure. She had provided that, hadn't she? Simply by not falling at his feet, forcing him to convince her to give him a chance. And by being the complete opposite of the women he usually dated.

Andrew cleared his throat, bringing her out of her internal musings. "It's good," he said.

She blinked. "Excuse me?"

He flushed. "Dinner. It's really good."

"Thank you," she said slowly.

He helped himself to another slice of lasagna and added it to his plate, which was littered with the remains of mushrooms. "About what happened the other day…" He pressed his lips together, then raised his head. "When we were fighting and the condom and everything. I…I've made up my mind."

Her heart skipped a beat. Despite what she'd said about letting him choose to stay or go, she was still nervous. A part of her, a big part, didn't want to let him leave. But she couldn't live like this any longer. "Oh?"

"I want to stay," he blurted. "Here. I mean, with you, whether that's in Shady Grove, or if you decide to move somewhere else. Not that I want to live in your basement as an adult or anything. But until I go to college, I think the best place for me is with you. I want to be with you."

Relief flooded her. "I'm glad. I love you. So much, and I have faith you'll figure out all the things you've been dealing with. I'm here if you need me, though I won't be asking you about them all the time. You need to come to me. If you need help, with anything, you let me know, and if you think you'd like to talk to someone…a professional…about what you've been through, what you're going through now, we'll work that out, too."

"You mean like a shrink?"

"A psychologist. Or a counselor. Just someone you can open up to."

"I'll think about it." He fiddled with his butter knife. "It's okay with me if you want to date Coach…I mean, Leo. Not that you need my permission," he added quickly, obviously having picked up a few things from their talk. "I just wanted to let you know I won't be an asshole about it."

"I appreciate that." She sipped her wine, set it down carefully. "But Leo and I have decided not to see each other anymore."

"Because of me?"

"Because we're too different."

He frowned. "So? What are you afraid of?"

"Leo is all about living in the now, living for the moment, and I look to the future. I like to plan and take things slow and think things through. He jumps into situations, then figures it out as he goes."

Andrew sat back. "I used to be scared of the future," he admitted quietly. "I guess I still am sometimes. I'm scared of getting sick again. Of dying."

Her heart about stopped. "Oh, honey…"

"But I realized maybe there's a way to live in the now and have hope for the future. That's what you've taught me. To always have hope, no matter how bad things get."

Shocked, Penelope sat unable to move while Andrew dug into his second helping of dinner. Always have hope. But it was fleeting, so nebulous.

And oh, so necessary. What kind of life would she have, what kind of world would this be, if there were no hope? Hope for her son to have a healthy future and a long life. Hope that Leo truly did love her, that they could build a life together.

Hope that she could get Leo back.

LEO, GETTING READY to head into work for an extra shift, crossed the living room to answer the knock at his front door. The past week he'd taken on several extra shifts to get his mind off of Penelope.

It hadn't worked.

He'd keep trying. Something would eventually kick in and he'd stop thinking about her.

He opened the door, and his hand tightened on the handle. Of course, that would be easier to do if she wasn't standing on his porch.

"Penelope." He sounded calm enough, but his stomach flipped. She looked so beautiful, her cheeks flushed from the cold, her hair blowing in the breeze. He could hardly stand to look at her. "I don't mean to be rude but I was just on my way to work—"

"This won't take long," she said, her voice trembling slightly. She sounded and looked nervous. He'd be lying if he said he didn't take slight satisfaction in it. "Please. I just need a few minutes."

He sighed and let her in. "I hope you don't mind if I continue getting ready."

He didn't wait for her answer, but went into the other room and gathered the things he'd need for his shift.

"I—I wanted you to know that Andrew and I had a long talk, several actually, and we've worked out quite a few things. I think we'll be okay."

"I'm glad." And he was. He may be pissed at her for breaking his heart, but that didn't mean he wanted her and her son to be at odds.

"You were right. About a lot of things."

He froze. He hadn't expected that. She constantly surprised him. "Such as?"

"Such as how I shouldn't give up my life trying to make Andrew happy. How he needs to live by my rules."

He shrugged on his jacket. "Good to know. Now, I really do have to—"

"I'm sorry," she blurted.

He pressed his lips together. "Look, I appreciate it, but you didn't have to come over here to tell me. You're the one who decided we weren't good together, that we had no future."

She twisted her fingers together at her waist. "I may have been wrong about that. But my concerns were legitimate. For instance, if we are to try to stay together, we need to discuss some very important issues, such as what does us having a future together even mean? Marriage? Because I wouldn't feel right only living with you while Andrew still lived at home."

Leo was stunned. And confused. "What are you saying?"

"I'm saying there are things we need to decide. If we are talking the possibility of marriage, what about children? I'm unable to have any more, and I'm assuming you'll want at least one child of your own. I wouldn't be opposed to adopting, maybe an older child, but I don't want you to miss out on having a baby." She was rambling, her words coming fast and furious and all he could do was stare.

"And what about your job? It's dangerous. I would never ask you to quit it for me because I know how much you love it, but I'm not going to lie. I'd worry about you every day. And what about your family? They've been very nice to me and Andrew, but that was when they thought we were just another kid you coached and his mother. They probably want someone—"

"Whoa, whoa," Leo said, taking hold of her upper arms. "Breathe. Just inhale for me." He waited until she did so. "Good. Now let it out slowly. Better?"

She nodded.

"I don't have the answers to those questions," he told her, amazed and so grateful she was even asking those questions, that she was considering giving them another chance. "If we decide to do this, it'll work. We'll make it work. Together."

"I'm so scared," she whispered. "But I don't want to be. I want to be brave. For you. For us. I just... I don't want to hurt you again. It's so frightening, having this vision of a future, one that's so bright and shiny with so many possibilities. A future with you, making a family of our own, having a life I've never thought possible." She cupped his face and his heart swelled with hope. "But I want that life. I want it more than I've wanted anything in a long, long time. I'm terrified I'll get it only to have it snatched away."

"I can't guarantee Drew will never get sick again or hurt. Or that he won't make a mistake and piss us both off. I can't guarantee I'll never get hurt on the job, or we won't argue or have different opinions. Just like you can't guarantee nothing will ever happen to you, that you'll never be taken away from me and Drew or grow to hate winters in Shady Grove." His voice grew husky and he tugged her to him, reveling in the feel of her body against his. "But I can guarantee I will always love you, and I will do everything in my power to prove that to you each and every day of our lives."

She sniffed. Smiled. "It won't always be easy."

He grinned. "I thrive on a challenge."

She laughed and hooked her hands behind his neck, her fingers warm on his skin. "Being together will make all the effort worth it. You don't give up. You won't give up on me or us."

"Never."

"I promise never to give up on you. Never again. Life is too precious not to be with the person you love, to waste a single day. I know that better than most. I want to be with you, Leo. I want you to be my future. Forever."

Humbled and so grateful his knees were weak, he kissed her. Leaned back and stared into her eyes. "Forever."

* * * * *

*Look for the next*
*IN SHADY GROVE book by Beth Andrews!*
*Coming in 2015 from Harlequin Superromance.*

# LARGER-PRINT
# BOOKS!

**HARLEQUIN** *Presents*

PASSION
GUARANTEED
SEDUCTION

## GET 2 FREE LARGER-PRINT
## NOVELS PLUS 2 FREE GIFTS!

# LARGER-PRINT BOOKS!
## GET 2 FREE LARGER-PRINT NOVELS PLUS
## 2 FREE GIFTS!

**✦ HARLEQUIN®**

*Romance*

### From the Heart, For the Heart

---

**YES!** Please send me 2 FREE LARGER-PRINT Harlequin® Romance novels and my 2 FREE gifts (gifts are worth about $10). After receiving them, if I don't wish to receive any more books, I can return the shipping statement marked "cancel." If I don't cancel, I will receive 4 brand-new novels every month and be billed just $4.84 per book in the U.S. or $5.24 per book in Canada. That's a savings of at least 19% off the cover price! It's quite a bargain! Shipping and handling is just 50¢ per book in the U.S. and 75¢ per book in Canada.* I understand that accepting the 2 free books and gifts places me under no obligation to buy anything. I can always return a shipment and cancel at any time. Even if I never buy another book, the two free books and gifts are mine to keep forever.

119/319 HDN F43Y

Name _____
(PLEASE PRINT)

Address _____ Apt. # _____

City _____ State/Prov. _____ Zip/Postal Code _____

Signature (if under 18, a parent or guardian must sign) _____

### Mail to the **Harlequin® Reader Service:**
**IN U.S.A.:** P.O. Box 1867, Buffalo, NY 14240-1867
**IN CANADA:** P.O. Box 609, Fort Erie, Ontario L2A 5X3

### Want to try two free books from another line?
### Call 1-800-873-8635 or visit www.ReaderService.com.

\* Terms and prices subject to change without notice. Prices do not include applicable taxes. Sales tax applicable in N.Y. Canadian residents will be charged applicable taxes. Offer not valid in Quebec. This offer is limited to one order per household. Not valid for current subscribers to Harlequin Romance Larger-Print books. All orders subject to credit approval. Credit or debit balances in a customer's account(s) may be offset by any other outstanding balance owed by or to the customer. Please allow 4 to 6 weeks for delivery. Offer available while quantities last.

**Your Privacy**—The Harlequin® Reader Service is committed to protecting your privacy. Our Privacy Policy is available online at www.ReaderService.com or upon request from the Harlequin Reader Service.

We make a portion of our mailing list available to reputable third parties that offer products we believe may interest you. If you prefer that we not exchange your name with third parties, or if you wish to clarify or modify your communication preferences, please visit us at www.ReaderService.com/consumerchoice or write to us at Harlequin Reader Service Preference Service, P.O. Box 9062, Buffalo, NY 14269. Include your complete name and address.

HRLP13R

# *ReaderService*.com

## Manage your account online!

- Review your order history
- Manage your payments
- Update your address

---

*We've designed
the Harlequin® Reader Service
website just for you.*

---

## Enjoy all the features!

- Reader excerpts from any series
- Respond to mailings and
  special monthly offers
- Discover new series available to you
- Browse the Bonus Bucks catalog
- Share your feedback

*Visit us at:*

# ReaderService.com